LEGACY

BY

CORINA ZURCHER

NeverMore Publications, LLC

Library of Congress Cataloging-in-Publication Data Available

Library of Congress Control Number: 2014900501

ISBN: 0991172442
ISBN-13: 978-0-9911724-4-3

Printed in the U.S.A.
First American edition, June 2014

"Do not go where the path may lead, go instead where there is no path and leave a trail."
- Ralph Waldo Emerson

THE ELEMENTS

I

"They pierced the heart of my queen, brother. They have severed her heart in two."

"Then let them rot for all they've done…and all they have failed to do."

"How could they have not guessed? How is it they don't know? It is true of what the old ones say, 'You will reap what you sow'."

"Reaping and weeping, its song is the same. They forgot all about us, the Creators of the game."

"Then let us remind them, my brother, who dominates this land. For even our sister weeps at the works of their hand."

"Come Fire."

"Come Ice."

"Come Wind and the Earth."

"Entwined altogether, dismantle hope of new birth."

"*The Lion.*"

"The Wolf."

"*Gorilla and Bull.*"

"These kings and their sons will no longer rule."

"*Only the noble can summon the queen's return.*"

"Until that day comes, dear brother...we shall let the realm *burn*.

ONE YEAR AGO...

BODIES

II

"Tell it to me, Reginald. Tell me about the Old War."

The ivory feathers that adorned the crown of the eagle warrior's head stood on end the moment the queen issued her request. It was not quite a command, but knowing its words breathed forth from his queen's mouth, he knew he was more than obligated to tell the tale — a tale that had been bred within him from the very beginning — one he had sworn to never forget. But why she asked this of him now, when she had never bothered to command him of it before, troubled him greatly. For this particular story was filled with a darkness that still stained the clan with a deep, suffocating shadow of shame, a shame they all bore under the weight of its shadow — including his beloved queen.

"And do not tailor it the way the historians have done. I do not want to hear a skewed report drowning in political correctness. I want to know the truth. And I want to hear its horrors, its victories — both brutal and kind. And if there is no kindness, then be vicious in your storytelling. I need to see the past and understand it from the eyes of the clan."

He breathed in deeply, attempting to calm the angst that had settled in his mighty heart. When he finally exhaled, it was almost a sigh as he weighed his words in warning to his queen, "It is a difficult story to tell, my queen. My version of the tale will be quite different than the one woven by the ravens and the wolves. Perhaps, it would be best told by King Ivan or Queen Tatiana."

Her bright, gray eyes slowly began to dim until they were as black as onyx-colored stones. The feathers on his head slowly lowered in fear as the transition in his queen's demeanor suddenly shifted, for Reginald recognized the sign of his queen's anger.

"I don't want the wolf king and queen to tell me their version of it. I want *you* to tell it to me. I want to know how the eagles remember it, for I have heard the whispers on the wind, and only the eagles speak the truth. Tell me the secret tale then, Reginald, that which you know, that which you fear, that which you've been sworn to remember by those who have come before you."

Reginald looked into the jet-black pools on his queen's face and desired nothing more at this moment than to see their shining gray again. He nodded in respect to his queen, shifting uncomfortably as he attempted to find the words, "I shall do my best, my queen. Forgive me, I did not mean to upset you."

She rose from her chair and moved swiftly toward him. As her young form approached, Reginald knelt down before her and lowered his head.

"It's not you that's made me angry, Reginald."

Queen Rebekah laid her hand down on the top of his feathers and stroked them affectionately. Upon touch, he lifted his large head and saw that the color behind her eyes was slowly lightening. She rested her hand on his cheek, staring into his fierce, raptor eyes with a look that was almost sad.

"There are bodies, Reginald, bodies piling up along the borders."

Reginald narrowed his regal eyes never having heard this bit of news before. "*Whose* bodies?"

"Warrior beasts from the *other* side of the realm." She lowered her hand and looked out toward the far corner of her room. "Tell him."

From the shadows, a deep raspy voice answered, *"Bullssss and amphibianssss...."*

Reginald craned his neck around and looked into the shadows. Through the darkness in the corner of the room, he could make out the raven assassin's enormous form.

"Are you sure?"

"Quite sssure..."

The raven remained hidden in the shadows as Reginald rose to his full height of eight and a half feet tall; he turned around to face the cloaked being.

"Why was I not informed of this sooner?"

"Tok...tok...tok..." Only the sound of the raven's warble answered him in reply.

"Answer me, Poe!"

Poe's scarlet eyes illuminated against the darkness. *"I had to be sssure that what I had ssseen wasss true. Ssso I have waited and watched from the treesss near The Lair to sssee how they come here..."*

"And?"

"The bodiesss are as ssstiff and hard as rocksss...dead before arriving..."

Reginald turned around to face his queen. She was seated once again in her chair, watching his reaction closely.

"I know what you're thinking, Reginald. Why are they coming here? What is it they seek?"

She tapped her long fingers on the wooden armrest rapidly thinking about what the answers could possibly mean.

"These warriors have never ventured past Mariner Dam in almost two-hundred years — and they are weaponless upon arrival. This mystery has troubled me greatly, which is why I need you to tell me about the war. There's a key to this mysterious door, and I have yet to find it."

"There isss nothing for the eaglesss to sssay, my queen...Palimusss wasss our greatest king..."

Rebekah kept her eyes on Reginald as she answered her raven, "So it has been said, Poe."

"Tok...tok...tok..."

Rebekah's eyes bored into Reginald's, "What happened, Reginald? What happened in the Old War? What did King Palimus really *do*?"

Poe did not rattle another word as he waited to hear his captain's version of the tale, the eagles' version. The eagle warrior took a deep breath, feeling the weight of this moment on his enormous chest. "As you know, my queen, the Old War was a bloody war, a war that ripped our realm in two. And it is one that I hope we shall never live to see again."

She nodded at him encouragingly, but before he continued, he paused, remembering the words the old eagle chief, his mentor, had spoken to him the first time Reginald himself had learned about what happened those two-hundred years ago. It was the reason, he was told, as to why he could never fly across Mariner Sea Dam, only alongside it from the north to the east, having to turn back around the moment he had gone too far south. It was why borders had been built between the territories in order to keep the other clans out. It was the reason he had never seen the other kingdoms on the opposite side of the realm — the Lion's Den, Gorilla Jungle, Bull Valley, and the Amphibian Swamps — only to remain in Bird Kingdom, soaring across the skies over the Wolf Lair, Critter Country and Reptile Desert.

He was a young fledgling when the old chief had told him about the lion, toad and gorilla warriors from the Old War.

"They were our allies, Reginald, legends and heroes from long ago...their

acts of valor have never been repeated but in the stories we tell."

And it was why, the chief had said, that Reginald would never see such beasts again in his lifetime.

"It's because of that war, Reginald. Our king, Palimus, cursed us all."

Looking at his queen's beautiful face, he heard the old chief's words echoing forth from his memories from long ago. Speaking life into the visions from his youth, Reginald began the horrific tale of the clan.

"In the beginning, there were seven kingdoms, seven kingdoms to rule one land. Each king had his queen and along with it a people to shelter and care for. Of the seven, each had their own unique gifts and qualities to bring forth an abundance of strength, prosperity and beauty throughout the land, all of which were meant to be shared with all.

"But not every king and queen developed such gifts or brought forth the abundance their land had to offer. Instead, they relied on the efforts and work of the other kingdoms. And over time, their reliance turned to weakness, envy and resentment as certain kings rose above the rest, for they had more resources of which to share, more fruit of which to grow, more talents of which to offer, and in turn, needed to protect. And it was on these grounds that the land shifted and the balance of what was once meant to be equal became a valley divided."

The words poured from Reginald's mouth like a flood, "The birds ruled the north while the west was ruled by the lions. The wolves ruled the east, and the gorillas dominated the south. The other kingdoms — the mariners, amphibians, reptiles and bulls — served the four kings that equally ruled the realm.

"Tired of their reliance on the other kingdoms to survive — a fault all their own — the mariner king convinced the kings and chiefs of the lesser clans that their valley was the lifeline of the realm. Without the valley and the sea, the kingdoms to the north, south, east and west would fall."

He looked at his queen, the pupils of his pale-colored eyes shrinking to the size of tiny dots. He could feel the heat in his heart rising. It was pounding inside his massive chest. "So the lesser clans united and rose up as one to bring down the other kings and queens, for those that ruled over them would rule no more…"

THE OLD WAR
III

"*T*he lion and bird clans were allies, having been so as far back as time began. They had agreed that the lion king would lead the ground battle along with the gorilla and wolf kings, while the bird king would lead the aerial attack. Only the ostrich warriors would remain in Bird Kingdom, ordered by their chief to annihilate any lesser clan warrior that crossed the Great Mountains into the north."

Large nine-foot-tall warriors with the heads of lions, tigers, cheetahs, jaguars and panthers raced down the grassy hills of the Lion's Den, each on their two animal legs and on toward the valley — the center of the realm. The Lion King Luther led his pride across the plains toward Mariner Sea while, overhead, enormous eight-foot-tall beings with the heads of eagles, owls, hawks, falcons and ravens filled the sky. The Bird King Palimus led the flock, riding atop the raven chief; the Golden Eagle warriors — the Thunderbird Guard — were directly behind him. On the heels of the lion king and his den, they followed, ready to attack from the sky above.

The Wolf Pack had already reached the sea, having stormed the beaches from their lair in the east. The Wolf King Feyedor led his gigantic seven-foot-tall soldiers made up of wolves, hyenas, coyotes, jackals, and foxes as they battled it out with the bulls, rams, and buffalo soldiers. Joining the wolf king's side was the Gorilla King Brock. He wielded his bone scepter down upon the bull and buffalo soldiers, bludgeoning skull after skull, piercing spine after spine, as he drove the edge of his scepter down into the beasts' backs as they charged him and the band of his tribe. Robust six-foot-tall silverback, baboon, orangutan and chimpanzee warriors followed their king as they swung down from the trees and stormed the valley, riding the waves of blood from the streams their king had sprung.

Rising up from the mounds and burrows, scampering from branch to branch, were the Critter Clan warriors made up of gophers, squirrels, possums and chipmunks. They battled it out with the amphibians and reptiles as they collided between the east and west.

The four kings followed the river's tide that poured forth from Mariner Tower, driving their troops upstream, back to the source of its font, back to the beginning, back to the sea.

"There was only one plan that the four kings agreed upon, knowing it was the only way to end the battle: Capture the mariner king, win the war. But the king of the sea was not waiting for them to do battle in his home court. He was bringing the battle to them, and he was using the streams and rivers to do it."

Rocketing and jetting forth from the waterways were the mariner warriors — beings with the heads of devil rays, eels and octopi. They blasted out from the rivers and streams, landed ashore, and immediately engaged in battle with the Lion's Den, the Wolf Pack, the gorilla soldiers and bird warriors. Joining them were the kings, nobles, and warriors of the bull, reptile, and amphibian clans.

Cassius, the mariner king, rode the tide on the backs of his shark warriors, leading the revolt onward and upward. The moment the lion king saw the mariner driving toward them, he roared toward the warriors in his den, *"TO THE TREES!!!"*

"It was a massive, violent battle for rule of the valley."

The Wolf King Feyedor and Gorilla King Brock continued to fight side by side against the bull and reptile clans, and their herd of champions: black angus, rams, and buffalos, cobras, Komodo dragons and lizard soldiers. Brock was relentless with his bone scepter, Bane, as he wielded it like a sword, a hammer, and a spear.

The bulls were just as relentless, ramming and tearing the gorillas from inside out as they charged and gutted them with their massive horns and powerful forms. But little by little, the wolves and gorillas made more headway, forcing the bulls and reptiles back toward the center of the valley, and back toward the sea.

The Lion Guard made up of panthers, jaguars, cheetahs, lynxes and tigers were now the only clan viciously battling the mariner and amphibian armies.

The amphibian king led his pool of toad and frog soldiers, completely undeterred by the size and number of the warriors of the Lion's Den.

"NOW!!!"

Answering their king's command, the toad warriors unleashed their lethal venom, spitting it out onto the faces of the Lion Guard warriors that came crashing forth. The catlike warriors went down, choking on the poison within.

Seeing the mariner warriors emerge from the streams, following the Lion Guard to the trees, Palimus commanded the Thunderbird Guard to attack the mariner warriors down below. The golden eagles swooped in and out of the sky, hurling the bodies of shark and eel warriors miles away from the waterways. Within minutes, the soldiers began to suffocate and die, unable to stay ashore without being near their lifeline of the water and the sea. Eagles continued to storm the battlefield, careening the mariners into the trees and rocks, and into the mouths of the vulture soldiers waiting in the sky. They tore the mariner soldiers limb from limb, ripping them to shreds; not a single body part hit the ground.

In the field below, the critter chief commanded his

porcupine archers to unleash their quills onto the lesser clans. The turtle and tortoise warriors watched the sky grow dark as the quill arrows covered it in shadow.

A black tortoise warrior commanded his army to shield itself. The turtle warriors immediately shrunk inside their shells as the quills rained down, and the critters stormed in. The moment the turtles and tortoises emerged, they were beheaded — and heads began to roll.

The Lion King Luther wound through the trees, circling back around to the river's tide. Cassius had dismounted from his shark warriors' backs and was battling it out with a tiger warrior. The moment Luther saw him, he knew victory was his for the taking.

He looked to the sky and saw Palimus and his ravens directly overhead. As he crept forth from the shadows of the trees, Luther saw a large man barreling toward him — it was the bull king.

Luther whipped around, changed direction, and charged toward the burly man — but the bull king did not run. He merely lowered his head and sneered at the lion king. It was then that Luther realized his mistake.

Too many trees.

From the shadows within the forest, the buffalo soldiers emerged. They charged toward Luther, surrounding him on all sides, but the lion king did not surrender. Wielding his sword, the lion king ran even faster, barreling through the throng of approaching buffaloes, gutting them and slashing their Achilles tendons from underneath them. The buffaloes went down as Luther bulldozed through them, continuing his relentless pursuit of the bull king.

The bull king turned and sprinted toward the forest, and Luther followed. Another grave mistake. Luther cursed himself for his zealousness and pride as he now found himself in the Old Forest. It was an old, haunted fortress that bordered Bull Valley — the bulls' home turf — and Luther was all alone.

Luther slowed his step, looking all around the forest for the bull king, but the king was nowhere to be seen.

SNAP!!!

Luther whirled around just in time to see an enormous buffalo warrior charging toward him — but he did not turn fast enough. The buffalo soldier's horn swiped the lion king across his fighting arm, slicing straight through his bicep. Luther dropped his sword and roared in pain just as another buffalo soldier attacked him from the other side, slicing the king in the ribs as he turned on his hoof and wound back around the trees. The lion king could do nothing but fall to his knees.

Seething in pain, the lion king looked out into the forest beyond. A dozen buffalo soldiers slowly emerged, circling the lion king. Seeing their size and number, he knew he did not stand a chance, but the lion king refused to go down this day, for he knew he had one last card to play.

Luther looked up through a clearing in the trees and saw the ravens flying directly overhead. He roared to the sky, *"PALIMUS!!! SEND ME YOUR RAVENS!!!"*

From above, Palimus heard Luther's cry, but he made no movement in reply. The bird king and his ravens hovered in the sky for what seemed like an eternity until the raven chief craned his neck around, awaiting his king's command. But Palimus remained absolutely still, refusing to answer the lion king's plea.

Luther shouted once more, *"PALIMUS!!!"*

Too late.

The buffalo soldiers lowered their horned heads and stormed toward the king. Like a cyclone, they came at him from all sides, winding on their heels, turning their horns toward every muscle, every organ, and every piece of flesh they could find. When they had done all the damage they could do, they slowed their merciless spin — and the lion king fell.

With his face in the ground, blood spewing from his lips, Luther cried out one last time, *"PALIMUS!!!!"*

But it was not Palimus who answered the king.

It was then that Luther heard the lions and tigers of the guard. Their cry thundered across the realm as they answered their king's pitiful shout. From up above, Palimus saw the panthers, jaguars, cheetahs and lions charging from the valley and through the forest toward their king.

The Thunderbirds rose up from the valley alongside the Lion Guard, and launched into the sky, also having heard the lion king's painful shout. Seeing the raven battalion hovering up above, the eagle captain called out to Palimus, *"KING!!! THE LION ROARS!!!"*

Palimus shifted his gaze from the lions to his eagles. And as the eagle captain looked at his king, the feathers on his head stood on end. It was a look of pure darkness — almost as if a shroud of bitter cruelty had surrounded his king like an eclipse, blotting out the light of the sun. The eagle captain shuddered as he looked into his king's eyes — they were as black as the ravens and the crows.

Turning his onyx-colored eyes to the raven battalion, Palimus finally issued the command, *"ANNIHILATE THE BUFFALOES! TO THE LION KING!!!"*

The Thunderbirds and ravens immediately dove down, joining the Lion Guard as they charged toward the lion king's side. The lions and tigers reached their king first. They raged through the trees, annihilating every buffalo soldier in sight as the Thunderbirds rocketed the beastly soldiers off of the lion king and into the mouths of the vultures. The ravens flew low to the ground, stealthily winding between the trees as they hunted for the bull king.

The Gorilla King Brock continued to fight the reptile king hundreds of meters away from the Old Forest, completely unaware of the lion king's demise. The reptile king — a cobra warrior — heaved his ten-foot long tail at Brock, lashing it out at him from all sides. The gorilla king leapt for the branches in the trees, dodging the attack. He climbed the branches and swung swiftly back around to come head on with the reptile king. The gorilla king swung down from a branch, smashing his bone scepter against the reptile king's skull.

He wielded Bane down again and again until he felt a presence emerge from behind him. He whirled around, only to come face to face with the mariner king.

Cassius was aiming his hooked spear right at the gorilla king's heart. On either side of him stood his shark warriors, aiming two more spears at the mighty king. Taking in the size of the beasts, along with their weapons, Brock knew he was outnumbered; yet he did not allow the idea of defeat to sink in. His only thought was, *The sun will not go down on me today.*

Quicker than they could react, the gorilla king took his scepter and swung it down upon the shark warriors' feet, knocking them to the ground with one fell swoop. Without breaking stride, he twirled the bone weapon around and plunged it deep into one of the warrior's gills, before clubbing it down upon the other shark's nose.

From the burrows in the ground, the gopher warriors plunged their swords up through the shark warriors' hearts and up through the mariner king's feet. Cassius roared in pain as he fell to his knees. Gripping the ground with his fists, the pool of black blood from his warriors spilt all around, surrounding him like a large bulls-eye.

As Cassius slowly looked up, the gorilla king was standing over him holding his bloodied scepter. All around the gorilla king, the critter warriors, hyenas and wolves emerged from the forest. With his body racking in pain, the mariner king attempted to rise. He was suddenly grabbed by the back of the head and pulled to standing.

The Wolf King Feyedor looked at him with his ice-cold eyes. *"Fool…"*

It was then that the king heard his wolf captain howling in the distance. Feyedor's eyes grew wide, understanding its meaning. He looked at Brock, *"The lion king!"*

Feyedor took off, dragging the mariner king by the hair. The Wolf Pack followed closely behind as the gorilla soldiers shouted across the valley, answering the lone wolf's howling cry. The warriors raced through the Old Forest following the howls through the trees.

Palimus dove down into the woods and landed a few feet from where the Lion Guard stood. As he moved forward, he could hear a low growl coming from the lion warriors, a sound of tremendous mourning and woe.

Palimus stepped between them and saw the lion king's body on the ground below — but it was no body. It was a bloodied mound of torn flesh that looked like nothing more than a pile of meat. All eyes were on the lion king — all except the eagle captain's. Palimus looked up at his captain, feeling the raptor eyes on him, daring to meet the eagle's challenging stare.

From behind Palimus, the raven chief emerged, standing behind his king at over nine feet tall. He leveled his eyes at the eagle captain, speaking his unspoken warning with a single look from his ebony eyes. The eagle captain held his ground as he looked between the raven and his king, but he spoke no word that revealed the thoughts and questions swirling in his head.

Swinging down from the trees, the gorilla king emerged, followed closely by the wolf king and the critter chief. The moment the gorilla king saw the mound of flesh, he fell to his knees. Feyedor was bowled over at the sight of the remains of the great lion king.

"King..."

Feyedor looked at Palimus for any sign of understanding, but Palimus merely lowered his head; an act the wolf king interpreted as a sign of mourning and respect to the lion king. When Palimus looked up, only the mariner king was left staring at him, not so much in defeat as in wonderment.

The Lion and Tiger Guard roared to the sky, and a great cry was heard across the land, unlike any that had ever been heard before.

"The lesser clans were punished severely for their uprising. Weapons were stripped from their possession and banished from that moment on. A dam was built upon the sea so that control over the water was no longer left to the Mariner Clan. The titles of kings and queens of the lesser clans would remain in name alone, for power was no longer theirs to wield. The lesser clans were now to be governed more closely by the four most powerful kings in the realm.

The lions would rule the bulls. The gorillas would dominate the amphibians. The wolves would reign over the reptiles. And the birds would protect the critters. But that was not all…"

On Judgment Day, the Mariner King Cassius stood before the Lion Queen Alana and the other three, powerful kings. The lion queen showed no emotion as she stared at the king from the sea. She silently stepped aside as Brock advanced toward the rebel king.

Taking his bone scepter, he smashed the mariner king's skull in two. When the king's body dropped, he flipped the scepter over and plunged its sharpened edge through the mariner king's heart.

"The other kings and chiefs of the lesser clans were brought forth without any judge, trial or jury. They were hurled into a large fire, burnt alive as the other kings and queens watched on in silence.

"After the rulers of the lesser clans had been eliminated, the wolf, gorilla and bird kings approached the throne to where the lion queen stood. One by one they bowed before her in mourning and respect. The last in line was King Palimus. He moved toward the lion queen, reaching out to her to take her hands in his. That is when they saw it, my queen. The lion queen had reached out to take his hands in hers when her right arm suddenly jerked. A dagger fell from her sleeve. And before King Palimus could react, the lion queen plunged her weapon of vengeance deep into our king's heart.

"There was chaos then. Stunned by what the lion queen had done, unsure of what our king's true role was in this tragedy, the kingdoms argued and fought with one another over what to believe, over what was just. The result is what we seen now, my queen — a realm split in two.

"With the assassination of our king, an alliance between the lions and the gorillas formed against the wolves and the birds. Only the Mariner Sea and the once-rebellious mariner king separated the neutral territory dividing the four ruling clans.

"And for almost two hundred years, these alliances have remained, and a blood meridian separates the two most powerful kingdoms in the realm, dividing them as enemies — that of the lion and that of the bird."

After Reginald had finished speaking, no one said a word. The air in the room suddenly felt heavy, as if the spirits of those whose names he had spoken of filled it, weighing it down with rage and woe. Queen Rebekah's face was completely ashen, as if the blood from her body had completely drained itself out. She looked like death itself, sitting in her large chair, as she pondered the perspective the eagle had shared. She was utterly silent, staring out across her balcony and into the moonlight.

"Thank you, Reginald."

The queen leaned over and reached for a large scroll that was spread out across the table beside her. She stared at it for a long while before she finally spoke, "What would it mean to you, Reginald, if I told you that the lion king of our era desires to unite the realm once more?"

Reginald's pupils contracted into tiny points, shocked at the news. Even Poe emerged from the shadows by what he had just heard. Rebekah looked up at both her eagle and her raven, taking in the stunned looks on both her warriors' faces.

"I know…utterly shocking, with or without the eagles' tale."

She handed the scroll to Reginald and Poe. They immediately began reading it in unison.

"Now you understand why I wanted to hear the eagles' side of the story. I wanted to know if this kind of treaty could be trusted." She looked at Reginald, suddenly feeling very tired. "What do you think?"

Poe turned his large black head toward his captain waiting to see what his response would be. Reginald's face looked fierce as he stared at the writing on the scroll. He slowly began to pace the room. Rebekah watched his eight and half foot tall frame walk back and forth as the wheels in his head were rapidly spinning.

"He claims there's a *famine*, my queen?"

"Yes, on the lion king's side of the realm. And he claims it has spread into Bull Valley, Amphibian Swamps and Gorilla Jungle. He claims the clans are starving and need our help." Rebekah shifted her eyes to Poe. "It would explain the bodies. You said they were stiff before they arrived, Poe, yet you have not seen *how* they have arrived, let alone how they died. Perhaps, they are crossing here to find food, dying of exhaustion by the time they get here, having starved to death."

Reginald stopped pacing.

"I do not think ssso, my queen. They have woundsss…"

Reginald caught the slightest dimming again behind his queen's eyes once again. "What kind of wounds?"

"Weaponsss have killed these beastsss…but weaponsss unlike the onesss on our ssside…"

Rebekah rose from her chair, her eyes were now nearly black. "Does Ivan know?"

"Ssskoll has informed the wolf king…and the prince. King Ivan thought it best to address it after he returned from Mariner Sssea…he does not agree with my assessment of the sssituation. He does not believe there isss any foul play."

"Not if his wolves are the ones who attacked." Rebekah looked at Reginald, "The lion king wishes to have all the clans meet in The Den to discuss this treaty. He is desperate for an answer, claiming that without our help, his side of the realm will perish." She shifted her gaze to Poe, "Have the crows and the owls watch the borders on the west near The Lair. Tell Ume to add more ostrich guards along the mountain range. I need to know how these warriors are dying."

Poe nodded to his queen.

"Until I know exactly what's going on, I have no choice but to honor this treaty." Poe was about to protest. "Thank you both. You may go."

Both Poe and Reginald bowed to their queen and exited the chambers. As they walked down the long corridors to the garden gate, neither warrior spoke. The moment they reached the doorway to the outer realm, Poe turned his head toward Reginald, his ebony eyes glistening in the moonlight. Reginald met his gaze, waiting for the raven assassin to speak.

"The eaglesss dishonor Palimusss with their tale...tok...tok...tok..."

"Poe, it's merely the tale that was told to me. Our queen wished to hear it."

"The lionsss are not to be trusted. Thisss treaty isss not to be trusted. It isss a trick to destroy our clan."

"You have no proof to back your claim."

"Yesss, I do. There's something we ravensss have also burnt into the memoriesss of our mindsss about the old lion king. Sssomething the eaglesss could not sssee..."

"And what was that?"

"He cursed...the Sssun...he dishonored Fire...vowing to desstroy all who honored the Sssun...Palimusss knew...Palimusss chose...Palimus' heir must rule the sssame...she must ssstay clear of the lion..."

Reginald's regal stature froze the moment the raven spoke the words.

"Then we must find proof that this new lion king is false and means harm through the ruse of peace before our queen signs the treaty."

And without another word the eagle headed toward the light and the raven dove into the dark.

THE LION

IV

"**Y**ou fight like your sister!"

"Shut up, Brandon!"

Brandon, the tiger baron, roared in laughter as he watched the panther lord, Maximillian, battle it out with the lion prince in open sport — not with the grappling of limbs but with the clashing of swords. The panther lord swung his weapon hard and fast as he tried to outperform the champion of The Den.

"He'll never beat Nathan."

Brandon looked down at the lion prince's eight-year-old sibling, seeing the twinkling look of pride behind the younger prince's amber eyes; he could not help but smile.

"I know, young cub, but Max is a rather prideful lord, unlike your brother Nathan who uses his humility as a mask to draw his prey in just before the slaughter. Poor Maximillian."

"OW!!!"

Maximillian dropped his sword and gripped his forearm tight. Blood ran between the bulging veins of his muscular arm as he attempted to put pressure on his wound. Nathan, the lion prince, tossed his sword into the dirt and grinned at his unfortunate opponent.

"Come now, Max, it's merely a scratch."

Maximillian glared at him with his electric green eyes. Even in the day, they would mirror like his panther warriors' did at night. Maximillian was not used to defeat, let alone having it be witnessed by his rival, the tiger baron. Seeing Brandon walking toward him with a smug look on his face made his blood boil.

"Some scratch, Max. It's more like a paper cut. You panthers never learn — you must linger a little longer before you pounce."

"And what do you know of lingering, Brandon?" Nathan added, "You're always running around in circles before getting a good swipe in. And even then…you miss."

Marcus giggled in reply.

Maximillian saw his opening. "It's a wonder the tiger clan stands so close to the lions within the guard."

Brandon continued smiling, "Well, when one sees a panther lord fight like you did today, all wonderment surely dies." He elbowed Maximillian in his wounded arm. The panther lord cried out in pain. Having no one else to take his anger out on, he turned to

Marcus and shouted, "Stop gawking and get me a dressing!"

Marcus dashed around the corner and raced inside the Lion's Den.

Nathan's smile slowly evaporated, "Now, now, Max, no need to take it out on your prince. What do you need a towel for when you can merely lick your wounds?"

Brandon watched the blood as it dripped down Maximillian's arm, shaking his head in reply, "I blame the maidens of the Gorilla Clan for your legs going out on you today or Nathan would have done more than nick that arm of yours. If we were at war, they'd be the death of you."

The panther lord continued to nurse his wound, calming down with each breath he forced himself to take. "Bedding them is worth it, my friend, even if it does cost me. At least I'd die satisfied. If you weren't so afraid of their clan, you'd come with me to Gorilla Jungle and know I was right."

"Enough talk of beds. Young ears approach."

Marcus returned, catching the last bit of conversation. He looked forward to days like this when he could hang around and hear the young men talk. He always seemed to learn something new, knowing he would never hear it anywhere else. What he loved listening to the most were their stories about the other kingdoms and clans — Bull Valley, Mariner Tower, and Amphibian Swamps. But lately, all they seemed to talk about were their visits to Gorilla Jungle.

Brandon's grin finally faded, "I'm not afraid of the clan, just those nasty baboon warriors. All that whooping...I don't know how you can concentrate."

Maximillian's voice deepened, "There are *other* sounds that have my attention."

"What other sounds?"

Nathan grabbed the cloth from Marcus' small hand and tossed it to Brandon. "Never mind, Marcus."

Nathan turned to the tiger baron, "Brandon, you're afraid to go anywhere outside of Tigerland. I still remember the time Max dared you to stay out in the woods of the Wolf Lair for *one* night."

Maximillian laughed, "The tiger didn't even last an hour. My panthers still jest about it."

Brandon retorted, "At least I tried it! You wouldn't have lasted ten minutes. That place is a fortress of spooks and spells. Besides, I wasn't going to wait around for the Wolf Pack to slaughter me."

Nathan laughed, "The Wolf Pack? You know you were more worried about being torn to shreds by the bird queen."

Marcus looked at Brandon in confusion. "How could the bird queen tear you apart? Aren't tigers stronger than birds?"

"Stronger? Try less weak."

"Shut up, Max."

Maximillian nodded to Marcus, "Tell him, Nathan."

"Tell me what?"

Brandon's face turned ghost white as he whispered his reply,

"The curse of the bird clan…from the Old War."

Nathan shook his head. "No, he's too young to hear it."

Maximillian sneered challengingly, "*You* weren't too young to hear it." He looked at the young lion prince. "As a matter of fact, Nathan was your age when he went into the woods in The Lair. And Brandon only went a few months ago."

"Shut up, Max!"

Marcus looked up at his older brother with pleading eyes, "Tell me, Nathan! You're the only one who tells me the truth!"

"It'll give you nightmares."

"No, it won't! I promise!"

Maximillian could not help but smile, "Tell him, Nathan. If you don't, someone else will and they'll probably exaggerate more than we do."

Nathan sighed deeply in resignation, "All right, but if you can't sleep…"

"I'll sleep!"

"All right. Well, after the Old War, when King Palimus was assassinated by our queen out of vengeance for King Luther's death, a curse was placed over Bird Kingdom."

Brandon finished dressing Maximillian's wound, adding to the story, "It was the tigers who cursed them."

Maximillian lowered his head in rebuttal, "It was the *panthers!*"

"*Tigers!*"

"It was the lions."

Both men looked to their prince with no further retort. Nathan continued, "The curse was passed on from generation to generation within the bird clan."

Marcus was fascinated, "What was the curse?"

"They say that the royal line was cursed, destined to become more animal-like in appearance, resembling their warriors, becoming less human-like as each generation was born."

Marcus' eyes grew wide, "You mean…the bird queen looks like a *bird*?"

Nathan nodded his head, "That's what they say."

"It's true. My panthers have seen her."

Everyone turned their attention to the panther lord.

"One night, a few years ago, my panthers were patrolling the canals along Mariner Dam. They were admiring the moonlit sky, walking along a path they had crossed many times before, when they came upon a trail they did not recognize. So they decided to walk its path, and before they knew it, they had walked straight inside The Lair."

Marcus gasped while Brandon laughed. "And you're still wondering why the panthers aren't the second-best warriors in the Lion Guard? Crossing into The Lair without knowing it…*pathetic!*"

Maximillian glared at Brandon. "Let me finish."

"Fine."

"So they found themselves in The Lair near a blackened lake. That's when they saw her."

"Who?" Brandon asked.

"The *bird* queen, you idiot!" He looked back at Marcus. "They say she stands on the banks of Wolf Lake night after night, just before the dawn."

Marcus asked, "What for?"

"They say she honors the sun. Anyway, just before the dawn, the queen turned her head having heard the panthers behind her. When they saw her face, it was just like a vulture's! She had a beak, and large beady eyes! She also had talons instead of fingers!"

Brandon's face was whiter than Marcus'. "Nuh-uh."

Maximillian looked Marcus dead in the eye, "With one flick of her finger, she can tear a pound of flesh from your body to eat. And she'll peck your eyes out with her razor-sharp beak! She eats her own people for food, but little boys are her favorite."

Marcus turned to Brandon, "And *you* went into the woods anyway?"

"Shocking, isn't it."

"Shut up, Max."

Maximillian continued, "Every member in The Den must prove his bravery somehow, little cub. Some choose to go to The Lair."

"But why is the bird queen in the Wolf Lair?"

Nathan replied, "They are kin clans — especially the wolves and the ravens — they are bound to one another."

Marcus looked at his older brother. "And *you* went into the woods when you were my age?"

Before he could reply, Maximillian answered, "Of course he did. Your brother is the bravest of us all. And in battle he's to be commended; he fights on even though his legs give out...*often*."

Marcus, completely oblivious to what had just been insinuated, shouted excitedly, "I want to go to The Lair!"

"I don't think so."

Maximillian grinned snidely. "Why not? Are you saying young Marcus isn't brave enough to do it? Is he a *cowardly* lion?"

Nathan stepped toward the panther lord so that they were eye to eye; the pupils of his eyes slit to a cat. "There is no lion in The Den who runs from fear. They run toward it to come face to face with their terrors, not to be mastered by them but to own them and be called Master."

Brandon watched this exchange in utter silence, seeing the small tattoo marking around Nathan's neck darken. The panther lord had crossed the line with his prince.

Maximillian's snide look faded upon seeing Nathan's eyes, "I was only joking, Nathan."

"I wasn't."

Marcus wedged his tiny body in between them and looked up at Maximillian. "I *am* brave! If Nathan can stay the whole night, so can I!"

Maximillian stepped back away from Nathan and smiled down at Marcus, attempting to feign bravery himself. "I agree with you. Too bad your brother won't let you go."

Nathan looked down at his younger brother, "Marcus, you're not going into those woods, and that's final."

Marcus pleaded with him, "Nathan! *Please???* I'm ready!" He stood proudly, puffing out his little chest.

"You even take one step in the direction of The Lair, I'll beat you so badly, Marcus, you'll never walk again. Now go inside!"

Marcus' face fell in disappointment.

Maximillian shook his head in mock sympathy. "Poor little cub, branded a coward so young. How shall such a one as this lead and rule The Den when no one respects him, thinking him weak?"

Brandon chastised him, mumbling under his breath, "Max…"

Nathan's eyes glowed the color of golden amber, but before he could move in on Maximillian, Marcus erupted in anger and ploughed straight for him. The panther lord, however, stepped quickly aside just before Marcus tackled into him, pushing Marcus further forward and into a pile of rocks.

Nathan immediately rushed the panther lord and decked both Maximillian and Brandon in the face, laying them both out flat. He turned to help Marcus up, but Marcus ran from his brother's outstretched hand and straight out of the courtyard. Nathan watched as his younger brother raced across The Den, carrying his pain and bruised pride along with him.

Nathan crouched down to the panther lord and tiger baron. He grabbed Maximillian's dark head of hair, yanking the panther lord's head up from the ground until their faces were inches from one another.

"You ever insult my family again, and I'll string you up from the highest tree in The Lair and let the vultures rip you to shreds. Better yet, I'll leave you for their queen."

He released his grip, and Maximillian's head hit the ground with a loud thump. Nathan turned from the courtyard and strode out toward the Great Halls that led inside Lion's Den Castle.

Several moments passed with neither Maximillian nor Brandon saying a word until Brandon finally asked, "I don't get it. Why did he hit *me?*"

"Shut up, Brandon."

There was something mysteriously comforting about the burden of sadness — even in all its woe — and the queen of the Bird Clan felt it. She had always felt it, almost as if the world itself had chosen to write its grief upon her heart in order to give her a deeper insight into the pulse of the world through the eyes of weary tears.

It was a night darker than all the others that had ever come before, yet the queen refused to cry. She refused to acknowledge the shadow of melancholy that followed her footsteps as she walked the corridors in her kingdom halls, completely alone with nothing and no one but the thoughts that were storming inside her head. For now she knew. She knew that there was a just reason to despise her clan, not the other way around as all the kings and queens had said before. For the clans on her side of the realm had blamed the old lion queen for slaughtering the once great bird king for no other reason than needing someone to blame for the lion king's demise. Yet, Rebekah now understood that innocence was not a banner that could be waved by her side anymore — it was shame. And shame had woven a veil of shadow over her clan, keeping all others out. And there was a name to the shadow…and his name was Palimus.

"Why did you do it?"

Rebekah stood before his portrait, staring into his handsome face. Looking into the king's dark, brown eyes, they were shining, speaking forth an invitation and a warning with the underlining of a dare. He was a handsome man with his olive skin and jet-black hair; and he was a raven through and through.

Looking into the eyes of this king, Rebekah's eyes filled with tears. What a tragedy it all had been. Centuries of separation out of fear and loathing — and her clan did not deserve it — they did not deserve to be hated for so long. She knew how difficult a task it must have been for the lion king to ask for her help. Thus, he must truly be desperate in order to ask. *But a famine?* How could there possibly be a famine? The mariner king of old was an utter fool, for he had forgotten one, tiny, little fact: that whether he controlled the sea or not, it was the bird clan that ensured that there was rain enough to fill it. Had Cassius won his war, he would have lost in the end, for there was no doubt in Rebekah's mind that Palimus would have held back his warriors from carrying water from the earth and sky back to the sea. The rain had never ceased. And what bothered her the most were the bodies on the borders. What were they *really* doing there? And *who* put them there?

"I thought I sent you to The Lair."

Rebekah stood before King Palimus' portrait, but her words echoed into the shadows of the corridor.

"You are sssad, my queen…I feel it."

Rebekah turned and looked at Poe, seeing his scarlet-colored eyes glowing in the darkness. Her face softened at his words, needing to speak her thoughts aloud, if only to be heard rather than be answered. She breathed in deeply, turning her gaze back to the great king.

"I know what it isss you ssseek, my queen. You sssearch for an answer. You long for the 'Why.'"

She nodded silently, speaking no other word.

"We ravensss cherish Fire. We admire the Sssun…even in the dark. The lion king did not ssseee, Queen, he thought he could master Fire. He thought he could rule the Sssun…"

Rebekah turned her head and looked at her raven assassin standing in the dark. The weary look on her face shifted into tight lines, until the softened look of kindness hardened into a vicious look of anger.

"Go on."

"He did not believe in the Creatorsss of our world and sssought to banish their veneration and adoration by the clans once the war was won. The lion blamed belief in the Invisible Onesss for the mariner king's belief in the exalted ssself and purpose for sssomething more...Ssstrip the belief, chain the believer, massster the realm. Palimusss knew...Palimusss chose...Palimusss wasss right..."

The queen looked at her raven, "Why did you not tell me this before?"

"You never asked me, my queen. You assumed you had the answer from all the talesss before. You listen to your eagle, but the eagle's voice isss not the only one that must be heard. There isss light and there isss dark, and there are advantagesss to both. We ravensss sssee the sssecrets in the night...truth to the real ssself that hidesss in the shadowsss away from the light. But you, Queen, you have no sssecrets. You are the light and the dark. Just...like...Palimusss..."

She stood there in silence, pondering his words. That was when the assassin emerged from the shadows and stood beside his queen. He looked up at the portrait of the great king and spoke with a tone that resembled a sigh, *"We ravensss revere him. The crowsss long for him. The vulturesss ssstill mourn him. And the eaglesss...the eaglesss wish to forget him. Now you know it all, my queen."*

He swiveled his head and looked at his queen, *"I do not wish for you to be sssad when you ssstand before our king. I do not wish you to fear when facing the unknown. I am beside you and the clan isss behind you. I will fight the battlesss you do not sssee and bend to no one'sss will but yoursss. You are not alone, Queen. You are never alone."*

Rebekah lifted her hand and gently rested it against Poe's cheek. "You have reminded me of something I had long forgotten, Poe. That it's not what others call you, but what you answer to. And I have focused far too long on the call."

'No, you have longed to give your answer. I sssseee you, Queen. You champion the clan. You wish to resurrect usss once again. Do it, my queen. Let your fire burn within, but not without asking the question…alwaysss the question…How do you want to be remembered?"

Poe swiveled his head and took one last look at the portrait of King Palimus.

"Tok…tok…tok…"

He turned and bowed to his queen before disappearing into the dark. Rebekah stood there, surprised by the feeling she now felt, stirred by the words of her raven.

How do you want to be remembered?

That was a question Rebekah had been asking herself all her life. And for that reason, she had always had an answer. The queen walked swiftly down the hall, through two solid oak doors, and was immediately inside her personal chambers. Never breaking stride, she grabbed a long, dark-hooded riding cloak draped across a nearby chair and strode toward the balcony just outside her room. She stepped up onto the railing and looked up at the moonlit sky.

So Luther despised belief in the Creators...

She whistled sharply into the darkness.

How do you want to be remembered?

She dove off the railing speaking the answer she had always had.

Better than this day.

She fell toward the garden below, weighing the eagle and the raven's advice.

Wiser than the others.

Knowing she would never swear an oath she would never keep.

Kinder than the rest.

She vowed not to hold back what she promised to give.

An eagle that soars rather than the scavenger who settles.

She would not fall prey to siding with one side of the clan or the other, but be a balance between them.

To do something great. To be someone unexpected.

She thought of King Palimus, and how he was not the balance within, but one who sided with the dark over the light. And for that reason alone, Rebekah vowed one, last thing: that she would be...*different than Palimus.*

THE LAIR

V

"**D**on't be afraid...don't be afraid..."

Marcus kept repeating the words to himself as he crossed the border into the woods of the Wolf Lair. Trees surrounded him on all sides as he moved through them. But the more silent he tried to be, the louder his footsteps became as they crunched loudly on the cold, hard ground.

In all his studies at The Den, this was the one lesson he wished he had paid more attention to — the climate in the different kingdoms of the realm. His little body trembled as he crept between the massive trees as his breath fogged on the icy air.

"HOOT! HOOT!"

Marcus froze at the sound. His teeth began to chatter — out of cold or fear, it was hard to tell — as he looked up at the surrounding trees seeing nothing but interlocking branches reaching up to the moonlit sky. The trees, however, seemed to be moving; shadows growing and shrinking all at once as his eyes roamed the foliage. Their branches looked like twisted fingers that no longer resembled crooked wood but skeletal bones…and they were all reaching out to him.

"HOOT! HOOT!"

The sound was directly behind him. He spun around, pointing his tiny sword toward the looming shadows that seemed to be dancing amongst the trees. Marcus began walking backward, on guard for the owl warriors that seemed to be following him from tree to tree. In his studies, his guardian — a lynx warrior named SinJin — had told him that the owl warriors were known for their magic. The more they hooted, the more confused their prey became, often losing their sense of direction the more the owls spoke their audible warning. It was at this moment that he understood what SinJin meant as he continued to look all around for the owl soldiers.

A wolf suddenly howled in the not-too-far distance.

Marcus whirled around and accidentally tripped over his own feet. He fell and tumbled down a large hill, careening into an enormous tree. His leg smashed against the thick wood of the trunk with a loud CRACK! Marcus cried out in pain.

His hand shook as he reached out to touch his leg. He gasped the moment his fingers felt a hard object sticking out from between the flesh. He adjusted his eyesight, seeing a sticky substance running down his leg, before realizing that the hard object he felt was his bone.

He tried to move; a sharp, shooting pain ripped through his tiny body. He cried out again and fell backward. Marcus looked all around the woods, only seeing large shadows moving amongst the trees. The owls were no longer hooting. All he heard was the silence as he sat there all alone. And with that realization, his tiny chest began to rise and fall rapidly as the panic and fear set in.

"How am I going to get home?"

Trembling uncontrollably from the pain and the cold, he sat up and took a closer look at his broken leg. He began to sob harder. "Nathan's gonna kill me."

SNAP!

Marcus froze as his heart plummeted to the floor. He could hear his heart hammering inside his little chest as he looked into the darkness from where he thought the sound had come from. His breath fogged endlessly as he grabbed for his sword amongst the heaping snow mounds…but he could not find it.

"Young lion, do not be afraid…"

It was a woman's voice.

The young prince looked all around for the source of the voice. Adjusting his cat-like eyes to the night, he looked before him and saw a hooded figure walking up the hill towards him. He frantically searched for his weapon. He spotted it lying a few feet above him further up the hill. Through the pain, he leaned backward and pulled his body up the hill as the figure continued moving toward him. He scrambled the last few inches, reached for his sword, managing to grab hold of it. He wielded it over his head and pointed it shakily at the approaching form.

"Stay back!"

The hooded figure reached inside her cloak and pulled a small silver object from inside. She hurled it straight at Marcus' hand, disarming him as he dropped his sword without so much as a fight. The small weapon shot past Marcus and wound back around the trees and into its shooter's hand — it was a small boomerang. As soon as she had it, the woman put the weapon back inside her cloak without once breaking stride.

"I'm not going to hurt you, young cub." The woman crouched down in front of Marcus and looked at his leg. "From the looks of your leg, it appears you've already done that yourself."

Marcus shouted in defense, trying to scramble back up the hill. "Stay back, She-wolf!"

"I am no wolf."

He stopped and eyed her suspiciously, "Then what are you doing in The Lair if you aren't from their pack? Who are you?"

"It is I who should be asking you those very same questions." She extended her gloved hand in an attempt to examine his leg. Marcus pushed himself backward, breathing hard in pain. He heard the wolves again and noticed they were getting closer.

"Young prince, I am not going to hurt you! Your blood has

seeped through your clothes and is dripping onto the ground. The wolves can smell it, as can the vultures."

Marcus looked up at the sky and saw a swarm of large bird warriors circling above him as their forms swirled across the moon.

"They're coming for you and they will have you unless you let me help you!"

He looked back at the woman, "Why did you call me prince?"

She lifted her gloved hand and pointed to the lion crest embroidered on his cloak. "Only members of the royal line wear such insignia. Either you are a prince or a thief to have such a cloak in your possession."

Marcus remained silent, admitting nothing.

"Tell me...what is your name?"

He refused to answer her.

"So you're a mute now, is that it?"

He growled slightly. "I am no mute! My name is Marcus. *Prince* Marcus of the Lion's Den. And if anything happens to me, my brother and my father and the whole Lion Guard will come to The Lair and avenge me!"

"I see."

The woman quickly searched the ground and sky, watching out for the vultures and the wolves. "And what is a lion doing crossing into enemy territory during the wolves' feeding hour? Hmm?? Either you are very brave or very foolish."

Marcus fell silent once again.

"Well, I hope it wasn't on a dare that you came venturing into the Wolf Lair. I have heard of many young lions that have crossed into these woods spurred by such an idea, but none of which have ever made it home. You are very lucky I was here or you would have been attacked already, but not by a wolf."

She stood and moved out of his line of sight so that all Marcus could see behind her was a large black tree. From the shadow at its base, a shape slowly came forth. Marcus gasped as a seven-foot-tall raven assassin emerged.

Marcus' eyes roamed the warrior's body, taking in his lethal humanoid form coloring his muscles with coal-colored feathers. His arms were bicepped like Nathan's, but wings jutted forth from beneath his triceps. His hands had five black, fingers — all of which were clawed and taloned. As Marcus' eyes flowed down to the raven's legs, he was reminded of the lion warriors from The Den. They were legs like humans, but far more muscular. Unlike the lions and tigers whose quadriceps and calves were thick with muscle, the ravens were long and lean.

Marcus whispered under his breath, "A bird warrior."

He looked up at the raven's face and saw the raven assassin's beak glistening in the moonlight — sleek and sharp. Marcus did not lose sight of the fact that the raven's eyes glowed red as they took in the sight of him sitting on the ground in enemy territory. The young woman stood calmly, listening to the sounds of the woods.

"Poe, we have a visitor from The Den."

"Tok...tok...tok..."

The raven's voice was one continuous rasp. Marcus was paralyzed as he watched Poe pull a dagger from his sable breastplate. His voice was gravelly and low, *"My enemy comesss tapping, rapping at my kingdom'sss door."*

He advanced upon the prince. Marcus froze in shock, unable to react.

"Poe..."

Poe halted.

"Put away your dagger. The shadow of death shall not touch Prince Marcus this night."

Poe stared at Marcus with his ruby red eyes.

"Yesss, my queen."

Marcus' eyes grow wide, *"QUEEN?!?"*

"You see, the prince only comes this once and will trespass these grounds no more...will you, young cub?"

Marcus shook his head fervently.

"Good."

She removed her black leather gloves from her hands. Marcus' eyes grew even wider the moment he saw what lay underneath. The queen caught his look. "Did you think I had talons?" She waved her fingers at him.

Marcus looked up at her dumbfounded; his cheeks already having turned pink from the cold, turned a shade darker.

"Oh yes, I've heard the stories. I'm sorry to disappoint you. They are merely fingers."

She moved toward him, looked up at the sky, and aligned her body with the moonlight. She crouched down to Marcus and gently laid her hand over his broken leg. He immediately tensed at her touch.

"Please don't eat me!"

She paused, "Why would I eat you?"

"My brother Nathan and his friends said you eat your own people, but little boys are your favorite."

Poe scoffed, *"Idiot lionsss! Your tongue should be pecked from your mouth for that insult to my queen!"*

Marcus looked between Poe and the queen, "So you don't have a beak?"

Poe lifted his dagger, gripping it tightly in his blacked-out talons. *"Let me do it, my queen."*

The queen looked over her shoulder and up toward the moon. "No, I don't have a beak, young lion, and am I not a cannibal. All I want to do is help you get home."

The queen closed her fingers around his bloodied leg. Marcus winced in pain.

"Now, hold very still."

She raised her hooded face to the moon and touched a golden medallion hanging from her neck. Marcus saw that it resembled the sun, and on opposite ends of the orb were the heads of an eagle and a raven — one head faced east and the other west. Poe stepped toward her the moment he realized what she was about to do. Still clutching his dagger tight, the feathers on his head rose and morphed into the shape of a mohawk.

"No, my queen! You are the remnant! Think of the clan!"

The queen leveled her eyes at him. "I *am*, Poe."

Poe's feathers lowered at the tone in her voice. She shifted her gaze toward Marcus, speaking in a softer tone, "This is going to hurt me more than it's going to hurt you."

Marcus nodded, although he did not understand what the queen meant by her words or what was about to happen. He stared at her long fingers as they rested gently over his bone. He breathed a little easier knowing that they were not clawed talons ready to rip him to shreds. He looked up at her cloaked face and saw her ruby-red lips smiling at him.

He smiled back, relieved in knowing it was not a beak, but a gentle acknowledgement of kindness. The queen's smile faded and Marcus could sense her body relaxing as he heard her inhale deeply. Poe stood behind her; his body tensed as he watched his queen with a look of dread.

The queen lifted her head to the sky…and the world seemed to answer her. Marcus immediately felt the wind blow through the trees, swirling around them faster and faster — and around them alone.

Marcus looked at Poe and saw the raven warrior close his eyes and bow his head, in reverence or respect, Marcus did not know. He felt the ground underneath him begin to shift and move, although the queen and the raven remained still, barely even noticing, if at all. He looked down at the twigs and the snow and saw movement beneath them. Suddenly frightened, he looked up at the queen and saw her lift her head to the moonlight. She stretched one hand up to the light while the other rested on Marcus' leg. With the wind and earth moving all around him, Marcus' focus shifted to the queen's medallion. It suddenly began to glow. It continued to shine brighter and brighter until Marcus had to turn away from the glare as the medallion suddenly ignited in flame. A white light struck down like lightning, followed by a loud SNAP!

He shut his eyes and cried out in pain...but nothing happened. There was no pain. Marcus opened his eyes, moving his leg all around, rubbing his hands up and down the new skin. In disbelief, he stood up and began jumping up and down to test his weight.

"You fixed it!"

Marcus looked down and saw the queen crouched down holding her arm in pain. Poe was beside her, clutching the same arm as he shared in her pain. He was breathing hard. *"I feel it, my queen. I beg of you, do not wassste your gift on the unworthy. The clan cannot take it."*

Marcus knelt down beside her, "Are you hurt?"

Poe shifted his scarlet eyes to Marcus; his eyes were accusing as he looked at the prince.

The queen answered, her voice very faint, "Only for a moment."

Poe's feathers rose straight up as his head spun around toward the direction of the trees. *"The wolvesss approach."*

He swiveled his head back around toward his queen. Without saying a single word, they locked eyes. He nodded his head in understanding, completely in tune with what her will desired. Poe immediately rose and spread his arms wide; his feathers unfolded around his muscular arms as he vaulted into the sky. The queen watched as he flew north toward the vultures. The moment he reached them, they scattered like flies. She continued to watch as Poe flew north toward her kingdom.

"What is your name, Bird Queen?"

She looked at the young lion prince as he knelt beside her. "My name is Rebekah."

Marcus stood and bowed low to her. "Thank you, Queen Rebekah of the Bird Clan. I, Prince Marcus of the Lion's Den, am forever indebted to you. This night, you are no longer my enemy. I shall call you...friend."

He rose and extended his little hand to help her up. She grabbed onto it and stood. "I thank you for your gratitude and accept your offer of friendship Prince Marcus of the Lion's Den. You are brave."

The moment he heard these words, Marcus beamed at her. She curtsied to him in return. He could see her ruby-colored lips smiling from behind her hood. But as she rose from her royal gesture, he could see her smile slowly begin to fade. She moved swiftly past Marcus and up the hill where she saw two torches in the distance.

"Your people...they are coming for you..."

Marcus turned and saw the flames winding between the trees. "How do you know?"

Her eyes never left the torches. "Who else would come to The Lair at this time of night? Their fire will be the death of them!"

A lone wolf howled closely behind them. Hearing the sound, Rebekah recognized the call of the captain.

Rebekah whirled around; her hood fell back down onto her shoulders, revealing her very human face. Marcus gasped in surprise as her dark hair and gray eagle eyes illuminated in the moonlight.

"You must go! *Quickly!* Get to your people! The Wolf Pack is coming!"

Marcus' eyes grew wide, *"THE WOLF PACK?!?!?"*

"Go!!!"

Marcus turned and raced up the hill faster than he had ever run in his life. His eyes focused on the torches up ahead. As he raced across the snow, the wolves' howling and growling seemed to rise up around him all at once. He could see the trees swaying in the distance as enormous shadows seemed to be moving between them...and fast.

"Tok...tok...tok..."

Poe.

Marcus looked up into the sky as he ran, seeing the raven assassin overhead. He could not tell if the large warrior was there to protect him or lead the wolves directly to him. Remembering the Old War, he decided to run faster.

Rebekah turned from where she stood and saw the Wolf Pack racing forth on their two legs as they bounded down from between the trees. Having seen Poe's return, she whistled sharply to the sky, summoning a different warrior. She ran down the hill toward a large, black lake. The moment she reached its shores, she jumped. Reginald swooped down and caught his queen as he dove underneath her. She straddled his back as they vaulted into the sky just as the Wolf Pack rushed past.

Marcus continued charging up the hill. He slipped on the snow-covered landscape and slid back down the way he had come.

"Marcus!!!"

Marcus immediately recognized the voice. *"NATHAN!!!"*

He heard a lion roar. Storming down through the twisted trees were Apollo, captain of the Lion Guard, and Roman — a tiger warrior.

"Apollo! Over here!"

A cacophony of wolves growling and barking echoed forth from the shadows of the trees.

Apollo charged down the hill, dropping on all fours, sliding down the hill at Marcus' feet. "On my back, young one!"

Marcus replied, "I can run!"

"There is no time!"

Roman was suddenly at their side bearing a torch and a sword in his massive paw-like hands. He immediately growled and bared his teeth as he stared into the darkness behind Apollo and Marcus. Marcus, terrified, slowly turned his head. Looking over his shoulder, he saw the silver and golden glow of several pairs of eyes mirroring in the moonlight.

Apollo slowly turned around and came face to face with the Wolf Pack.

Between his legs, Marcus could feel the heat rising up from the lion warrior's body. A low rumble rose from the lion's chest as he stared at the pack. Marcus looked out into the darkness and saw the movement within as the beasts moved through the trees as they crept and leapt between them. It did not take any of them very long to see that they were completely surrounded as the shadowed forms of the Wolf Pack emerged. They were on all fours — hyenas and wolves of every kind. At the head of the pack was the alpha — the largest wolf in the group — the captain — a timber wolf named Skoll.

His yellow eyes were seething in utter fury as he took in the lion and tiger warriors.

"*Lions!* Coming to pay homage to the Wolf Lair! More and more continue to cross where they do not belong..."

Approaching quietly from behind the trees, Nathan emerged.

Upon seeing the lion prince, the hyenas began to bark and the wolves growled lowly. Nathan stood in front of his warriors and faced the wolf captain. He shouted over the barks, "We mean no harm!"

Nathan's voice thundered across the woods, commanding power and respect. Skoll's sharp fangs dripped with saliva, prepping for the slaughter as the claws on his paw-like hands emerged. Nathan moved his hand toward the hilt of his sword.

Skoll spat out the words, "Lions always mean harm! Mercy is never spared in The Den…nor shall it be in The Lair! *Enemy…mine!!!*"

Skoll barked once…and the pack responded.

A wolf named Freki and three hyenas lunged from the shadows of the trees and pounced on Apollo, while the remaining six wolves advanced on Roman. Marcus was knocked violently to the ground.

"Behind me, Marcus!"

Nathan grabbed Marcus and shielded him as Skoll lowered his wolf head and lunged at them.

Just as Skoll was about to tackle Nathan and Marcus, a large golden eagle warrior swooped down and snatched up Marcus, followed by a second golden eagle that grabbed for Nathan. Skoll slammed into the icy ground and rolled down the hill, careening into a tree.

He rose onto his two hind legs, reaching over eight feet tall, and saw that both princes were no longer there. He raged to the sky as the Thunderbirds soared across the moon carrying the princes west.

Another golden eagle dove down and headed straight for the tiger warrior, snatching him up from the wolves. Apollo alone remained, battling it out with the hyenas as they continued to tear the flesh from his powerful body. Skoll saw the lion captain and bounded up the hill to join in the attack. He was almost to the top of the hill when a loud shrill echoed across the moonlit sky.

The pack looked skyward, their teeth completely covered in lion fur and meat. Skoll growled viciously the moment he saw the bald eagle's form fly past the moon.

"Reginald…"

He barked to his pack.

The wolves and hyenas howled as he approached, relinquishing their merciless attack on Apollo. The pack slowly retreated back into the forest as Apollo watched them go. The lion warrior was badly beaten; blood soaked through his fur in several places as much of his muscle and flesh had been torn away. His breath fogged on the cool night air as he struggled through the pain. A low, pitiful growl was his only reply as he collapsed onto the ground. Breathing hard, he tried to remain conscious as his breathing slowed bit by bit. He could see a pair of eyes mirroring from a nearby tree.

From the shadows, Skoll's lethal voice echoed from across the forest, "Dare to trespass again, *cat*, and I'll rip your throat out...just as your king's was long ago."

The lion warrior passed out.

Reginald suddenly dove in and lifted Apollo's body from the woods and carried him across the moonlit sky. From the trees, Poe watched as his captain headed toward The Den.

Reginald heard the painful moaning of the lion warrior draped across his back. They were about to cross illegally into enemy territory. It was the first time Reginald had ever been on this side of the realm — and his heart was pounding. He led the Thunderbirds as they soared silently toward The Den. Watching the moon, he knew the dawn would soon be coming. He flew even faster.

Looking off in the distance as he flew past Mariner Tower, he could see the landscape changing. The colors shifted from white to green to a pale brown as he entered the Lion's Den. The trees had vanished, going from the bare bones of winter, to the forests of spring, to the flat ground of summer with nothing but dirt and grass-filled plains.

He dove down just as the sun's rays shone on the horizon. Following their captain's lead, the Thunderbirds swooped down into the courtyard and gently laid the princes, Roman, and Apollo down onto the ground before any lion soldier in The Den could react. They soared silently back into the sky; not even the flap of their enormous wings could be heard. Marcus watched them go just as the sun began to rise. A jaguar soldier guarding the gate caught sight of the bodies lying in the courtyard. He growled up at the sky and banged a loud drum. He jumped down from the gate and rushed to his princes' sides.

"My lords!"

He and other clan warriors, having heard the drum, raced toward their princes and guards. Nathan sat up and watched the eagle captain fly past the rising sun as Reginald and the Thunderbirds headed north. He watched in silence, too stunned to say a word. It was the first time he had actually seen a bird warrior — his enemy — and he had not been devoured by it. He had been saved.

Marcus rushed over to him, "It was the bird queen, Nathan. She saved us!"

Nathan looked down at his younger brother, the sudden realization of what had just happened hitting him full force. He grabbed his brother's cloak in his fists. *"Marcus!"*

Apollo's pained growl sounded as the jaguar soldiers tried to stir him. Nathan looked over at the captain of his guard. He released his hold on Marcus and scrambled over to Apollo. Taking in the massive injuries Apollo had sustained, Nathan could barely speak.

Seeing the look on his prince's face, Apollo whispered, "Fear not, my prince. I will heal."

Apollo closed his eyes, feeling his prince's strength flow through his veins. Nathan commanded the jaguars, "Take him to the infirmary."

A loud roar sounded from behind the courtyard gate. Nathan closed his eyes, recognizing the tone. Two panther and two cheetah warriors burst through the doors; storming behind them and heading toward Apollo was his father — the lion king.

The panthers and cheetahs rushed toward Apollo. The panther chief examined the lion captain's wounds. He rested his blackened hand over the great captain's chest. He growled low and deep, nodding to the other soldiers.

The Lion King Gunthar roared upon approach, *"OUT OF THE WAY!!!"*

The king stopped the guard and examined the captain. Seeing the brutal wounds, he shouted across The Den, *"WHO IS RESPONSIBLE FOR THIS?!?!"*

Roman looked to Nathan. Nathan shook his head in warning. The tiger nodded in understanding and remained silent.

Nathan moved toward the king, "Father…"

Gunthar continued to shout as he took in the wounds, "I haven't seen such marks in ages!"

His eyes slit to a cat the moment he recognized the marks, "Only hyenas could take a lion down!"

He whirled around and shouted at the panthers, "They've

breeched the borders! *GUARDS!!!*"

A battalion of tiger and cheetah soldiers vaulted and leapt over the courtyard walls, summoned by the call of their king. They surrounded Gunthar, awaiting his next command — one of retaliation and revenge. Seeing the lustful look of battle behind their feline eyes, Nathan placed his hand on his father's chest, "Father, the hyenas did not breach the border. It was *I* who crossed over into theirs."

Marcus rushed up behind Nathan to protest, but Nathan shoved him back behind him. Gunthar took in his handsome son's strong face. "*You?* You crossed over into The Lair?"

"It was foolish of me, I know. But with the treaty...all the stories of The Lair...curiosity got the best of me." He lowered his head. "I deeply regret doing it. Especially with the pain it caused Apollo."

The lion king grabbed hold of his son's face and lifted it so that they were eye to eye. He looked him dead in the eye, as if by this fierce look alone he could will the truth out of a lie, but Nathan offered up no further explanation. Gunthar pulled his son's head toward his and patted him hard on the side of his face.

"My son..."

Moments passed before the king suddenly broke out into a large grin followed by a deep, roaring laughter. He turned toward the soldiers still waiting for his command.

"HA! Your prince ventured into The Lair!"

The feline warriors growled their approval in reply. Still holding onto Nathan's head, he spoke lowly at his son, "You are brave, yes...you are brave. What other son of mine could have crossed into the Wolf Lair and come back alive. Yes...a strong king you will be."

He turned back toward the guard, "Ha! A king to rule all! Look to your brother, Marcus! Bravery in the face of death is the mark of a king!"

And with a wave of his hand, Gunthar called off his guard.

"But Apollo..."

Gunthar rested his hand on Nathan's shoulder in understanding at his son's concern, "Apollo will heal, Nathan. That lion is chief of his own clan. He will heal."

The king looked west. "I'll have to send an explanation to the wolf king that it was all a test of bravery. With that rascal of a son of his, Alexander, he'll understand."

Nathan alone nodded in reply.

Gunthar smiled at his sons, "Not to worry. I won't say a word of this to your mother." The lion king headed across the courtyard leading his soldiers back inside The Den. The jaguars carried Apollo back to the infirmary; Roman followed swiftly behind leaving Marcus and Nathan alone.

Nathan was utterly exhausted. He rubbed his head, realizing his adrenalin had suddenly slowed. His limbs dropped in heaviness, suddenly refusing to move upon command. He was overcome by fear, by guilt, by anger, and by surprise. He looked up at the sun, still in shock that he was alive at this moment to see it again. It was the most beautiful sunrise of his life.

Marcus stared at Nathan, "Why didn't you tell him that Queen Rebekah saved us?"

Nathan looked down at his little brother, seeing the innocence behind his eyes as he had yet to understand the repercussion of his single act that had caused a ripple effect across the lives of all involved. How he wished to be that unaffected, only seeing the good of what truly lay beneath it.

"Marcus, Father would never believe it. I don't even know if I believe it."

He shook his weary head, trying to make sense of it.

"The Bird Clan is our sworn enemy. Father and any one of the other kings and queens this side of the realm would take this as a sign of attack against our family if you mention that clan — with or without the treaty."

Nathan could feel his anger rising as he relived the moments in The Lair where he saw Apollo and Roman getting torn apart.

"They would call for retaliation that would lead to war. I don't want to be held responsible for the deaths and slaughter of innocent people just because you decided to spend the night in the woods! Father is trying to seek peace. Look at what happened to Apollo! That could have been you! That could have been me! And for what?"

Marcus' lip began to tremble. "I just wanted to show you...that I was brave...like you."

He started to cry. Nathan pulled him close and wrapped his arms around him, picking him up in his strong, muscular arms.

"You are brave, Marcus...braver than me."

He turned and carried his younger brother back inside The Den with no further argument.

THE WOLF
VI

Queen Rebekah sat on the marble floor of her personal chambers setting up a chessboard for play. Reginald stood silently in the corner watching her without really seeing her; his powerful arms were crossed over his powerful chest; he was deep in thought.

"Reginald, you've been quiet all day."

"I am deeply troubled, my queen."

She leaned back against the large velvet cushion propped up behind her. "Speak your mind, my friend. I'm inclined to hear it."

Reginald immediately began to pace the room, "Those lions are not the first to have crossed where they should not have ventured."

"You're referring to the murders along the borders."

He stopped dead in his tracks.

"Yes, my queen. This talk of hunger and starvation, famine on the lands of the lesser clans near the Lion's Den and Gorilla Jungle, but my eyes have searched the borders, and I have found nothing of the sort. The land is healthy."

She smiled coyly at him, "When did you do that? That's illegal, you know."

The white feathers near his beak turned a shade of pink.

"I thought it would be wise to take advantage of last night's unfortunate event, especially since you have asked for proof."

"And wisely so. I'm glad you surveyed the borders, it helps me understand the kind of people and kings I am about to deal with. I hate the unknown, especially when I have a thing or two to say about it."

He nodded gratefully at her.

She continued, "And what of the lands further *in* The Den and jungle?"

Reginald smiled shyly, "I did not venture that far into enemy territory. Only as far as the dam and canals go as they lead out from Mariner Sea."

Rebekah tapped her finger against the old, oak table, deep in thought. "And yet so many bulls and amphibians are crossing over onto our side of the realm." She leaned forward, taking in the pieces of the chessboard. "Strange...they're slaughtered before finding solace here according to Poe. Ivan, Khan and Rayford swear no one from our clans is responsible for it, which means there's only one conclusion if Poe is right…they were killed by their own clan and dropped here for us to find." She stared at the king piece on the opposite end of the board. "But what for? If not for food, why would so many dare to cross illegally onto our territories to then kill their own kind?"

"I do not know, my queen. Perhaps the famine is true. That is why the lion king has called for a truce amongst the clans so that a new treaty can truly be written."

Her gray eyes narrowed. "Yes, a treaty for my clan to feed the rest."

A deep frown settled upon her face.

"What is it, my queen?"

"The rumor of famine arising from drought would only be true if there was no water. My birds bring the rain that fills the sea…"

"And we have never stopped bringing it. The mariners have no control over the dam or the canals — the gorillas and lions do."

Her eyes locked onto his, "Correction. You mean the amphibians and the bulls. Gunthar and Brutus ordered the lesser clans to take on the responsibility almost a year ago. And they also allowed them *weapons*."

Reginald lowered his large head, "Forgive me, my queen. I had not recalled that."

"You were growing a new beak then. There is nothing to forgive." She grabbed hold of her medallion and held it gently in her hands as she stared at the shape of the sun. "I wonder…"

Reginald tilted his large head inquisitively in her direction, wondering what it was she was about to say. He loved moments like these when his queen was working out some problem inside her head. She always seemed to come up with just the right answer at just the right moment. Her wisdom was one he relished in, feeling as if the eagle within her was most alive at such times as these.

"Tell me, Reginald, what are the water levels in the Mariner Sea like?"

Reginald's pupils enlarged, understanding her meaning.

"Perhaps, we should send Ratatosk to the dam. Have him report the sea levels there. He will be safe on our side."

"And if the levels are normal, my queen?"

She sat back against her large cushion, "Then we know it's the *canals* that are the problem, Reginald."

Reginald smiled proudly at her, nodding in agreement at her unspoken thought. "As always, you are very wise indeed. I shall have Chief Rayford send him immediately."

He bowed, extended his enormous wings, and flew across the room and out through the balcony. Rebekah continued to stare at the king piece on the opposite end of the board.

She spoke softly to herself, "What kind of kings am I dealing with?"

The cock guard outside her chamber doors crowed twice, sounding the arrival of her guest.

A deep, masculine voice shouted from the halls, *"REBEKAH!"*

A dashing, athletic-looking young man with jet-black hair and striking blue eyes burst inside the room. He threw his riding cloak and leather gloves down on the floor and continued over toward the queen.

"I come home from a long, unwanted trip to find a mob of angry wolves at my father's door. What happened?"

The Wolf Prince Alexander immediately sat down across from Rebekah and moved his pawn forward.

Rebekah smiled at him, "I missed you."

Alexander did not even bother to look up from the board, "Don't change the subject, woman, spill..."

"Princes from the Lion's Den crossed the borders into your father's woods."

Alexander lifted his ice blue eyes and stared at her steadily. She moved her pawn.

"Go on."

"*Wolf*, didn't you hear me?"

"How do you know they were royalty?"

"They were wearing the royal emblem. Your wolves were on the hunt. I have a feeling they wouldn't have bothered to look at the crest before they attacked. Then we'd be talking war at this moment."

Alexander's face remained set, "What were they doing on my land?"

Rebekah sat back and took in the serious look on his face, "The youngest cub ventured into your woods on a dare."

"What kind of dare?"

Rebekah tried to hide her smile, "A quest of bravery. Either that or to see if I really had a bird beak for a nose."

"You're joking."

"Apparently, I have talons for fingers and I eat my own people for dinner."

Alexander suddenly burst out laughing. "Why, that is sheer treason, Rebekah! You should have let my wolves eat him alive for that remark!"

"Poe wanted to peck his eyes out. Poor young prince...he was terrified. And I'm glad. I doubt his experience last night would be anything he would ever want to repeat again."

Alexander looked at her pensive face. "What's with the look, bird?"

The jovial expression on the queen's face slowly dissipated. "Seeing that lion in your woods and everyone's reaction to the entire episode made all the history of the last two hundred years come forth." She looked up at Alexander, "All I've ever wanted is to raise my kingdom up again. To be known as a clan of honor — one that can be trusted by all. Yet I've never done anything to make that happen. And now my enemy, the lion king, is the one giving me the opportunity to do it...and I am hesitating. I don't know that signing his treaty is something good. It's too easy a victory."

Alexander reached across the board and took her hand in his. "Building your house?"

Rebekah smiled faintly.

"Trust your instincts, Rebekah. They have always served you well, even saving that young lion's life. You did the right thing, no matter how many wolves howl and scrape at my door. Besides, that's why I'm really here tonight. I need some peace and quiet."

He moved his knight. She leaned in and moved her horse.

"Oh, and sorry."

"For what?"

"I was the one that started that rumor…about you having a beak."

"Alexander!"

"How was I to know that only ignorant lions would be the ones to believe it. Besides, it was years ago."

"Speaking of rumors, how was your trip?"

Alexander stared at the board, refusing to look up. "Long."

"For good reason from what I hear."

Alexander slowly lifted his eyes, "And what did you hear?"

"Oh, nothing much…"

"Bird…"

She tried not to smile. "Well, there's a rumor going around of a certain engagement. Care to confirm?"

Alexander looked back at the board. "Nope."

He moved his knight again.

Rebekah continued to bait him. "Marriage to the princess of mariners, cousin...that is quite a bit of news. No wonder you're tired...a life-changing moment."

He eyed her. "My parents may be your godparents, but we are not kin. Stop calling me cousin."

She moved her other pawn. "So moody...does your bride-to-be have fins and gills that are making you so cross this evening?"

Alexander sat back against his matching cushion. "No more than you have talons and a beak. Keep mocking me, Rebekah, your time will come soon enough."

Rebekah's gray eyes grew wide. "Ha! There's no man in the realm I wish to marry!"

Alexander raised his eyebrow, *"None?"*

Rebekah leveled her eyes at him, "I am destined to remain single in my queendom."

Alexander sensed her annoyance and decided to now bait her. "Well then, you should know that your godparents would never allow it. They feel responsible for you and your happiness. And they think happiness is only found in marriage."

Rebekah tapped her finger on the board in annoyance, "Why do they think that?"

"Because they're old. Now that they're marrying me off, I'm sure my mother and father are dying to draw up a contract for you as well."

He suddenly captured her pawn.

Rebekah did not see the move coming. "I am a *queen*! They are not entitled to act on my behalf. I am of age and have ruled my clan for quite some time. If and when I wish to marry, it will be the man of my choosing!"

Rebekah pursed her ruby-colored lips and tried to concentrate on the board. Seeing her worked up, Alexander continued to goad her, relishing in the moment. "King Brutus?"

Rebekah looked at him in disgust, "*Brutus?* That man already has a dozen wives. Not to mention a harem of a dozen others in that jungle of his."

"Well, beak or no beak you *are* harem material. And a harem isn't as scandalous as you think, Rebekah."

She threw a small cushion at him.

He laughed as he knocked it way, "I didn't say *I* wanted one. Besides, Brutus is the only king still on the hunt for more queens."

Her face contorted into a further look of abhorrence. "Are there any men left in the realm who are actually noble and, and…respectable?"

"Noble and respectable? Rebekah, you sound like a poem only a woman would write."

"This is so disheartening."

Alexander stared at her pensive face, all mischief dwindling from behind his eyes, "Well, if you don't want to marry him, there's always the alternative…"

She continued to stare at the board. "Hmm?"

Alexander's eyes never left her face. "Marry me."

She slowly lifted her eyes and looked into the wolf prince's handsome face. After several moments of silence, she tapped her finger on the table and began nodding her head. A small smile spread across her face, "Oh, I see..." She sat back against her cushion.

"What?"

She pointed her long finger at him, "Your ploy. You're not getting out of your engagement that easily."

Alexander crossed his lean arms over his muscular chest; he exhaled angrily, "We are not officially engaged, Rebekah. I haven't signed the contract."

"Why not?"

He leveled his eyes at her, "You're not the only one building your house."

She leaned in toward the board and captured his knight. "And what is the cornerstone upon which you will build yours?"

He reached across the board and took her hand in his. Slowly, he brought it to his lips. His ice-blue eyes seemed to glow as he spoke, "Passion, dear lady. Passion." He kissed her hand softly.

"There's more to life than your kind of passion, Alex."

He smiled wryly, "No, woman...there's not."

She pulled her hand away. "Well then, if your lady is anywhere near as beautiful as that sea she lives in, you should sign your contract and get on with that passion."

"Bird, do you think me so shallow?"

"Alexander, you're a *wolf*. Of course I think you're shallow."

With the moment now gone, Alexander sat back in defeat, "Then I'll have you know, that although a mariner from a beautiful sea, she's the princess of apes."

Rebekah roared in laughter, "No! You lie!"

Alexander gritted his teeth, "You'll see soon enough when we go to The Den. Marry me...marry me now, Rebekah."

She laughed long and hard. "Oh, Alex…"

Alexander could not help but smile at the sound of her laughter — she was the only one who could bring it out of him — a smile. He had missed her. Being around her was the only time he was truly happy. And being near her now, he was at peace.

"Speaking of lions, you could always marry that lion pup you found in the woods and accomplish your goal of changing the clan's name from enemy and betrayer to champion and friend."

"Or cradle robber."

Alexander's smile broadened at her retort.

"But you do bring up a good point."

"How's that?"

"I do hear he has an *older* brother."

Alexander's smile faded fast. "You can't mean *Nathan*."

"Is that his name?"

Alexander refused to say another word. He knew all about the handsome lion prince. All the women in Gorilla Jungle talked of nothing but the lion prince. How charming he was. How manly he was. How powerful he would one day be when he took the throne. This was not the conversation he hoped to engage in when he arrived this evening, and he was in no mood to continue on its path now. So he suddenly rose from the floor and began walking back toward the hallway.

Rebekah looked up in surprise, "Where are you going?"

"I'm tired."

"But the moon is still out."

He shouted back at her as he picked up his gloves and cloak from the floor, *"I'm tired!"*

He left the room and headed down the hall toward the designated quarters he assigned himself when he and Rebekah were children. Rebekah watched him go, mumbling under her breath, "Somebody's cranky this evening."

Alexander yelled from across the hall, *"I can hear you, Rebekah!"*

She smiled faintly and whispered even lower, "That's because you're a big cranky wolf."

"I can still hear you."

Rebekah continued to whisper, "Good night, Alexander. I'm glad you're home."

In a lighter tone he replied, *"Good night."*

Ratatosk — a squirrel warrior — and a few other critter clan soldiers reached the outer rim of Mariner Dam on the border of Bird Clan territory. The river was flowing powerfully forth from the sea and out through the canals. Ratatosk and his squadron of chipmunk and raccoon warriors looked up at the massive dam and their connecting canals that stretched out across their side of the realm.

Ratatosk took in the height of the wall, feeling uneasy about what he saw before him. "These walls are higher than when I saw them last. Wait here."

He began to climb the wall while his soldiers stood watch, bearing small torches in their furry hands. They seemed to wait for what seemed like hours as Ratatosk climbed to the top of the dam.

While standing guard, one of the chipmunks suddenly caught an unfamiliar odor lingering in the air. The whiskers around his nose began twitching as he attempted to decipher the scent.

A raccoon warrior noticed him sniffing, "What is it?"

"Not sure."

A low snort sounded behind them. The chipmunk and raccoon soldiers whirled around, pulling their swords from their sheaths as they looked out toward the direction of the sound. The odor was stronger now, causing each of the warriors' whiskers to rapidly twitch as they, too, tried to decipher the scent.

Even from the roaring sound of the sea, they knew that whatever it was, it was close enough for them to have heard it so clearly. It was almost as if the beast's breath infected them as they faced the unknown.

Squinting into the darkness beyond, all they could see was a dark shadow blending in near the base of the dam. They listened closer. One of the soldiers decided to hurl his torch into the darkness. It slammed into a large black barrier before dropping to the ground. The critter soldiers gathered closer together, wielding their weapons tight. It was then that they saw the beast's enormous hoof step over the torch, and his full ten-foot-tall frame emerged.

The warrior beast lowered his horned head and charged straight for the critter soldiers. A loud screech pierced the silence, slicing through the cool, night air.

Ratatosk was crouched low, having heard the loud shriek. He looked down but could only make out the small flames burning on the torches. They reminded him of small matches. Seeing no further movement, he leapt swiftly across the top of the dam and over toward the first canal. He looked down into the sea, feeling uneasy as he scaled to the top of the wall. He crouched down, gripping his small dagger in his tiny fingers. He had felt them — the eyes, eyes that watched him from the sea.

Ratatosk squinted into the murky water, waiting for confirmation. He searched down below, watching the darkened waves rise and fall. He knew they were there. And because he knew it, he knew he had to act fast. Ratatosk glided swiftly across the top of the wall and over toward the canal. The moment he reached it, he looked over the ridge from where the water poured out from the sea. His eyes narrowed, and his face grew grave at the picture he saw before him. *"King..."*

SPLASH!

Ratatosk whirled around and faced the sea. His eyes quickly scanned the top of the wall from where he stood, looking to see if the mariner warrior had emerged from his home, but he found nothing and no one; only the rolling waves of the darkened waters below. He crept slowly across the top of the dam, checking for any sign of the mariner warrior. Far out in the center of the sea, he could see Mariner Tower rising up from the rolling waves. It was lit up from all sides; the fire reflecting off of its ivory walls. It was beautiful yet ominous at the same time, like morbid beauty often was. The guardians of the tower roamed the sea, for the gate to the kingdom was underwater, only able to be breached if one could swim long enough to fight their way inside or ride the waves toward the tower in order to swiftly break through its guarded doors.

Where are you?

Ratatosk continued to search for the shark warrior.

He was about to turn back toward the canal when he saw them. There was not just one warrior, but a fleet of them. Barely rising up to the surface of the water were twenty shark fins. And they were not circling as they were often known to do, but were perfectly still, all facing Ratatosk, watching him from the murky waters.

It was a face-off, and Ratatosk was outnumbered. But being a squirrel warrior, he was fast, faster than a shark if he could make it to the nearby canal before they vaulted out of the sea to attack — and he knew within his very bones that that was exactly what they were aiming to do.

Ratatosk waited, not even breathing as he watched the fins. One of them suddenly disappeared, sinking slowly down into the sea. He knew it meant the warrior had dove down into the depths of the sea to gain momentum. One by one, the fins began to sink down into the sea. Without waiting to see what would happen next, Ratatosk dove off the top of the wall just as a great, white shark leapt up from the sea, followed by three more warriors. Ratatosk landed in the canal, plunging underwater as the force from the tide carried him away from the dam. He popped his head up, trying to catch his breath. That was when he saw all four warriors dive into the canal after him.

They were catching up quickly as they wove underneath the water, gliding with the tide. They were going to catch him.

Ratatosk looked all around him as he passed a multitude of rocks and trees, barely recognizing the landscape. He grabbed for a branch overhead but lost his grip as the force of the tide continued to pull him down and away from Mariner Sea. He grabbed for another branch and held on tight.

He back-flipped out of the water and landed on the branch of the tree. He flew from branch to branch, tree to tree as he tried to veer away from the waterways. He felt a spear zip past his head. Then another. And another. He leapt for another tree and felt the tip of the spear skim the armor on his underbelly. He landed on another branch and turned around to face the mariners.

Standing atop the canals were the shark warriors. On their two massive legs, they reached over nine-feet-tall. Ratatosk had never seen a shark warrior standing, for they never ventured beyond the dam. Seeing one of the spears embedded in the trunk of one the trees nearby, he realized, they did not just learn to use their weapons. They had been using them all along.

The shark warriors dove back into the canals and swam upstream back toward Mariner Dam. It was then that Ratatosk breathed a sigh of relief, but it was only short-lived. As he looked around at the land beyond the trees, he saw that it was flat ground with no foliage for coverage. It was then that he realized which canal he had jumped in, and where the canal had taken him — straight into the Lion's Den.

RATATOSK
VII

Ratatosk was exhausted. His small body could barely move, feeling the weight of his tired limbs as he trudged across The Den. He was delirious, half drunk, having had no sleep in the last two days.

Get to Ume.

After landing on the Lion's Den side, Ratatosk ran as fast as his four-foot frame could carry him as he attempted to find cover in the grass-filled plains. With very few trees and barely enough grass tall enough to hide behind or conceal him, he sprinted and crouched over and over again, hoping to gain ground in the moonlight before the sun rose. Using a small compass his father had given him, he continued moving north to the Great Mountains that bordered Bird Kingdom.

Get to Ume. Get to the ostrich chief...

Once the sun had risen after that first night, Ratatosk had a hard time travelling long distances, laying low to the ground amongst the grass as the day wore on, moving inch by inch, trying not to draw attention to himself while the female lioness warriors were out hunting during the day.

He had crossed the Lion's Den fortress unseen, passing through Panther Prairie; he was now in Tigerland. From there, he would reach the Great Mountains. The ostrich warriors lived closest to the rocky domain — and they were fierce. Guarding the border, the twenty-foot-tall warriors could cover ground almost as swiftly as the cheetahs, attacking their enemy and their prey with the swiftest of movements; their only weakness was their long necks. It made them easy targets for beheadings.

Being a squirrel warrior, he covered ground quickly where he could, but now that night had fallen, he could feel his body running out of steam. He had not eaten in two days, and had yet to find any nuts or berries to feast upon as he crossed The Den.

It was almost dawn.

Ratatosk dragged his body slowly up a grass-covered hill, feeling as if his body moved slower than time as he inched his way up the mound of dirt. He tried to focus his mind on the task ahead. Even if he never made it back home, he had to report what he had seen. He had to let the bird queen know.

"Get...to...Ume..."

He took one step more when his heart skipped a beat. Before his tiny ebony eyes, he saw them, he saw the mountains.

Almost there.

He felt the rush of blood pump through his veins as his limbs slowly came back to life, resurrected from the dead as he saw the light at the end of the tunnel. He would get there. He would cross the mountains and border. He would tell Ume all that he had seen.

He was going to make it.

Ratatosk moved forward, his body fueled by a renewed sense of purpose. The sky was changing from dark to light blue. The sun was rising, which meant only one thing…feeding time.

Must hurry…

He clasped the compass in his hand, willing the help of his ancestors to protect him and give him the strength to push on. From the hilltop to the mountain border, there was only open ground — it would be a Russian roulette game to make it to the border before the sun had completely risen. Gathering up all the strength he had left, Ratatosk knew there was no other choice but to take his chances…and run.

Ratatosk shot down the hill, sprinting faster than his body had ever gone. His ears were attuned to the sound of approaching danger, and his eyes were set on the mountains ahead.

Get to the mountains.

There, he could climb and leap faster than a tiger. There, he could hide and scamper within a make-shift cave. There, he would be in his element. There, he knew he would make it home.

His heart was pounding against his tiny chest so hard, he feared the tigers would hear the thumping. The blood was now circulating all throughout his muscles, pumping through his small body, fueling his limbs as he raced on — that was when he felt it, that was when he sensed it...*the eyes of an unknown enemy.*

Don't stop!

He could feel the dry air burning inside his lungs, but he ran faster and faster still. And as Ratatosk raced across the plains, he could see that the ground beneath him was all the same — flat and brown. Realizing he could see color, he looked at the sky and saw it had turned from blue to peach.

The sun was rising — and the tigers would soon be coming.

Only in paintings did these things exist. Only in books had she read their histories and philosophies. Flying atop of Reginald, soaring over borders she had never crossed, Rebekah's heart was filled with excitement, wonder, and yes — a little bit of fear.

"Reginald, look! The Amphibian Swamps!"

Both the queen and her captain peered down at the dark crystal waters and bamboo forest below that housed the inhabitants of the lesser clan. The lion king, ensuring welcome and safety if they came by way of the swamps and through Bull Valley in route to

The Den, had paved the road for their crossing.

Led by the Thunderbirds, Rebekah felt both guarded and free as she breathed in the unknown world before her. The strangest feeling fell upon her, it was almost as if this world, this realm, were a part of her and she a part of it. And the realm seemed a little less scary, a little less big, but a place where she felt a deep connection. As if every clan and every kingdom were somehow a part of who she was and she a part of them. It was a feeling she breathed in and pondered in her heart as she flew past the swamps and onto the rocky terrain of Bull Valley.

"Crittersss, my queen..."

Rebekah looked down at the pale-colored cliffs below. Rayford, the Critter Chief, and his tribe of warriors marched through the thinning path molded between the rocks. The bird clan, being guardians to the critters, were sworn to protect them seven times over since the Old War. Although this was a peaceful march to The Den, no one was taking any chances. Especially since Ratatosk and his mighty men had yet to return from Mariner Dam.

Rebekah noticed the critters had stopped their march as a few disheveled squirrel and raccoon warriors scaled down the rocks and headed toward their chief. It was those warriors Poe had seen.

"Poe, see if everything is all right."

"Yesss, my queen..."

Poe dove down with a battalion of ravens behind him.

"Those are Ratatosk's men, my queen."

Rebekah's heart suddenly froze as she peered down at the vagabond group. "And yet…no Ratatosk." She looked behind her and caught sight of the Wolf Pack. They marched behind the reptile clan. Alexander and his parents, King Ivan and Queen Tatiana, followed with their band of warriors below. Instead of following the critters down the narrow winding path, they were hiking and climbing their way over the cliffs, forging their own path to see high above the landscape rather than remain crowded and surrounded down below by the massive rocks that left them vulnerable to attack. They had yet to encounter any warrior beings from either the swamps or the valley, and Rebekah wondered if this path was cleared more for the other tribes than for their own. Either way, seeing Alexander was a relief to Rebekah, knowing that she had champions in her corner with the Wolf Pack. Alexander, however, was against the treaty — and had told her so every day since his return from Mariner Sea.

"The lions and gorillas cannot be trusted."

"I'm sure they're saying the same thing about us, Alex."

"But your clan is the key to their survival if the famine is true. Your birds bring the rain, and your crops yield food that could feed the realm forever."

"What's your point?"

"If you're going to sign the treaty, don't do it without getting something in return. A king or queen should never give away the key to their power without exchange of a gift equal to it that could level the other side. You leave yourself vulnerable to attack if you do."

But what did she need that she did not have?

Only that one thing. That one thing that she had been wanting from the beginning.

How do you want to be remembered...

Rebekah looked back at the critter clan, seeing the tribe gathered together in a large crowd all along the cliff. They had completely stopped their march. This could not be good.

"The Den, my queen."

Rebekah turned her head and saw the pantheon-looking fortress ahead. Thousands of warriors had gathered outside its massive gate to get a glimpse of the arrivals of all the clans from the other side of the realm. Her heart was beating rapidly as she took in the sight of the panther, jackal, cheetah, tiger and lion warriors gathered outside its gates.

Only in paintings...

They were just as menacing as the Wolf Pack.

The crowd parted as Khan, the reptile king, led his tribe through the gate. On their heels came the wolves. The moment the wolves and lions caught sight of one another, Rebekah did not know what was going to happen — especially after the occurrence in The Lair.

Reginald's feathers suddenly stood on end. "I feel it, my queen."

Rebekah suddenly realized she was not breathing. She let out a small exhale. "I couldn't help it, my friend."

You could slice the tension in the air with a knife. Having all the clans in one arena, may not have been the wisest choice the lion king could have made. And for that, Rebekah had to give him credit. It was a bold and daring act. She wondered even more about this lion king the closer they came to his den. Seeing the warriors below sizing each other up, one could see that they were ready to attack any second if there was call to do so.

They dove down toward a large stone arena. From below, Rebekah saw a robust, powerful looking man waving to her — it was the lion king. Rebekah breathed in deep as they soared toward the ground. She climbed off of Reginald and moved toward Gunthar.

He was a handsome man with a large, athletic frame and deep yellowish-green eyes — just like his lions.

What kind of king am I dealing with...

Apollo, Roman and a few other Lion Guard warriors stood beside their king. Apollo's fur was bald and scarred in a few places, but he was healing quickly. Gunthar grinned widely as he approached the queen. He bowed to her as she curtsied to him.

"Queen Rebekah! Who would have thought that this day would come where two enemies now stand as friends."

He extended his arm to her.

"Thank you."

She graciously took his arm, feeling the strength of his form as she held onto his muscular arm. He led her toward a set of stairs that wound upwards toward a large chair that overlooked the arena. As they walked toward it, Apollo and Roman approached

Reginald.

"Eagle, I owe you my life. You protected our princes against the wolves, your kin. Why?"

Reginald swiveled his large head toward Rebekah. "Because of my queen. It was her command."

The lion and tiger warriors watched as their king walked arm and arm with the enemy. Gunthar was smiling as he entertained the queen while the other clans began to arrive.

Reginald watched the lion and tigers' reaction to what his words revealed and what this sight meant to them. Reading their faces, he knew what it was they felt. It was as if this moment was not truly real, yet there it was. It was a moment in time that did not allow hate to flow, hate that had been bred into all their hearts and minds from the beginning — an education that continued the banner of vengeance — and it was suddenly pulled out from underneath them and replaced by one commanding peace.

What does one do with pent-up emotion and prior perception one is no longer allowed to have and is unable to release? Where does it go? Reginald himself had his reservations about coming to The Den. He was on his guard like all the rest, but not because he had ever hated those on the other side of the realm. It was because he was unsure of what to believe with all the mysterious happenings on his side — all the bodies. He looked at the lions, seeing that their hearts were still filled with anger and fear as they looked at their king with the queen. He could see the turmoil of emotions on each of the warriors' faces even as they tried to conceal their thoughts. And by the look he saw behind their feline eyes, Reginald suddenly feared for his queen.

"Tok...tok...tok..."

Apollo and the other Lion Guard warriors spun around, never having sensed the raven assassin's arrival. The lion warrior's hair on his mane began to tingle as he looked at Poe. The raven's eyes glowed red; he was unlike any other warrior he had ever seen before. It was as if the raven could see straight into the powerful lion's heart, seeing the darkness within while the eagle could see a glimpse of the good. As the lion took in the eagle and the raven standing side by side, he understood that these two beings were a powerful balance of light and dark. And as Apollo turned to face their queen, he suddenly felt afraid.

Rebekah turned her head and smiled at them. Her smile slowly faded the moment she caught sight of her raven. There had been something she had seen beneath his fire-red eyes, and for a moment, Apollo could have sworn he saw her eyes fade from their glowing gray to a heartless black. He could sense that this queen held a power deep within that made the powerful lion's bones shudder inside his massive frame.

Like Palimus...

Apollo looked back at the raven and the eagle. There was a look of sorrow on the eagle captain's face, while the raven seemed to be smiling.

THE TREATY
VIII

Brandon and Nathan were side by side, lying on their stomachs, aiming their bows at two wildebeests up ahead.

"My aim is better than yours, cub. Don't the women usually do your hunting for you?"

Nathan smiled at the challenge, "Gives me more time to practice."

They both fired. Nathan's arrow landed directly in the beast's heart, killing it instantly. Brandon's arrow landed in the other beast's chest. He cursed in frustration as the beast squealed in agony as it lay paralyzed, slowly bleeding to death. Both men rose from their positions and walked toward their prey. Brandon whistled to his Tiger Guard. In reply, a Siberian tiger warrior named Konga dropped to all fours and charged toward the wounded beast; he dove his massive fangs into the beast's jugular and ripped its throat out, putting it out of its misery.

Brandon shook his head, "A lucky shot."

"NATHAN!!!"

Marcus called out from over the hilltop some distance away. His lynx guard, SinJin, was at his side.

"Nathan! Look what I killed!"

A four-foot tall squirrel hung dead from SinJin's claw — it was Ratatosk.

Brandon shouted back, "Not bad, little cub! Serves him right for crossing illegally!"

Marcus smiled at his approval; he jogged proudly back toward Nathan and Brandon.

Nathan, however, did not share in their excitement. He was deeply disturbed upon seeing the squirrel — not only on his land, but dead. "A critter warrior...what's he doing on our land?"

"Everybody's crossing borders these days from what I hear."

"The clans are about to sign a peace treaty! And my brother, a *prince*, is holding a dead critter warrior in his hand. Not exactly sending a peaceful message."

"Don't worry, Nathan. Nobody saw it. Just have SinJin eat him. Then there won't be any evidence that it was done."

But Nathan felt sick to his stomach as he watched the lynx warrior dangle the squirrel from his paw-like hand.

"Speaking of treaties, what did your father bribe you with to come all the way out here to babysit Marcus?"

Nathan looked at him oddly, "What are you talking about?"

"He must have given you a new sword or piece of land in Bull Valley. I, of course, was given an antique — one that I have coveted since I was a young boy. Come. I'll show you."

Brandon walked over to his tent and pulled out a large coat made entirely of wolf fur. Nathan's face paled the moment he realized what it was, "How did you get this?"

"After the Old War. The Lion Queen Alana gave it to my clan after the wolf king handed it over to her as a symbol of his sole alliance with the Bird Clan. I told my father he had to give it to me. There was no other way I would miss out on something so big if he didn't."

Nathan remained deadly silent as he saw this treasure so carelessly handed over to the tiger baron, as if it were a collector's prize rather than a clan's inherited relic.

Brandon ran his hand across the fur admiring it, "Over two hundred years and the kings and queens of the seven kingdoms are called to your father's court today, and we are going to miss it."

"*Today?*"

Nathan immediately dropped his bow and arrow just as Marcus reached the tent. He looked east toward the Lion's Den; his eyes slit to a cat; the tattoo around his neck suddenly darkened. "I'm not missing it." He charged forth with ferocious speed leaving a stunned Brandon and Marcus behind.

Marcus yelled after his older brother, *"Nathan!"*

Marcus immediately followed after him. Seeing the princes racing across the plains, the Lion Guard roared, dropped to all fours and chased after their princes. SinJin, still holding onto Ratatosk, bit down and devoured the squirrel warrior. He tossed the rest of the carcass to the tiger warriors, dropped to all fours, and chased after his prince, leaving Brandon alone with an empty hunting camp. Konga stood beside him, staring at his lord still holding the wolf coat in his arms.

"Konga, what did I say?" He cursed in the realization, "Nathan didn't know." He gritted his teeth at his blunder. "Don't tell my father about this. I'm not giving the coat back."

He put the coat back in the tent and shouted to his tiger guard. They headed to The Den.

The kings and queens of the seven kingdoms sat on their designated thrones that surrounded the outdoor arena. Each of the four kings and queens sat high above their tribes to distinguish class and rank even within each individual kingdom. Sitting highest above the rest was the lion king. Directly across from him on the opposite side of the arena was Queen Rebekah. Reginald and Poe stood on either side of her. The Wolf King Ivan and Wolf Queen

Tatiana were seated on their thrones to Rebekah's right; Alexander stood in between them looking lethal in his black, royal attire.

The Mariner Princess Lara was seated beside her father — the Mariner King Mar. None of the mariner warriors were in attendance since they were so far from the sea. Alexander turned his head and saw Lara staring at him. Her face lit up the moment they caught sight of one another. He nodded in acknowledgment and smiled politely back. The Amphibian King Archer was next to Mar — both kings were on the lowest level.

The Gorilla King Brutus, a lusty-looking man, sat closest to Gunthar, the legendary bone scepter, Bane, rested against his hip. He stared unabashedly at Rebekah. A silverback and orangutan guard stood to his right and left. The Bull King Rom sat below the gorilla clan; a crown of horns rested on his head. Rom was on the lower level with Mar and Archer, completing the hierarchy of the lesser clans.

A toad named Ikaki was showing the kings and queens the Tablet of Destinies — a large stone tablet with markings and symbols that reflected fire, wind, ice and earth.

"We have seen the future: the sun has changed direction. Its sudden shift has caused the lands in The Den and Gorilla Jungle to dry out faster than normal. The rivers in the Amphibian Swamps and Bull Valley have already floundered, and all the territories in the south and west will become a barren wasteland within five year's time."

The clans reacted to the devastating news. Alexander looked over at Rebekah and rolled his eyes; Rebekah ignored him. Her eyes were focused on the symbol for fire, the largest symbol on the stone tablet.

Gunthar's voice was low yet carried without effort across the arena, "The sun has changed direction. *That*...is the reason for the famine."

Ikaki bowed in acknowledgement. Gunthar looked at Brutus and shook his head in disbelief.

Rom, the bull king, snorted his reply, "That is why our crops are withered!"

The Wolf King Ivan shouted back, "That is why your clans are crossing illegally onto our lands...to steal food!"

Rom seethed at the tone behind Ivan's accusation, "What would you do if you were starving? My people should never be murdered when they're trying to find a means to survive!"

The clans erupted again. The Critter Chief Rayford raged across the arena, pointing his small finger at the bull king, "Our clans have murdered no one! If we had crossed into *your* territory, your bulls would have slaughtered us and they wouldn't have thought twice about it!"

Rebekah could see the anger in Rayford's face as he spoke. She glanced at the rest of the clan and saw Ratatosk's men beside him shouting with the rest. She glanced at Poe, seeing his large black head lowered as his red eyes stared at the bull king.

"Tok...tok...tok..."

He cackled lowly, but Rebekah and Reginald understood his tone.

The Reptile King Kahn was to the right of the Wolf Pack. He shouted in reply, "Non-citizens should never be allowed to reap the rewards of my people's hard labor! Where is the skill and mastery of their gifts to wield their own fruit! They eat all of mine and produce none! My people will soon starve as well with the changing direction of the sun, and we will all be in the same position!"

More shouts ensued. Rebekah glanced across the arena at Brutus, having felt his eyes on her. He smiled faintly at her. She had no idea he was so young and as good-looking as he was. He had that lusty animal magnetism in his demeanor that she knew meant trouble if you were a woman of no further virtue. All Rebekah kept thinking about as she nodded in return was how large his harem must truly be — and how willing the women must seem to go.

Gunthar's voice thundered across the arena as the clans quieted down. *"KINGS!!!"* He turned to Queen Rebekah and Queen Tatiana. "And queens...that is why we are here."

He looked at Rom, "Your people will not have to cross into other kingdoms to steal crops and hunt prey if the kings and queens on the other side of the realm agree to what is fair and what is needed, Rom. They shouldn't have been doing it anyway! You and your bulls are a disgrace to the realm!"

Rom held Gunthar's stare but said nothing in reply.

Ivan replied instead, "What is fair indeed, Gunthar. I know of nothing you have to offer that we don't already have."

Alexander smirked at his father's bit of philosophy, while the Wolf Pack barked their agreement to their king.

Gunthar tilted his head slightly in amusement. A faint smile curled at the corner of his lips, "I beg to differ with you, King. The one thing you do not have...that none of us has...is peace. And it can be guaranteed for your son and for mine if we choose to agree to the terms of the treaty I have written for all of us today."

Gunthar looked at all the kings and queens on the other side of the arena. "We kings hear the cry of our people — and we must answer for it. And my answer is this: that we reunite the realm as one."

Low murmurs rumbled across the arena.

"The treaty I wish to forge amongst the clans is designed to begin open trade amongst the kingdoms once again — the way it was established long ago by our ancestors."

Alexander looked at Rebekah. Her eyes were on the lion king; he could see she was not breathing as she listened to his words. He could tell she was listening for the truth behind them. By the look on her face, however, he could not tell what she was truly hearing, for her face gave nothing away.

From the lower level, the mariner king's voice rose up unexpectedly, "King! Before we start discussing trading of resources, I have a thing or two to say about this treaty before you continue...if I may."

"You may not."

Mar's face turned crimson. Rebekah could see the tightening muscles along his jaw. She knew it was taking every bit of effort for the mariner king not to speak what he was truly thinking as he looked at the lion king.

Brutus interjected, "Let him speak."

Gunthar kept his eyes on Mar, "He has no importance here. I only invited him out of respect to The Lair due to certain upcoming events." Gunthar nodded at Ivan. The smirk on Alexander's face immediately vanished the moment the words were spoken. He refused to look in the mariner king's direction.

Mar spoke regardless, "*Rain!* Rain pours by the grace of the Bird Clan. Rain that fills the sea to my kingdom and spills down upon yours and Brutus'! My clan perishes without the sea — as does the amphibians with their swamps. So this treaty affects my kingdom as much as any other!"

Gunthar waved his hand nonchalantly, "Fine. Speak."

Mar stood and bowed in mock respect to the lion king, turning his attention to Queen Rebekah. "I am neither against peace nor open trade, but let's call this treaty what it really is: a cry for help from all the kings on our side of the realm to the one clan who can give it. Nothing else matters as to what is needed or what can be offered if the Bird Clan has no desire to bestow mercy upon us."

He looked back at Gunthar with his turquoise-colored eyes, "If Queen Rebekah, your sworn enemy, agrees to send more rain to fill my sea, there will be no drought — with or without the changing sun. Your clans can continue to carry the water along the canals all throughout The Den and Gorilla Jungle. Crops will continue to grow and there will be no famine. And for those that are starving now, should the queen send food from the crops on her land, all will survive!"

Murmurs of agreement arose on all sides of the arena.

Gunthar held Mar's stare before finally answering, "Trade of resources was the will of our fathers. I aim to resurrect that idea once again."

Mar continued, "And it can be as long as this alliance is a true exchange that benefits all. I learned from my ancestors long ago that sole reliance and dependence on any one clan or resource is never a means to go about keeping the peace amongst the people."

Mar, now in command of the floor, looked at Rebekah once more.

"Everyone knows what we want and what we need. Now it's up to Queen Rebekah to decide what it is that *she* wants...should she choose to help us and keep her word in doing so — or we all die."

All eyes in the arena turned toward the queen. Alexander watched for her reaction.

Gunthar leaned forward, "Queen, what say you?"

Nathan and Marcus suddenly rushed past the Lion Guard and

headed inside the arena. They came up slowly from behind their father's throne, having heard their father's question. Nathan stopped and suddenly looked out across the arena…and saw Rebekah.

Rebekah shifted her gaze to Gunthar, "I commend you, king, for breaking down the walls of hatred and welcoming all the clans here today. You have reminded me of something very important — that the origination of the kingdoms was a cycle of giver and give — a flow of resource and prosperity meant to connect the clans as one."

Her voice was confident — strong yet kind. Nathan slowly stepped forward, unable to take his eyes off of her. Her presence was like a magnet. He moved forward, unable to resist her unknowing pull.

Rebekah shifted her gaze from the lion king to the bull and amphibian kings. She stared at them for what seemed like minutes. Murmurs rose up from the crowd at the uncomfortable silence as she continued to stare; and with that look, her gray eyes seemed to glow. Apollo watched her, recognizing the look he had seen in her eagle. He knew she was looking at the kings to see if there was any goodness within them.

Marcus tugged at Nathan's tunic, "That's her, Nathan! That's Queen Rebekah!"

"Shut up, Marcus."

Rebekah suddenly looked at the reptile king, "Kahn! Didn't our fathers tell us that before the Old War your clan's reputation for armor was the most sought after in all the land?"

He smiled proudly, "That and my people's working of skin for boots and belts for the armies of the four kings."

She turned to the critter chief, "Chief Rayford! Was it not the skill of your people to climb the highest of trees and dig into the deepest of mines to bring about the greatest treasures in the entire realm?"

"My people crafted the jewels and gold for all the kings and queens."

Rebekah turned to King Ivan and Queen Tatiana, "And was it not your pack's protection on the roads at night that guaranteed the safety of the kings and queens of the seven kingdoms?"

Ivan replied, "We wolves *own* the night, Queen."

The wolves barked and howled in reply. Nathan caught sight of the wolf prince standing beside his pack; he had not realized they were of the same age. All he had ever heard about Prince Alexander, was what he heard from Maximillian — all the tales of which he repeated from what he learnt from the women inside Gorilla Jungle.

Nathan looked all around the arena; it was the first time he saw all the species in the realm. He immediately recognized their similarities and their differences. The gorilla clan was filled with beautiful men and women with dark hair and tanned skin, warriors that were shorter in nature, yet powerful to behold. The bulls were lethal and extremely volatile, for anything would set them off. Seeing Rom with his crown of horns adorning his head, Nathan never realized their resemblance to the gorillas, only lighter-skinned in nature. Beside Rom was Mar, and from their immediate appearance, one knew they were mariners. Their hair was the color of ivory, their eyes were shades of blue, green and violet, and their frames were long and lean, for they were excellent swimmers. The amphibians resembled the mariners in frame, but their faces were wider, and their eyes were further set apart between their noses — giving them the appearance that resembled the look of their frog and toad warriors. And whereas the mariners were long and lean, the amphibian men and women were slim but more compact in nature. They could jump and vault like no other being Nathan had ever seen before.

Looking at the reptile clan, there was a slight resemblance to the amphibians. Odd to see, but Nathan could see it. Whereas the amphibians looked lean in frame yet bloated in the face, the reptile clan's builds were sleek and trim; their movements were fluid. He noticed that the men and women rarely blinked as they stared at anyone within their line of sight. They were all dark-haired — just like the gorillas. The moment Nathan caught sight of the critter clan, he grew sick inside. He saw the squirrel and chipmunk warriors standing beside their chief. Each man and woman in the clan was short and stout, barely reaching any height over five feet tall. And then there were the wolves.

Nathan's heart pounded the moment he saw Skoll standing beside the wolf prince. Taking in Alexander's frame, he could see the coldness behind the prince's eyes — the same coldness he saw behind the wolves and hyenas. Nathan could feel the blood in his body begin to boil. Looking at the wolf king and queen with their pale-colored skin and vibrant eyes, they looked lethal and strong. They were a clan to be reckoned with indeed, and from the looks on their faces, they knew it too. Standing beside the Bird Clan, Nathan suddenly understood what it must have been like long ago to have the wolves fight alongside the gorillas and lions — they balanced out the possibility of any threat to tear down the powerhouses of the four kingdoms. And with that thought, he was suddenly proud to have been a part of The Den, proud of his father for attempting to unite them once again, yet angry that he almost missed this moment — but he would deal with that later. He was too enthralled with focusing on the last clan…and its queen.

Rebekah looked at the kings on the other side of The Den, "Kings! Our clans can offer armor, gems and protection. What can you offer our clans in return?"

Brutus sat back against his large throne and grinned, spreading his large arms wide; Rebekah could clearly see his massive biceps as they flexed with each gesture. "Women!"

The gorillas grunted and beat their breasts wildly; Rebekah was not smiling, nor was Tatiana.

The gorilla king lowered his arms and continued, "And medicine. There are many plants in my jungle that can heal and save one from death."

Archer, the amphibian king, added, "And more can be found in my swamps. We can also foresee the future and speak to the dead; great wisdom lies with them."

Rom, the bull king, grunted, "My bulls can build and construct anything from the rocks in my valley."

Gunthar added, "And from The Den."

The bull warriors stomped in reply.

Brandon ran up behind Nathan and Marcus, completely out of breath. He keeled over, trying to regain his composure. "Nathan…"

He saw Nathan's face and followed his gaze. "My god! Is that the bird queen? I thought she had a beak!"

Gunthar continued, "My lions are the greatest hunters in the entire realm."

Rom sneered, "Don't you mean your *lionesses*?"

The bulls' laughter carried across the arena. Apollo and the Lion Guard roared, silencing the bulls.

Gunthar spoke to Rebekah. "My den is filled with killers, queen. And there is far less food upon which to hunt to trade in exchange for your crop. I have nothing to offer you but my hand in friendship."

She held the lion king's stare from across the arena. Apollo caught her look once again.

"King! Is it true that you throw the most magnificent balls in all the land?"

"The greatest, young queen."

Lions and tigers roared in reply. Gorilla soldiers pounded on their chests, and bull warriors kicked their hooves.

Rebekah looked around the arena at all the warriors, amused by what she saw. "I cannot speak for what the other kings want...but I would like a dance. A masquerade for all the clans held here at your court — as a symbol of our friendship. In exchange, I will sign this treaty, I will send more rain, and I will feed your clans." She looked at Mar. "*All* of them."

The entire arena was silent. All eyes were on the bird queen and the lion king.

Gunthar eyed her and then, slowly, a smile crept onto his face; he roared in laughter. "A masquerade! You shall have it, young queen! A ball in your honor!" The lion king rose and shouted to all the clans in the arena, "In a fortnight!"

The clans erupted in shouts of joy. It sounded like thunder, so much so that the columns in the arena began to shake. Gunthar stepped down from his throne as the other kings rose; the meeting was over. He turned the corner and saw his sons. His smile immediately evaporated, and a look of anger took its place.

"What are you doing here? I thought I sent you to Tigerland!"

Nathan did not shy away from his father's wrath. "Why didn't you tell me? This was the single most important event in the realm's history. I should have been here!"

Gunthar sighed deeply, "To protect you, my son — both of you. I didn't want your presence here to remind the wolf king about you illegally crossing into his woods. It would have been a great distraction against what was intended here today. I couldn't risk it."

Marcus asked excitedly, "Father, are we really going to have a masquerade with all the kingdoms?"

Gunthar ruffled his young son's hair, "By god we are! That queen could have asked for anything in the world and all she wants is a dance! Peculiar creature. We lions will show her how it's done! Ha!"

He strutted off down a long corridor; Apollo and Roman followed closely behind. Marcus wove through the crowd to find Queen Rebekah. Nathan shouted after him, *"MARCUS!"* He bulldozed his way after him.

"Queen Rebekah, this is Princess Lara."

Lara and Rebekah curtsied to one another upon Alexander's introduction; he looked completely miserable.

"I am so pleased to finally meet you, Queen Rebekah. Alexander spoke of no one else the entire time he was at my home."

Rebekah smiled kindly at her, "I, too, am glad to meet you, Princess Lara. I know we shall see much more of one another when your contract is finally signed and your wedding approaches.

I hope we become good friends."

Princess Lara was not listening to her; she was looking past Rebekah at Alexander. The smile on her face revealed a young woman completely in love. Rebekah turned toward Alexander to see his reaction. His face refused to smile as both women faced him.

"Well, I shall leave you two alone. I'm sure you have many things to discuss." Rebekah turned on her heel and moved toward the long hallway that led to the outside of The Den.

Upon her exit, Alexander bowed quickly to the mariner princess, "Excuse me, Princess Lara, but I promised to escort the queen home."

Lara's face fell in disappointment. "Of course. Please…I don't wish to keep you."

He finally smiled, "Thank you."

He bowed and walked swiftly away in utter relief. He could finally breathe again as he approached Rebekah's side. They walked side by side as Skoll, Poe, and Reginald followed closely behind.

Upon seeing Alexander, Rebekah scoffed, "Princess of apes...I knew you were lying. She's beautiful, Alex. And she's completely in love with you. I would say your trip to Mariner Tower went extremely well."

Alexander completely ignored her, "A masquerade? Rebekah, of all the things to ask for!"

"Well, what else was there to take? I don't need rocks, women or voices of the dead haunting my castle. I want to dance. There's nothing else I need or want that I don't already have."

He eyed her mischievously, "And what *kind* of dance would you be referring to?"

She suddenly slowed her step, just as he knew she would. She turned around and faced him. The smile on her face was replaced by one of warning. He loved it when she looked angry.

"Not the kind you're thinking of."

He crossed his muscular arms across his lean chest, a slow smile curling on the corners of his lips, "And what kind am I thinking of, Rebekah?"

She stepped closer to him so that no one could hear. Her eyes had dimmed to a cool brown. Yes, he loved moments like these when he knew he could evoke this kind of reaction out of her. There was something about how lethal she could look that made her that much more attractive to him. It scared him in a way that he knew she could match his own anger — unlike the way anyone else could. He loved that about her; he depended on that within her. And he knew that that particular quality could never exist in any other woman but this one.

"You promised me that you would never bring that up again."

He continued to goad her, "You know you loved it. The Fire Dance would be quite the hit at this king's party. We could take over the whole dance floor with those moves. Which means we'll have to practice. Say...around midnight? Large bonfire in The

Lair...your ravens, my wolves..."

He grabbed the golden medallion from around her neck and ran his fingers across the raven.

"Stop that!" She smacked his hand away. She lowered her voice and spoke sternly to him, looking all around to ensure that nobody could hear her. "That dance is forbidden! Reginald was furious with me for weeks when he found out."

Alexander grinned at her; his blue eyes dancing, "But Poe was quite proud — as was Skoll."

He moved past her without another word, and headed back toward the courtyard.

She turned and caught up to him, "Alexander..."

He continued walking, "Yes, a dance for the clans...yes, I see your ploy..."

Rebekah stopped and shouted at him, "Alex!"

He finally turned, "Yes?"

"You promised me."

"I promised you I wouldn't mention that night, not that there wouldn't be another one."

Rebekah looked at him in disgust, "You're despicable."

Alexander lowered his head and leveled his eyes at her, "That's what you get for putting me on the spot with a woman you know I don't want to marry. I'll see you tonight..."

He bowed mockingly and walked back toward his pack with Skoll following close behind.

"REBEKAH!"

Rebekah looked over and saw Marcus running excitedly toward her. Reginald stepped in front of him, slowing the young prince's step. Marcus stopped dead in his tracks as the eight-foot-tall eagle warrior loomed over him. "That is *Queen* Rebekah, young sire."

Marcus' eyes scaled up Reginald's body in absolute awe.

"You're an eagle! You're the eagle that saved Apollo!"

Reginald smiled, "I am, young sire."

"Tok...tok...tok..."

Marcus's eyes grew wide the moment he heard Poe's low, threatening sound. He looked behind Reginald and stared at the raven assassin.

Poe nodded to him. *"Lion..."*

Rebekah came toward him, "Prince Marcus! I wondered where you were. This is my eagle Reginald — captain of my guard."

SinJin ran up from behind and immediately joined Marcus' side. The lynx warrior sized up Reginald and Poe, moving between them and his prince to stand guard in protection.

Rebekah noticed Marcus' disheveled appearance, "Where have you been, young prince? Your garments are soaked through."

"I was out hunting with my brother Nathan."

Nathan watched the exchange from behind a pillar, feeling out the characters and the situation before him — like a lion on the prowl.

"Ah, yes. Your infamous brother. And how was the game?"

He answered excitedly, "I killed a critter warrior. He was as big as me with this white circle around his eye — almost like a bull's-eye. And he had this!"

Marcus pulled out a small compass. The moment he said the words, the queen's smile rapidly faded. Her eyes shifted from gray to brown. Reginald dropped his arms away from his broad chest. Poe's eyes glowed red, *"Ratatosssk!"*

Marcus did not understand their reactions. All he understood was that he had somehow done something wrong. Sensing the danger, SinJin placed his giant arm protectively around the young prince. He had seen the shift in the queen's eyes and suddenly felt afraid.

Rebekah's face was one of stone, "The critter warrior...was on your land?"

Marcus nodded. "Un-huh. He was running straight across the plain. SinJin said he looked good enough to eat, so I aimed my bow at him and shot him. I got him on my first try."

Reginald looked at SinJin; his pupils were the size of pins. Marcus saw the severe look on Rebekah's face; her eyes had turned almost black — like the raven. "What is it, my lady?"

She nodded toward the arena, "Do you see that clan over by the reptiles?"

Marcus looked over at the Critter Clan. Chief Rayford was surrounded by his soldiers: the possums, raccoons, mice, skunks and...*squirrels*. The moment Marcus saw the squirrel soldiers, his face fell into one of panic.

Rebekah continued to keep her eyes on Marcus' face as she watched his reaction as the realization of what he had done took shape.

Innocence...

She breathed deeply as she tried to control her anger and her sorrow; her eyes lightened to a cool brown. "There's a difference between animals and members of the clan, young cub. Recognize it. The future reign of your den depends on it."

He looked back at her; his eyes were suddenly filled with tears.

She nodded to him and walked off with Reginald and Poe in tow. She walked fast. Reginald and Poe sped up to follow her. Reginald attempted to calm her, "My queen..."

"Lionsss cannot be trusted. Lionsss mean harm, Reginald."

He chastised him under his breath, "Silence, Poe! We're still inside The Den."

"My lady!"

Rebekah turned to find Marcus chasing after her once again. He walked slowly up to her with his head bowed low. "I will right my wrong. Please, take this to the critter chief."

He extended the compass to her. She looked at the young prince with his head bowed in shame. She bent down, took her finger and lifted his chin so that his eyes met hers. Here eyes were now completely gray. "I believe you, young lion." She looked down at the compass. "You must keep that as a reminder, Prince Marcus, that when the world seems to come at you from all angles, forcing you to decide between right and wrong — confusing the lines between them — that you find your way onto the right path every time you look at that compass."

"I will." He smiled faintly at her in deep gratitude. "Queen Rebekah?"

"Yes?"

"Will you dance with me at the ball?"

She could not help but smile. "If you can find me, good prince." Rebekah winked at him and rose. Marcus and SinJin turned and walked back toward the arena as the queen watched them in silence. Reginald and Poe stood directly beside her.

Rebekah's eyes dimmed once more, "Drought. Famine. Ratatosk dead!"

She stood and faced her warriors, the look on her face was lethal, "After seeing these kings' faces today, I need an answer...and it lies in that sea." She faced Poe, "The night of the ball, fly over the lion king's side by way of Gorilla Jungle. And let Rayford know...his champion is dead."

"But you agreed to the termsss of the treaty."

The queen lowered her voice, "I have to, Poe. Ratatosk never returned to confirm what I had hoped would not be true. I only asked for a masquerade to give us an opportunity to cross onto this side of the realm at night. I need you to finish what he started."

Poe nodded and headed back toward the arena, *"Yesss, my queen."*

Nathan watched as Rebekah stormed toward the courtyard gate where her Thunderbird Guard awaited. When she reached the gate, the wind suddenly blew through the corridor and swirled around her. She stopped and slowly turned, looking in Nathan's direction.

Standing against the pillar, his muscular arms crossed over his sculpted chest, Rebekah caught sight of him. The sun's rays showered down upon him at just the right angle, setting his amber eyes aglow as his hair shimmered in the light. Reginald's feathers shot straight up the moment his queen caught sight of the prince. He swiveled his large head around until his eyes fell on Nathan.

"The lion…"

From the arena, Poe's charcoal-colored feathers also stood on end. He craned his jet-black neck around, lowering it like a bull the moment he caught sight of the prince. He had felt it. He had felt the stirring in his queen's heart — and because of the feeling, his eyes burned red. Alexander caught sight of Poe's chilling frame and turned to follow his gaze.

Without another word, Rebekah grabbed hold of Reginald's cloak and jumped onto his back. Reginald leapt into the sky and the Thunderbird Guard followed.

Nathan's eyes never left Rebekah as she soared across his den. Feeling other pairs of eyes on him, he turned his head and saw Alexander and Poe looking his way. Seeing the raven and the wolf prince standing side by side, Nathan finally understood what it was to catch sight of the dark.

Refusing to move or be intimidated, Nathan remained in his position, daring to look to the sky at the ascending queen. Alexander remained rooted to the spot, continuing to stare at the lion prince. Skoll approached his prince from behind.

"That's the one…the one who ventured into our lair."

Alexander took in the challenger's athletic frame. "If he ever ventures again, kill him."

Skoll nodded proudly at his prince. "As you wish, prince."

"Tok…tok…tok…" And Poe heard all.

A FORTNIGHT

IX

Rebekah was bent over the edge of her large, canopy bed, lacing up her boots when Alexander walked through her chamber doors, wearing an outfit identical to the queen's. Two weeks had passed since the clans had met inside The Den. In that time, nothing more had been revealed about how Ratatosk wound up in Tigerland. All that the queen had learned was that another bull had ventured into Critter Country the night Ratatosk disappeared. The bull had charged the critter soldiers, only to turn back toward Bull Valley without a further fight. The warriors had tracked him, finding he had returned to the valley. They had spent the next day and a half trying to track down Ratatosk but to no avail.

The guards from her side of the realm had reported no further crossings, and not even Poe had any complaints to relay. And even though the queen had signed the treaty, she could not help the gnawing feeling deep within her bones that the kings on the other side of the realm could not be trusted. But without proof to back her feeling, she knew she had no other choice but to help the other clans and sign the treaty. She could not explain why she had felt the way she did about the kings; all she knew was that something was amiss. A feeling she wished was not so.

Rebekah rose and walked over to a large mirror. She began fidgeting with her garments, adjusting her tie with no success. She turned to Alexander, "So...do I look like a wolf in this outfit?"

He frowned at her, "Come here."

"What?"

She moved toward him. He took her tie and unwound the mess she was attempting to create.

"Bird, have you never tied a tie before?"

"Yes, every day when I put on my dress."

He tied it roughly.

"Ow."

"There."

She turned back to face the mirror. "It looks exactly the same. You didn't do anything." Rebekah continued fidgeting in front of the mirror. She was nervous for a variety of reasons; the main one being what she knew her raven was going to try and pull off later that evening. She had hoped that whatever he found, it would be the opposite of what she had been thinking.

And although he was grateful for the chance to prove his theory right about distrusting the treaty, Poe was extremely unhappy with his queen. All day long, he informed her ten times over how difficult it would be to protect her from attack during the masquerade, to which she made him promise to dance with her in order to stay close. Rebekah could not believe it the moment she saw his feathery cheeks turn the color of his eyes.

She understood his concern, but she had no other choice. Rebekah had not slept well that last few nights, spending most of her moments at Wolf Lake staring out at the moon. She had even roamed her corridors staring at Palimus' portrait, wondering when he first felt that same unsettled feeling she had when she thought of the lion king. But there was no one to share her thoughts with, no one who understood the great risk she was willing to take in order to either carry on the way she began, or weave in an entirely different direction from where she now was.

Alexander watched her fidgeting in front of the mirror like a little girl. He knew she was nervous. He knew every look she ever had, understanding every emotion she tried to hide, even when she thought she was hiding it. He crossed his arms over his chest, holding them close to his body so as not to rush to her side and wrap his arms around her to hold her close and give her courage. He had been crossing his arms more often these last few months — up until he was forced to go to Mariner Sea.

"Alex, am I doing the right thing? Am I jumping too soon at the chance to make peace with the lion king? Am I walking..."

"Into the lion's den? You are, but you have not jumped."

Rebekah turned to face him; he could tell she needed reassurance from someone who would tell her the absolute truth. He loved knowing that that person was he. She looked so vulnerable at that moment. He could feel his chest begin to squeeze tighter and tighter as the ache and yearning continued to rise deep within his heart, for he loved Rebekah so — and had never said a word about it to anyone.

"Gunthar told the entire realm that he could only offer you his hand in friendship. And you have called him out to make good on his word." He moved closer to her and adjusted her tie once more. "And besides, it doesn't matter what I think. It doesn't matter what anybody thinks. Only you see the clarity of your vision, Rebekah. Only you can see it through the way that you want it to be. And I know you well enough to know that you will not stop, you will not rest, until you've accomplished your goal: to raise your clan up and deem it worthy once more."

She gently touched his hand, squeezing it tight. "Thank you, Alex. Your words mean more to me than you could possibly know."

There were tears behind her eyes as she looked at him. His chest seized even tighter. He lifted his hand and moved a strand of hair from her face, "Who else could get a lion to throw a bird a ball so she can dance in his den? It is I who should be thanking you. We finally get to show the realm the Fire Dance."

He could not help it. It was the only way he could stop himself from planting his lips on top of hers as she looked at him with her beautiful eyes. Ruining the moment was always his saving grace from being found out, and for once he wished he had chosen a different strategy.

She shoved him back and smacked his arm playfully as her eyes grew wide in surprise. "Alex!" She moved over to her bed. "We are not doing that dance!"

She began searching underneath it, moving across the room to the end table, then onto the rest of the room, still searching.

"Rebekah, they've never even seen it. They won't know what kind of dance it is."

Not finding what she was looking for, Rebekah moved out onto her balcony. "Oh, yes they will!" She rushed back inside. "Let me ask you something, when you have a daughter, are you going to let your wolves teach it to her?"

"No! *If* I have a daughter, I'm never letting her out of The Lair!"

"Well, I was someone's daughter. And I'm not doing it."

"You already have...what are you looking for?"

"My medallion." She continued her hunt all around the room. Alexander joined in. "And what do you mean you're not letting your daughter out of The Lair? Sheltering her from the world would be a great disservice for a queen in the realm. She wouldn't be prepared to rule if she didn't know what the world was really like. What *men* are really like…"

Alexander found her medallion draped over her chair near the mirror. He walked over to Rebekah as she rattled on. He clasped the chain around her neck. "I don't care. Let her be naïve and stupid. She probably will be. I'm marrying a mariner."

"Princess Lara does not strike me as being stupid or naïve. I've seen you in action. She probably thinks you're in love with her. What did you do to her, by the way? Sing a song to her? Write her some poetry?"

"I don't sing and I don't write poems, Rebekah."

"Well, whatever you did, she is head over heels for you."

She grabbed a navy blue suit coat and looked inside one of the side pockets. Understanding what she was looking for now, Alexander walked over to the chessboard and picked up her boomerang. He walked over to Rebekah and grabbed her by her lapel and placed the boomerang inside her corset.

"I can't help it if women find me irresistible. Which is why, if I have a daughter, she's never getting married. I'll send her to a convent. I'll send her to yours."

Rebekah slugged him in the chest before engaging in another search once more. "I feel sorry for your daughter already. You're not equipping her with knowledge of victory or loss or understanding other people's pain…"

"I don't even *have* a daughter! And you have no reason to feel sorry for her. I'd make a good father. Mine is pretty good and yours was even better. When the time comes for her to rule after me, she won't have to deal with loss or pain. Besides, you're not the only one building your house."

Rebekah stopped mid-step, having found her mask. Holding it in her hands, she let out a deep sigh. She stared at the mask in silence. When she finally looked up, there were tears in her eyes. She suddenly felt utterly alone. Keeping her deepest thoughts about the night's event from Alexander was taking its toll. Talking about his upcoming marriage was even harder — not because she did not wish him to be married, but because it meant another loss, another blow to those she called family.

"Alexander, you and your parents are my only family. What am I going to do when you are married with a family of your own living in the sea?"

Alexander moved toward her and took both of her hands in his. "First of all, I will never live near the sea. I can't stand water. And second…"

He took her face in his hands and kissed the top of her head, desiring nothing more than to have it be her lips. He looked into her gray eyes and felt his heart ache as he looked at her beautiful face.

"I'm not married yet."

She could barely look at him. He took his finger and lifted her chin so that they were eye to eye. "What's wrong?"

There were so many answers to such a question, but she knew

now was not the time to say them all. How she wanted to tell him the truth about why she asked for the ball, but she could not do it. He would not understand her motive. He would chastise her for not sharing her thoughts with him and his parents sooner. So she remained silent for fear of one thing: what if she was wrong? She could not risk the truth of her thoughts for fear of the repercussion of dismantling the excitement to which this treaty brought and represented.

"It's all changing, Alexander. Isn't it?"

"I thought that's what you wanted."

"I do. I just…if all that is happening is true, I'm not going to have any more excuses or barriers stopping me from dreaming the impossible…because it's happening. It's possible, and now there are no more barriers in the world…not even in my own mind. I'm scared, Alex. I'm scared to have what I wanted, what I've dreamed of, yet I want it all the same. And now that it's here…I don't know if I can trust it. It makes no sense, I know. Just know that these feelings I'm having, are more than what I'm saying to you in this moment."

Tears streamed down her face. Alexander had never seen her like this. Rebekah rarely cried; she loved to laugh, she loved to ponder, she loved to feel and think — even if what she felt was with no one but the company of her own mind. But the one thing Alexander knew was that when she did show her emotions, they poured out of her like the Mariner Dam — full force; a tidal wave of rage or woe — and there was no stopping it once it poured forth. He never knew her to fear anything, and this was one moment he was not prepared to handle — even if he had known her since they were born.

He pulled her into his chest and wrapped his arms around her, holding her tight. And for the first time in a long while, he could breathe. "Don't be afraid."

She buried her head in his shoulder.

"You deserve to have what you want in life. The great triumph of any given day is knowing that you made one small change that shifted the darkness of this world into light."

She lifted her head and looked at him, smiling faintly, "Why, Alexander, I thought you liked the dark."

He grinned at her as he wiped a tear from her cheek, "One can only admire the moonlight when standing before the sun. Now let's go to your dance so peace in the realm can begin."

Her smile slowly faded. She nodded silently as he offered her his arm, escorting the light of his life outside her castle and into the world beyond.

The entire realm was in attendance at the masquerade, disguised for the night's event. Nathan made his way through the crowd, wearing a black mask, dressed in the exact same black outfit Alexander wore the day the treaty was forged. Nathan searched the crowd, weaving in and out, trying to make out each person in order to find the bird queen, but she was nowhere to be found. Brandon and Maximillian stepped up beside him.

"Nice outfit. I suspect the wolf prince won't be amused."

Brandon, dressed as Maximillian, added, "I like your strategy, Nathan. Queen Rebekah seems quite fond of Prince Alexander. They're always at each other's side."

Nathan continued to search the crowd, "That's because they grew up together. Besides, Alexander is engaged to the mariner princess."

Maximillian's eyes glowed green, "Catching up on your clan gossip, Nathan. So does this mean the queen is off limits or does the best cat win?"

"Don't bother, Max. Queen Rebekah doesn't strike me as being into kittens."

Brandon laughed as Nathan walked off. Marcus was on the dance floor with a beautiful young baroness from the Jaguar Clan. Nathan could see his mother and father on their thrones in the upper balcony overlooking the dance floor. Apollo and Roman stood watch at their sides. King Ivan and Queen Tatiana stood on the top of the staircase that led down to the dance floor conversing with King Mar.

No Alexander…no Rebekah…

Nathan made his way to the balcony ledge that overlooked the ballroom.

A white tiger composer led the cat musicians as they played the enchanted music of the night's event — the beginning and end of which was countered by a lion's roar. All the nobles were dancing to an old courtly song as their partners wove in and out of one another as the melody played on.

The sound of the lion's roar ended the song as a new one began. It was a tune he did not recognize. It was dark and enchanting, a bewitching melody of mystery and magic. It was not a song from his side of the realm — it was one from the wolves' and the ravens'.

It was then that Nathan saw two identically clad dancers weaving in and out of the crowd, each gliding their way to the opposite ends of the floor. Gracefully, the two dancers moved like water as they wove through the crowd before joining each other in the center of the floor. Both dancers wore navy coats with white shirts, black pants and boots, while black masks covered their faces. The two dancers dressed as men as they stood shoulder to shoulder, linked arm to arm. They began their customary dance with a tap dance-jig that members of the wolf, reptile, critter and bird clans appeared to know. The clan members cawed, howled and slithered onto the middle of the dance floor, lining up in the form a square, while the twin dancers stood in the center. Nathan took in the lean, muscular physique of the taller dancer. He recognized the wolf prince. He shifted his amber eyes to the smaller dancer and zeroed in.

It is she.

And as the wolves, birds, reptiles and critters poured into line, the lions, gorillas, bulls and amphibians exited out. Noblemen, women, birds, wolves, critters and reptiles paired off and faced one another — females on one side, males on the other. Rebekah and Alexander faced one another and joined palms. They turned. Their right palms touched. They turned again, and the dance truly began. They ducked, spun, tapped, mirroring the exact same movements of the other dancer as they faced each other, weaving in and out of the rest of the dancers on the floor. Nathan lowered his head, focusing on their movements, concentrating and memorizing the beat and the step. The rest of the clans watched from the outskirts of the dance floor, seemingly enjoying the hauntingly beautiful tune. Rebekah and Alexander made their way to the opposite ends of the floor once more, linking arms to replicate the tap dance-jig as the next segment of the song was about to begin. They moved to different ends of the line as various partners switched positions.

Rebekah was busy admiring the other dancers as they formed a square once more, completely unaware of the dancer who stepped up opposite her. She turned her head and saw an athletic-looking man dressed in a wolf's attire with a black leather vest, black pants and white shirt that revealed his muscular arms. She could see the faint ink mark of a small tattoo creeping up from the collar as it scaled up his thick neck.

A lion…

Nathan stood before her — he was still disguised, but his golden hair and strong muscular frame gave him away as a member of the lion clan.

Amused that a member of The Den would be brave enough to join in, Rebekah leapt at the opportunity to test this man's bravery a little bit more. Hearing the chiming of the bells, Rebekah tap danced around Nathan and moved to the other side of the floor. He watched her steadily, focused on her from behind his mask, never taking his eyes off of her. They turned shoulder to shoulder — she looked forward, but Nathan's eyes remained on hers. They turned to face one another. The moment their palms touched, flesh-to-flesh, the birds reacted. Time seemed to slow with the beat of the drum. Gunthar immediately rose from his throne in the realization of whom his son was dancing with.

Reginald and Poe's feathers stood on end; a sudden chill moved from the tops of their heads to the bottom of their clawed feet. They felt it. They felt the heartbeat of their queen. And while the birds felt it, the lions saw it — they saw the look on their prince's face as he danced with the enemy queen; and they did not look happy.

Instead of mirroring his partner the way everyone else was doing, Nathan grabbed Rebekah by the waist and pulled her into him, spinning and twirling her in time with the beat. She followed his lead as he wove them between the other dancers. Nathan knocked into Alexander, forcing him off the dance floor.

Nathan moved behind her; their bodies became one as he lifted her and spun her body around to face him. He gently lowered her to the ground and continued on in the newly improvised dance. Brandon and Maximillian watched him from the sidelines.

Brandon shook his head in admiration, "Damn...he's good."

Rebekah and Nathan once again faced each other on opposite ends of the line — a playful smirk rested on Nathan's face as they stood shoulder to shoulder, touching palm to palm, their eyes glued to one another as if they were the only two people in the room. As the bells chimed to begin the next stanza, Rebekah changed the step in an attempt to throw Nathan off, but he rose to the occasion and mirrored her every move. The faster she led, the faster he followed. He matched her stride for stride, motion for motion, never missing a beat. The harder and faster she tried to throw him off, the more exact his movements became until he grabbed hold of her waist once more and pulled her body into his. He waltzed her all over the dance floor, twirling her, cacheing her, until they took over the entire floor. Rebekah could not contain herself as she burst out laughing every time he threw in the air. Nathan lifted her and swung her around over and over again. He lowered her down slowly so that they faced each other as the beat began to slow and the song was about to end.

Alexander stood at the bottom of the staircase — watching in silence.

The song ended and the lions roared.

Nathan bowed to Rebekah and, in return, she curtsied to him. As she rose up, he grabbed hold of her hand and kissed it in front of the entire realm.

Gasps were heard all throughout the room.

"Do you know what you're doing, lion?"

His amber eyes seemed to glow.

They rose together, hand in hand. Marcus stood on the lowest step of the staircase; his mouth hung open. All the nobles erupted in applause — all except the lion king.

A small smile formed on the corner of her lips as Rebekah sized up the lion prince. Nathan, still holding her hand, looped it through his muscular arm and placed her hand near his heart. Never once did he take his eyes from her face.

"You're just like your brother — a mute."

Nathan's eyes continued to glow. "I am no mute, good queen. I only speak when I have something worth saying. I choose my words carefully. And there is something I wish to say to you."

He led her up the stairs and out toward the garden gates, their eyes completely locked onto one another's. The owls, hawks, and eagles bowed as they passed; the wind blew gently through The Den, whispering its consent. Alexander watched them exit the ballroom in complete and utter silence. Tatiana placed her hand over her heart and touched Ivan's arm. "My goodness…"

Ivan squeezed her hand. "That's how I looked at you when I first saw you."

He kissed her hand.

Alexander could not stand it, he looked across the ballroom and over at the gorilla clan. Several women eyed him knowingly. He looked to the other side of the room and saw Princess Lara standing with a small group of mariner women. The moment she saw him look at her, she broke into a wide smile.

The walls were closing in on him as he looked all about the room and saw more of the same. Empty prospects good for the evening, good for the ego, but unworthy of a lifetime adventure. His heart had walked outside the ballroom doors on the arm of another man, a handsome man, a worthy opponent who many of the women in the room desired...just like him.

But unlike Alexander, Nathan was not set to be betrothed to another. He glared at his parents still in love after all these years, having fallen for one another long ago. Neither had been contracted to the other; there was no need. As far as Alexander was concerned, there was no need for him to be either.

"Tok...tok...tok...Prince..."

Alexander turned upon hearing Poe's familiar rattle.

"What is it, Poe?"

"There isss sssomething you must know about the night the lionsss entered your woodsss. It isss about my queen..."

REMNANT

X

Nathan and Rebekah strolled through the moonlight and into the Lion Gardens. Their eyes were locked on one another, lost in their own world.

"I had no idea lions were such good dancers. If your hair weren't the color of gold, I would have sworn you were a wolf."

Nathan took his mask off and dropped it onto the ground. "I like you."

"How do you know? We've never met."

He stopped and faced her.

"I was there that day when you came to my den. I could see the pride of each clan as their gifts and talents were spoken from your lips. Your voice stirred something deep within me and I haven't been the same since. I've been pouring over the histories of the clans since that day, and ours were always allies. *Always*."

Rebekah lifted the mask from her face, feeling a little uneasy of his recounting of the clans.

"Not always."

She looked into his amber eyes, feeling a warmth behind them, a confident strength resonating from his every fiber, one that she instantly knew she could count on.

"Yet here we are two hundred years later, dancing in your den."

"Because of you."

She laughed softly. "There really wasn't much to decide, lion. Not when all the realm desires the one thing you alone can give."

"You could have said 'no'."

Rebekah's smile faded. "No, I couldn't have."

"You could have. You're a good queen. If you weren't, the clans would not be laughing and dancing. I would be dead...and so would my brother. I owe you my life. Thank you for making sure I still have it."

"You're welcome, lion."

"Call me Nathan."

"Nathan."

He continued to stare at her, as if he were trying to figure something out; the answer to which rested behind her eyes.

"What?"

Nathan smiled faintly, "There is kindness behind your eyes —

and great strength. You have passion, lady, passion that mirrors my own."

"Hmmm…and what does your heart riot for, Nathan?"

His smile widened the moment she spoke his name.

"Peace. Peace amongst the clans. Our two kingdoms are the most powerful clans in the realm. My father has brought about a great change with this treaty, and I intend to maintain it. I am a champion of the cause."

He moved closer to her, standing before her until they were inches apart; he grabbed hold of her hands, holding them gently.

Rebekah's heart pounded wildly the moment he touched her.

"You are bold, lion. Your father and I have yet to shake hands in our newly formed friendship. Are you sure he would approve of what you've done and what you are doing?"

"I may be bold, but it's because I'm honest. My father is a good king. I have never known him to lie. Throwing a ball in The Den for you is his handshake. We are enemies no more. I am sure I have his blessing in my choices, not only because I am his son, but because I will be king of The Den one day."

"A king to be reckoned with, indeed."

His face at that moment looked vulnerable. His eyes seemed to twinkle as he looked at her. And her eyes could not help but twinkle back.

His voice lowered, "And what does your heart riot for, good queen?"

"Rebekah."

Nathan smiled and whispered her name, "Rebekah..." He lifted her hands and placed them on his strong chest. He let his hands fall to her waist as he leaned in closer. Rebekah could barely breathe as their lips were about to touch.

"REBEKAH!!!"

Nathan exhaled deeply as he recognized his brother's voice. Rebekah laughed and pulled away from Nathan's embrace as the young prince approached.

Nathan sighed deeply. "Marcus, it isn't polite to barge in on people unannounced."

Rebekah smiled widely, "Young lion."

"That's *Queen* Rebekah, cub!"

Marcus stopped and turned to see Alexander quickly approaching. The wolf prince gained on him and passed him. Nathan stood erect as Alexander approached. She could tell by the look on his face that he was furious. Completely ignoring Nathan, he glared at Rebekah. "I need to speak with you...*now.*"

His eyes glowed silver; they were wild with fury.

"Alexander, I would like to introduce you..."

"The older brother. We've met. Or haven't you noticed...he's wearing my outfit."

Marcus moved excitedly between Rebekah and Nathan, "Queen Rebekah..."

Nathan interrupted him, "Marcus, go back inside."

"But..."

Alexander shifted his focus to Marcus. "Ah, yes, Prince Marcus...my wolves told my father and me about you. I wouldn't creep into The Lair again if I were you. Treaty or not, they know your scent and think it means food."

Marcus paled at the wolf prince's tone. Rebekah could see the muscles in Nathan's arms and chest tighten at Alexander's remark.

Nathan crossed his arms over his muscular chest, leveling his eyes at his brother, "*Now*, Marcus."

Marcus sullenly walked back toward the castle, his head hung low. Rebekah called after him, "Young lion! Don't forget to save a dance for me!"

Marcus turned back and smiled widely, skipping back to the ballroom.

Alexander was now glaring at Nathan, "*Prince*, I don't like hearing how the remnant of the clan put herself in harm's way over a silly boy's broken leg! That blood alone threw my pack into frenzy!"

Rebekah's eyes grew wide. *He knew.*

Nathan's eyes narrowed at the mention of the word "remnant." "What are you talking about?"

Rebekah placed her hand on Alexander's arm, "Alex..."

Alexander grabbed Rebekah's wrist and shoved her sleeve up to reveal a deep burn where the moonlight struck her. Nathan's eyes softened at the gruesome scar; his arms fell away from his muscular chest. He delicately touched her arm and looked at her with deep concern. "Did my brother do this?"

Rebekah shook her head. "No." She shifted her gaze to Alexander; her eyes darkening to a cool brown. "My *cousin* knows exactly how this was done." She took her arm and pushed the sleeve back down. "Do not fret, lion...your brother was worth it. Thank you for the dance — and the conversation. Excuse us."

She nodded to him and grabbed Alexander by the elbow; pulling him back toward the castle. He shook his arm free from her grasp. They glared at each other.

"Queen Rebekah..."

She stopped and turned. Nathan approached slowly, now ignoring Alexander. "Thank you for dancing with me this evening." His eyes bored into hers as he reached for her hand, bringing it slowly to his lips. He kissed it. "It meant more to me than you know. I would like to see you again."

Alexander was about to protest when Rebekah hit him with her other arm, silencing him. "Come tomorrow. And bring the young cub with you."

"Until tomorrow."

Nathan bowed and watched her go as she walked swiftly back to the ballroom.

"Don't say it! Poe never should have told you!"

"Poe was right to tell me. That was a *stupid* thing to do! You are the remnant. The livelihood of your clan's existence depends on you!" He grabbed her by her arm and spun her around so that they were face to face. "Until you are married with children of your own...you must think!"

Rebekah tore her arm away, "Do not underestimate me or my confidence in you, Alexander. You overstep your boundary."

Her eyes were now dark brown.

Alexander's eyes, however, glowed silver, "If anything ever happened to you, I would never forgive you for it."

"Nothing is going to happen to me."

Alexander's jaw clenched into a tight grimace, "You don't get it, do you?"

Rebekah leveled her eyes at Alexander, "That prince would've been slaughtered, Alex. The choice was mine, no matter what it cost me. *End* of discussion!"

Alexander grabbed her arm once more. "Treaty or not...stay away from the lions. Stay out of The Den. And no more gifts for the unworthy."

A frog waiter with a bright yellow, fluorescent stripe down the middle of his forehead stuck a goblet of wine between them. He carried a tray of them. "A drink for the beautiful queen!"

Rebekah ripped her arm from Alexander's grasp. She turned to the waiter and smiled politely.

The frog waiter bowed proudly. "It is the specialty of my clan."

Alexander waved him away, "No, the queen doesn't drink."

Rebekah glared at him, "You are not my king."

She took a goblet from the tray and gulped it down entirely.

Alexander took the goblet from her and hurled it aside. Another frog waiter walked by. She reached for another goblet and turned to Alexander with a challenging look on her face.

"You drink that, and I'm not taking care of you when you get sick."

Rebekah smiled at him in defiance, "Who says I'm going to get sick?" She guzzled it down just as Princess Lara approached. Alexander cringed the moment he saw her coming closer. Shyly, she curtsied to him, "Prince Alexander, I was wondering...would you like to dance?"

Rebekah looked at him in satisfied amusement as she watched him trying to regain his composure.

He continued to look at Rebekah; the muscles along his jawline twitched. A smug expression spread across her face. Alexander turned and bowed to Lara. "I would be honored." Without another word, he escorted Lara onto the dance floor.

Nathan searched the ballroom floor for Marcus. The moment he caught sight of his younger brother, he crooked his finger, beckoning him to come forth — the look on his face was severe. Marcus walked over, and Nathan grabbed him by the back of the neck, driving Marcus into the nearby hallway.

"Ow! What did I do?"

"What happened in the woods the night you were in The Lair? Don't lie to me!"

Marcus, terrified by the angry look on his brother's face, blurted out, "I fell and broke my leg. Queen Rebekah fixed it to help me get away."

"How?"

"I don't know. She reached up to the moon while she was touching my leg. Then there was a bright light and a loud snap and my leg was all fixed. The light hurt her and her raven. He got mad, but it wasn't my fault!"

Nathan absorbed his words in deep reflection. He calmed, "No, it wasn't. But the wolf prince was right. She shouldn't have done it." He was speaking more to himself than to Marcus. "She is the remnant. If anything happens to her..." He looked back at the bird warriors gathered around the ballroom.

Marcus finished his thought, "The birds die!"

A shadow cast itself over Nathan's face, "Yes...the Bird Clan falls." A determined look came across Nathan's face. "Nothing must happen to the queen." He searched the crowd and saw Rebekah dancing with the Critter Chief Rayford; Alexander and Lara were dancing beside them.

Rebekah was absolutely hammered. The song ended and the lions roared. Alexander bowed to Lara, and just as he and Rayford were about to switch positions, King Brutus stepped up opposite Rebekah.

He was a massive specimen of a man, elegantly dressed in a half open shirt; his tanned skin accentuated the lines of the muscles on his chest. He bowed to Rebekah, "Queen…"

He extended his hand to Rebekah. Giddy from the alcohol, she smiled and lifted her hand, "King…"

As she was about to grab onto his, Alexander stepped in front of Brutus and pulled her off the dance floor and away from the gorilla king's grasp.

Rebekah could barely focus, "Alexander, the room is spinning."

Alexander clenched his jaw, "I knew it! I'm taking you home." He looped his arm through hers and headed over to Reginald.

Rebekah looked down at Alexander's arm, "Are we dancing? It feels like we're twirling."

"No, we're not dancing." He approached the eagle captain. "Reginald, the queen is too intoxicated to fly. She'll more than likely fall out of the sky in this state. I'll have my wolves take her home. Tell my mother and father, will you?"

Reginald nodded as he took in his intoxicated queen. She grinned at him; he could not help but smile back. She was happy.

"We will follow you from above. I shall gather the flock." He nodded and lost his balance, feeling slightly dizzy himself.

Alexander shook his head in disbelief, "Great…"

Reginald collected himself. "I'm fine, King." He nodded to Poe, silent communication passing between them. Poe snuck back into the shadows and disappeared. Reginald bowed to Rebekah and left to gather the rest of the flock. From the top of the staircase, Nathan reluctantly watched them go.

Alexander escorted Rebekah to the courtyard gates where members of the Wolf Pack awaited.

"Skoll, carry the queen home. I'll run beside you."

"Yes, my prince."

He dropped down on all fours. Alexander helped place Rebekah on top of Skoll's massive back. She lowered her head onto his fur. "Skoll, you smell nice."

Skoll looked at her sideways, amused by her current demeanor, "Thank you, Queen." He barked to the pack, and they took off across the plains. Alexander raced beside them as the entire flock of bird soldiers flew in protection from above. In the darkened sky, Poe soared across the moon, cloaked in shadow as he headed toward Gorilla Jungle.

CRAFTY KING

XI

The moment they arrived at Bird Kingdom, Alexander picked up Rebekah and carried her inside. Falcon soldiers lined up in front of the gates as Reginald soared past them and on toward the northernmost tower.

Rebekah's face was nestled in Alexander's neck as he carried her toward her bedchambers. "Alexander, the room is still spinning."

"You never listen to me."

"What? You know, if I weren't a queen, I would be a ballerina in another life. I'm happy, Alexander. And I didn't think I would be."

Feeling her so close, he was having a hard time concentrating. "Would you mind not saying my name like that? It's very distracting, Rebekah."

She lifted her head and whispered in his ear. *"Alexander..."*

He threw her onto her bed. She landed and burst into laughter. "Do that again!"

Alexander sat on the bed and unlaced her boots for her. She laid back against the pillow and beamed like a young girl. "We got to dance! And to see all the clans united together...laughing...I didn't expect it."

He tossed her boots onto the floor and started to unlace her shirt. She swatted his hand away. "Stop that! I can do that myself."

He unlaced his shoes. She leaned back against her pillows, her head in the clouds. Alexander started massaging her feet as she continued to relay her thoughts on the evening. "And Nathan is an unbelievable dancer. Who knew lions could move like that."

Alexander brought his feet up onto the bed.

"Rub."

She started massaging his feet while he rubbed hers. "That feels good. You have good hands, Alexander. And I know why. A large bird told me about your ventures in Gorilla Jungle."

He froze. He had no idea she knew about that. She looked at his feet, suddenly mesmerized by them. "Alexander...you have very big feet."

"Your birds are watching where they don't belong."

She looked up at him, "Ah, but I see too."

He could feel his chest tighten.

"And what do you see, Rebekah?"

She looked at his face and took in his features.

"Right now...three of you."

Alexander threw her feet off him and crossed his arms over his muscular chest, trying to stop the pounding in his head. He rested his head against her bedpost and closed his eyes. "You don't see much. Keep rubbing."

"Yes, I do." Her voice softened, "I see that you love me. That's why you haven't signed that marriage contract."

He opened his eyes and looked at her; his heart thundered in his chest.

"There's been something I need to say to you, and I need you to hear me, wolf." She stopped rubbing his feet and moved closer to him.

He could barely breathe. Rebekah took his hand and stared at it, trying to find the words. She knew it was a copout telling him this way. But this night had changed many things for her, although this one thing had always remained the same — her feelings for him, but not the kind she knew he wanted.

"You are so fun. Brave. You listen to me. Even though I don't listen to you."

Alexander touched her face. She took his hand away and placed it in hers.

"You challenge me. You even wear matching outfits with me." She looked at him. "I love you, you know."

His heart exploded at her words. He had no excuse anymore not to say it — what he was truly feeling.

"Then marry me."

Rebekah looked at the earnestness in his face. "Oh, Alex…I would marry you in a heartbeat, but…"

"No…no buts…"

He moved in for the kill. He grabbed Rebekah's face in both hands and kissed her passionately, years of desire pouring forth from his very being. He ripped her shirt open and moved his hand inside, taking her boomerang from her corset. He threw it onto the floor. He moved her further back onto the bed, kissing her face, her hair…

"Alex…"

"Rebekah…"

She tapped his shoulder.

He kissed her again. "Don't interrupt me." He kept kissing her. She tapped him on the shoulder once more. He pulled back and looked down at her.

"Alex…I don't feel very good."

She closed her eyes and passed out. He could not believe it. How he had wanted this moment to come — all these years of waiting, wanting, desiring. In every woman he saw, he saw Rebekah. With every woman he had, he wanted her. He touched her ruby lips with a deep longing. "Woman…" He almost cried as he looked at her. "I have always loved you."

He laid his cheek against her chest, closing his eyes as he listened to her heartbeat. "Always…ever…you…" After several moments, he finally decided to get up and tuck her into bed. He kissed her softly and put the covers over her, moving her hair from her forehead as she slept peacefully. She looked like a little girl sleeping in her enormous bed. His heart ached the longer he looked at her. Ever since he was a boy, he knew it was with her that he belonged. And from this night on, he vowed silently to never leave her side. Tomorrow he would tell his parents to break the contract with the mariner king. Tomorrow he would propose to Rebekah. Tomorrow his dreams would come true. He moved around the canopy bed and toward his self-claimed quarters, feeling a sense of peace, even though the night had not gone the way he expected or hoped.

He heard Rebekah shift in her bed as she mumbled, "Thank you, Nathan..."

He froze. Every muscle in his body tightened at the sound of the lion prince's name. Alexander looked back at Rebekah sound asleep in her giant bed.

He waited there, waiting to her if she would speak his name again. But she was utterly silent, fast asleep in her giant bed.

She had not meant it. No, she's merely drunk.

But what if she had?

In utter frustration, he swiped at one of her bedposts, hacking it clean off. The post slammed into the far wall, smashing in half. A falcon soldier burst inside the room just as Alexander stormed past him and down the hall. Tomorrow could not come soon enough.

Poe flew over the great dam by Mariner Sea. The land below him was burnt out and yellow; no sign to deter anyone from the idea of the existing famine the realm had come to accept — but not Poe. He remembered the bodies. He knew what he had seen. The markings, the weapons. The owl warriors had watched and listened. They had seen the shadows as they crossed into The Lair and into Bird Kingdom. Lions could not be trusted. Palimus had been right from the beginning. He alone had known that the lions wished to rule the realm, and he had known that to bring the lion down was the only way the realm would truly be at peace. Subdue The Den, relish in peace. It was the sworn oath of the ravens from the time of the Old War — and he was chief of his clan.

He landed atop the dam and crouched down over its ledge. His red eyes scanned the water levels, clearly noting their height. He tilted his ebony head as the sight of the water levels confirmed what he had believed from the beginning.

Poe moved to the lion and gorilla king's sides and looked down at the rivers flowing from the dam, over the canals, and into their lands. His eyes narrowed as he focused on the canals.

"Tok...tok...tok..."

His eyes glowed a menacing red.

"Crafty king..."

Poe suddenly heard a splash in the water. He looked down into the sea and saw a shark fin circling near the edge of the dam. Poe took a pebble from an opening in the rock wall and tossed it down onto the ground on the other side of the canal. The shark fin sank into the murky waters. Within seconds, a shark warrior vaulted out of the sea, landing directly beside the pebble. The shark warrior was crouched, scanning the grounds all around with his spear at his side. Poe was above him, blending into the shadows with his darkened colors that absorbed his form into the colors of night.

"Tok...tok...tok..."

The shark warrior whirled around, searching for the raven assassin. The gills around his large head moved up and down as he continued to search the shadows all around.

"Marinersss...protecting the bullsss' ssside...just like the Old War..."

The mariner whirled around again at the sound of Poe's raspy whispers, only to come face to face with the darkness. The shark's doll-like eyes were not meant for night vision — they were meant for the sea. And for that reason, he never saw Poe coming as he drove his dagger through the shark warrior's heart.

The shark gasped as the raven warrior attacked from behind. Poe's massive arm was wrapped around the mariner warrior's large neck, holding him close as he drove his weapon deeper still. The moment Poe felt the shark warrior's body go limp, he hurled the soldier's body back into the sea — a sign and a warning to the mariners that they would not get away with what they had started.

Poe launched into the sky and out toward the woods near the Wolf Lair. He headed toward Bird Kingdom.

His body seethed with anger as he soared across the valley, for now he had the proof his queen needed — the proof she had wanted from the beginning.

Lionsss could not be trusted. Marinersss could not be trusted.

Like the Old War.

He was almost to Raven Territory when a painful caw escaped his ebony beak; Poe faltered. He clutched his heart, wincing in pain. *"My queen...I feel it..."*

He fought to remain in the sky as his eyes began to droop; he was losing consciousness. Poe cawed loudly one last time before falling through the clouds, plunging down to the ground below.

THE DAWN
XII

Alexander stepped into the hallway and called out to Rebekah, "*Bird*, I'm leaving! How's your head?"

Rebekah did not answer. He moved inside her chambers. "I know you didn't go flying this morning. I told you not to drink. You should have listened to me."

He looked inside but did not see her. The covers on her bed were disheveled; several pillows were on the floor.

Alexander looked around the room and stepped out onto her balcony. The sun shown brightly, but there was no warmth in the dawn this day. Even the flowers in the garden below seemed to be wilting. A cold wind suddenly blew through the courtyard, chilling Alexander to the bone. And that's when he noticed it. Not a single bird could be heard in the entire kingdom.

Something was wrong.

His heart plummeted into his stomach. *"Rebekah..."*

"Alex..."

It was the faintest whisper, but he head heard it. He whirled around and saw Rebekah's outstretched hand on the floor. Lying on the ground near the chessboard, she was pale and sweaty. Her eyes were open, looking at nothing and no one. She was holding onto Alex's king piece in her other hand.

"Rebekah!"

He rushed to her side, scooping her up in his strong arms. Her body trembled violently, *"The wine..."* Her eyes rolled into the back of her head; she began convulsing.

Alexander shouted to the sky, *"REGINALD!!! SKOLL!!! POE!!!"*

Reginald flew in from the window and crashed into the wall near the queen's bed. Skoll burst through the hall rapidly taking in the situation.

He growled as if he were in pain the moment he saw Reginald's crippled form lying in the corner, *"Eagle..."*

Reginald was breathing hard; he struggled to rise, but it was useless. He collapsed onto the floor as his feathers began to rapidly wilt before Alexander's eyes as they fell from his body and onto the floor.

Alexander roared, *"Reginald!"*

Skoll growled at the unknown force that had infected the birds and their queen. Reginald struggled to breathe, he could barely keep his eyes open, "I am weak, good prince. My queen... I can feel the poison." His massive body began to convulse; his eyes closed as he fell flat to the floor. Skoll rushed to Reginald's side, his fur stood on end as he tried to rouse the eagle captain.

"*SKOLL!* Get my mother and father! *NOW!*"

Skoll snarled and leapt from the queen's balcony, barking to the other members of the pack on the grounds below. It was then that the bird soldiers began to fall from the sky. Alexander saw them from the balcony, plunging to the gardens below, colliding into the kingdom walls. The entire castle began to shake and rumble upon impact. He looked down at Rebekah, "No! *No!* Rebekah, hold on!"

But the birds kept falling.

Rebekah's body went still.

And all was silent.

Alexander shouted, *"REBEKAH! NOT YET! YOU'RE NOT ALLOWED TO GO! YOU'RE NOT DONE! NOT YET!"*

He laid her on the ground and began to give her mouth-to-mouth.

"YOU'RE NOT ALLOWED TO LEAVE ME BEHIND!"

He breathed into her, trying to revive her, pumping her chest over and over again.

"WAKE UP! DO YOU HEAR ME, BIRD?!? WAKE...UP!!!"

He continued to breathe into her. And then he heard it...her heartbeat, it was faint but steady. He sat back and watched her as her chest rose and fell. Tears of relief streamed down his face as he continued to watch her breathe.

He grabbed his head in his hands and let out a cry of anguish. Alexander lifted his head and looked at Reginald's slumped body in the corner of the room. Although she was revived, the poison was still inside of her; he had to get it out. But how?

Gathering his emotions, he leaned down near Rebekah's ear and spoke the words, "You are not going out this day, nor any other day that strips away what you have yet to do. You have not fixed it. You have not done what it was you were born to do. I'm not going to do it for you. I'm not going to lift your banner for you to see it through. You're the one, you're the one who's going to have to do it. You're going to have to fight through this blow in order to shine on. *DO YOU HEAR ME, BIRD?!? YOU'RE NOT DONE YET!*"

He listened for her heart, but it did not pound any stronger or any louder at his words — it pounded even less. He grabbed her medallion and clutched it in his hands. Staring at the emblem of the sun, his body shook as he shouted, *"HELP ME!!!!"*

A slow wind blew.

Nathan, Marcus, SinJin, Apollo, and Roman crossed the mountainous border toward Bird Kingdom. Marcus was carrying a bouquet of dandelions in his tiny arms. As they took in the enormous peaks before them, they could not help but take in the utter sight of majestic beauty as they headed north. Nathan breathed in the height of the Great Mountains, taking in their majesty, just as the wind swirled slowly through his light wavy hair.

He stopped short the moment he felt it. The tattoo on his neck darkened, and his eyes slit to a cat the moment he saw the large ostrich warriors lying all across the ground. The Lion Guard growled; their manes stood on end, seeing the still bodies of the bird warriors. Marcus dropped the bouquet in horror.

"What's wrong with them?"

Nathan searched the sky. All that could be heard was the wind. There were no birds anywhere. His head shifted to the direction of the queen's castle. Without another word, he took off racing across the landscape toward Bird Kingdom. The Lion Guard roared and everyone in the party followed.

The moment they reached the castle gate, they were leaping over bird warrior bodies, trampling through them as Nathan and the Lion Guard stormed inside. SinJin held Marcus back and remained in the queen's garden.

Nathan and his guards burst inside the queen's chambers. The moment Alexander saw Nathan, he seethed. In hyper-defense mode, he rushed Nathan, diving into him, slamming him against the wall. Nathan tried to fight him off as Alexander continued to relentlessly attack him. Apollo ripped Alexander off of his prince.

Apollo lifted his massive claw to swipe at him when Nathan shouted, *"NO!!!"*

Apollo lowered his claw as Alexander moved backward, whipping out his sword as he stood protectively in front of Rebekah's bed, guarding the queen.

Nathan saw Rebekah's unconscious, pale form lying still on the bed. All color drained from his handsome face. "What happened?"

"She's been poisoned by one of the frogs at your ball!"

Nathan moved toward Rebekah. Alexander immediately pointed his sword at Nathan's chest. "Get away from her!"

Apollo growled viciously. Nathan put his hand up as a sign of peace. He looked at Alexander, "She's dying, Alexander. Let me help her. Tell me which frog. What did he look like?"

"I don't know!"

"*Think!* He must be found!"

Alexander tried to remember. A flash of the frog's face came rushing forth. "He had a bright yellow stripe down the middle of his forehead."

Nathan roared to his guard, "Apollo! Find him! Search every home in the swamps until he's found! Roman! Get the gorilla king! *NOW!!!*"

A wolf howled in the distance.

Apollo and Roman roared in reply to their prince and burst over the queen's balcony just as the wolf king, queen and Skoll leapt through the room. Queen Tatiana rushed to her goddaughter's side; she touched her goddaughter's forehead. "Alex, get me some cool towels and heat your dagger. We have to get her fever down and bleed her to get some of the poison out." She looked up and saw Nathan. "Prince Nathan!"

He bowed slightly, trying to contain his emotions. "Queen, I've sent my guard to hunt down the frog responsible for this. They are also summoning the gorilla king. He must have something in his jungle to counteract the poison. He has to. I don't know what else to do." He stood there helplessly.

King Ivan marched inside, "Lion, your father must know of this. The Amphibians were once enemy to The Den as well. Skoll!!! Have the pack guard these gates!"

He bowed, "King…" Skoll barks over the balcony, calling to the pack.

Tatiana examined Rebekah. Alexander could see the fear stretching forth across his mother's face. "Ivan…"

She looked up at the wolf king. Tears filled her eyes as she whispered the words, "I don't think she'll make it another sunrise."

Even from her low tone, Alexander heard it all.

Ivan looked down at his wife with confident reassurance, "Tatiana…she is not going to die. Do you understand?"

She nodded her head, collecting herself as she began the task of rubbing Rebekah's legs to draw the fever away from the queen's head.

King Ivan looked at his son, seeing the pain in Alexander's eyes.

"Alexander..."

Alexander looked up at his father. "Don't speak a truth to me you do not dare to believe." He returned to the task of helping his mother care for Rebekah.

Nathan could see the slightest look of fear behind the wolf king's eyes as he looked at the bird queen. He knew Alexander was right. With one last look at Rebekah, Nathan followed Ivan out the door with Skoll. Skoll and Nathan eyed one another as they charged through the gardens and out toward The Den. Nathan shouted to the lynx warrior, "SinJin! Take Marcus inside with the wolf queen and prince!"

Marcus watched as his brother raced toward The Den with the Wolf Pack at his side.

Nathan and Ivan raced through the Lion's Den. They burst through the courtyard with members of the Wolf Pack howling their arrival. Nathan and Ivan headed toward the throne room. Nobles and guards rose, alarmed as they passed.

Nathan roared to the king, *"FATHER!!!"* Nathan burst through the throne room doors. Gunthar looked up as Nathan and Ivan rushed inside. The Bull King Rom was with him. Gunthar's eyes grew wide upon seeing King Ivan.

Nathan was breathing hard as he exclaimed, "The bird queen's been poisoned!"

Gunthar rose from his throne, *"What!"*

"Last night...by one of the frog waiters."

Gunthar looked to King Ivan, "Are you sure?!?"

Ivan nodded gravely as Nathan continued, "I just left her kingdom. The birds...they were falling out of the sky."

Rom watched for Gunthar's reaction. Gunthar slammed his fist into his chair and rose, "Wolf! The bird queen can't be dead!"

Ivan replied, "She isn't, lion."

Gunthar sat back down in his chair. "She lives?"

"Yes, but I don't know for how long. She needs protection at her gates against the amphibians. Some of my pack is there now."

Roman and the Gorilla King Brutus stormed inside. Brutus looked at Nathan. "I got your message."

Gunthar turned to Brutus, "What do you know about this?"

Brutus gripped his bone scepter in his massive fist. He did not look happy. "All I know is that the amphibian king has no cause to attack the queen. It was a sole individual who attempted this! Not the clan."

Gunthar's eyes darkened; his own tattoo grew dark, "The amphibians may be under your protection, Brutus, but you can't be certain what a king will and will not do!"

Brutus challenged the lion king, "I can when *I* am the king that rules over them!"

Rom continued to remain silent as he watched the entire exchange between the kings.

Brutus looked to King Ivan, "King Archer has a chief, a medicine man...the toad named Netapheha. I have commanded the king to send him to Queen Rebekah immediately."

Ivan nodded to him in respect, "Thank you, King."

Gunthar spat out the words, "A toad...superstition."

Brutus' eyes darkened.

"And if Archer doesn't obey?"

Brutus gripped his scepter tight, the veins in his massive muscles bulged beneath his shirt. "Then I'll kill Archer myself and any other king who gets in my way. Then I'll find the toad chief and send him to her anyway. If the queen dies, we all die."

Gunthar held the gorilla king's stare, but said nothing in reply.

King Ivan warned the kings, "We must all be on guard for attack against our heirs in case Brutus is wrong. The amphibians were almost wiped out by both the birds and the lions during the Old War."

Gunthar nodded and turned toward his son, "Nathan, make sure Marcus is taken to Bull Valley immediately."

"He's at Bird Kingdom with Queen Tatiana and Prince Alexander."

Brutus and Rom exchanged a look. Gunthar's eyes slit to a cat and his tattoo darkened to pure black. "What were you two doing there?!?"

Nathan looked at him in confusion, "Carrying out the treaty, Father..."

Gunthar took in his son's words, his voice remaining low and lethal. "Go get your brother."

Apollo suddenly burst inside and threw the frog waiter down onto the floor. The frog was absolutely terrified and badly beaten. Behind him walked the mariner king.

"He wasn't hard to find. The frog was in the swamps on the south side of the dam. Your guard came to me immediately to help hunt down this murderer!"

Nathan lunged for him, but Gunthar vaulted in front of him, grabbing him by the shoulders; he threw him against a pillar, "His fate is for *kings* to decide!"

He released his son and turned back toward the frog. The frog tried to scatter backwards on the ground away from him, but the gorilla and mariner kings were behind him, blocking his escape. Gunthar crouched down to the frog. "Now tell me, frog...who put you up to this?"

The frog shook his head profusely. Gunthar lowered his head; his eyes glowed a hue of gold. His crouched shadow loomed over the frog's terrified face.

From the grounds of The Den, the lion roared.

THE STONE
XIII

The Toad Chief Netapheha was a sight to behold. With his scholarly-looking robe and large golden crown on his head, Marcus was absolutely mesmerized. In wide-eyed awe, he watched the chief waddle back and forth, murmuring to himself before suddenly shouting a command for any one of those in attendance to obey.

He had arrived with two frog warriors, using a coral staff that helped aid his hobbled gait. They had arrived swiftly at the gorilla king's command, and upon seeing Rebekah's pale form, even the toad's mustard skin had turned white. Netapheha hobbled over to Rebekah, gently touching her forehead. That was when he saw the queen's medallion laying gently against her chest.

"They don't know, queen…they don't know what it is they do…A POT! I NEED A POT!"

His voice echoed throughout the room as he shouted at everyone and no one. Tatiana immediately rose and exited the room to obtain one. Alexander never left Rebekah's side, holding her cold, pale hand while she remained unconscious.

Nathan had returned along with King Ivan. The wolf king had ordered his pack to gather up the bird warriors who had fallen from the sky, bringing them inside the kingdom gates. They were all unconscious like their queen, having felt the deathblow dealt to the remnant of the clan.

Marcus watched in fascination as the chief jumped into action. He had taken the clay pot Tatiana had brought back and began feeling its insides with his webbed fingers, murmuring to himself all the while as if he were testing the pot's durability. He walked all around the bed, sprinkling gold dust all around the covers, having pulled a mysterious small bag he had taken from inside his fuchsia, velvet robe.

The moment he reached the side of the bed Alexander was sitting on, the toad chief suddenly stopped murmuring and shifted his bulbous eyes to the wolf prince. Taking in his forlorn appearance, he suddenly spoke the words, "Yes, yes, heartache and pain within your rage will quickly bring your demise." He reached into his bag and grabbed for more dust. He tossed it once in Alexander's direction as if dismissing him with a single flick of his webbed hand.

"May your cornerstone light your way…yes, yes…"

Without anything further, he hobbled back to the other side of the bed, leaving Alexander completely befuddled. Without looking at anyone in particular, Netapheha shouted once again, "LION CUB! COME HERE!"

Marcus looked at Nathan standing alone in the corner, unsure of whom the toad chief was speaking to. Nathan nodded at him, and the young prince approached. Netapheha handed him the pot, barely glancing at him as he removed the crown from his head.

"Watch, watch...you need to remember..."

Netapheha pulled a magenta stone from the center of his crown and dropped it into the pot. He pulled a small group of berries from another hidden pocket inside his robe and tossed it into the pot as well. He lifted his large bulbous eyes, looking intently into Marcus' own.

"This borax stone is from outside the realm. It will heal the queen. Remember...remember..."

The toad chief took the end of his coral staff and touched it lightly to Rebekah's head.

"She needs her raven. SEND THE WOLF! Send the wolf to pick up the pieces."

Poe.

Alexander had forgotten all about him. He looked at his father and watched as Ivan quickly left the room, answering the toad chief's command.

"Angry she will be...wrath of the raven cannot be...good queen, good queen, peace…"

He took the stem of his staff and plunged it into the pot, crushing the wild berries, hammering his staff down against the stone as Marcus continued to hold onto it.

"A gift, a gift, a gift for me…it is what the earth gave to me. Remember, young lion, you will see…"

Clutching the pot within his tiny arms, Marcus tried not to drop the pot as Netapheha kept hammering away at the stone. How the chief was strong enough to break it, Marcus had no clue, but he looked at the old chief with the gold dust and robe filled with mystery, never knowing that such things existed — especially *outside* the realm.

Satisfied with his concoction, Netapheha took the pot from Marcus' hands and moved closer toward the queen.

"HOT WATER!"

Nathan jumped at the toad's sudden shout as he made his way across the room to the large hearth in the far corner of Rebekah's bedchambers near the chessboard. Nathan took the small cauldron hanging over the fire and brought it over to the toad chief.

Netapheha explained to Marcus what he was doing. "This is from the juice of a wild berry that grows near the tide pools. Yes, yes…slow acting." He looked at Nathan, "POUR!"

Nathan poured the water into the pot. The toad chief mumbled to himself, watching as the stone dissolved. He looked up at Queen Tatiana, "Dear lady, this is an antidote for the poison, but it will be

a long while before the queen recovers. She will be quite weak. Her birds will recover much slower than she. The queen must marry and have an heir if the clan is to survive another attack."

The toad looked at Nathan, "Soon…soon…GOBLET!"

Tatiana grabbed for one of the goblets near the chessboard and handed it to the chief. Netapheha took a spoonful of the antidote and dropped it into the goblet to cool. He motioned for Alexander to lift Rebekah up so she could swallow it; she was still unconscious. Alexander lifted the goblet to her lips and helped it go down.

Several moments passed without any movement from Rebekah. Nathan stood in the corner, frozen to the spot, watching for any sign of stirring. Alexander held her hand, listening ever so closely to the sound of her heartbeat. Neither prince was breathing as they waited.

Then, suddenly, they heard the faint sound of a crow cawing in the distance. Once. Twice. Until the sound of cockerel cries echoed across the garden and throughout the queen's chambers. Nathan closed his eyes in silent relief, while Alexander watched Rebekah's chest rise and fall into a rhythmic cycle of deeper breaths. Marcus looked back at Nathan with a huge smile on his face.

Queen Tatiana let out a cry of relief as she rushed to Rebekah's side, "Oh, my dear…"

Rebekah slowly opened her eyes and saw her godmother beside

her. Tatiana took her free hand and held it tight. Rebekah looked over at Alexander.

"Alex..."

Tears of relief streamed down his strong, handsome face as he kissed the top of her forehead and stroked her hair. She looked around the room, catching sight of the toad chief. Her voice was barely a whisper, "Thank you."

He nodded in respect. "It is the lion prince you should thank, young queen, for you see...you see..."

Netapheha looked over at Nathan standing in the back corner of the room. Rebekah followed his gaze. They stared at one another in silence.

"Lion...you came..."

He smiled faintly at her from across the room.

Marcus approached her side, "I brought you flowers! But then I dropped them..."

"Young lion..." She was too weak to say anything more. She fell back asleep.

Queen Tatiana moved a piece of hair from her goddaughter's forehead. "She needs her rest now, Alex."

His eyes never left Rebekah's face, "I'm not leaving her."

Tatiana touched her son's cheek, wiping the tears from his strong, handsome face. She walked over to Netapheha, leading him out with his frog warriors.

Nathan called out to his brother, "Come on, Marcus."

"Is she going to be all right?"

Nathan looked at Rebekah's sleeping face and nodded silently. Marcus reluctantly joined his brother's side as they turned and headed for the door.

"Lion..."

Nathan turned at Alexander's call. Still looking down at Rebekah, he finished his statement. "Thank you."

Nathan nodded silently as the princes headed back to The Den.

Brutus was seated on a chair in the throne room inside The Den; Gunthar was pouring himself a goblet of wine. "So the birds were falling from the sky...kill the remnant, annihilate the clan. Worried? Seeing as how you have that in common with the queen."

Brutus ground his teeth together. "Should I be?"

Gunthar smiled at the gorilla king as he drank his wine down.

"If not for your son, Gunthar, we'd all be dead. We need her. We need her birds."

"Don't be ridiculous, Brutus. And damn my son! He was only giving in to his lust by going to see that queen."

Brutus rose in anger, "Damn *him*? *Damn that frog!* How suicidal can one be to think that killing the queen would alter the past when the birds are the ones that bring the rain!"

"Because it's a myth! Superstition and hocus-pocus!" He slammed his goblet down. "That ball of fire in the sky we call the sun hasn't and will never change directions!"

Brutus moved closer to the lion king. "So you believe that the amphibians' prediction and my belief in it is..."

"*IGNORANT!!!* Toads telling me how to live by reading a rock! Ha! My den was once a desert and now, centuries later, it is turning into one again. The elements, which I cannot control, bring the rain. *Not the birds!* The only thing I can control is whether or not I bring my people food! And I would've had it...I would've had her lands if not for my son!"

Brutus' face darkened as he realized what Gunthar had just revealed.

Gunthar took another drink from his goblet. "It's The Den that will unite this realm! *We* will bring the peace! And if it means I have to kill a queen to do it, I will! And I'll do it to get her land so she can never withhold her food from any of us...because that's what her clan always does when you least expect it. They turn on you. Never forget it, Brutus!"

Gunthar finished his wine.

Brutus' voice was low and lethal, "It was you...you dare take it upon yourself to decide the fate of my clan!"

Gunthar hurled his goblet across the room. "And why not! At least one of us kings decided to act! If not for me, there would never have been a treaty! There wouldn't have been an opportunity to bridge the gap between what I want and what I need! And if I need it, you need it. *I* lead, *you* follow!"

"You are *not* king of my jungle!"

Gunthar looked at him with a venomous sneer, "Then *be* king of your jungle instead of ruling off of fear carved upon stones."

Brutus clutched the hilt of his bone scepter. "I don't want to war with you, Gunthar, but a battle it will be if you try to kill her again."

Gunthar scoffed, "You're taking this too personal, Brutus. I'm not after a war. I want peace. What I did was for the best. And I would do it again in a heartbeat. But if you want to fight, we'll fight. My den fights to win. And we always do, Brutus."

The kings held each other's stare.

"Send word to Mar. I want to see him."

"What for?"

Gunthar sat back down on his chair. "It's about my son."

A NEW DAWN

XIV

Rebekah lay awake watching the sun rise over her balcony. Dandelions filled her room. Alexander's head rested in her lap as she gently stroked it; he was fast asleep. As the sun's light moved across her bed, it gently reached out and kissed Alexander's weary head. She stroked his dark hair with her pale hand. Upon feeling her touch, he slowly opened his eyes and looked at her.

"Rebekah…"

Her voice was barely a whisper, "It's quiet."

Alexander swallowed hard, "The clan fell ill with you."

Rebekah did not reply but continued to stare out at the sun. Pools of tears filled her eyes, but she remained silent, staring out at the light. Alexander understood how she was feeling, knowing exactly what this news meant to her. She suddenly covered her face in her hands and started crying. "Alexander, I'm so stupid. So stupid..."

He was distraught at seeing her so vulnerable, "Stop it, Rebekah...how could you have known such a plot would be set against you under the guise of peace?" He chastised himself, "I should have been more on my guard in protecting you."

"It's not your job to protect me. I am a queen. I'm supposed to be wise and vigilant. I'm supposed to protect my clan. And I failed. I never wanted to bring harm...to my...people...I let my guard down. Just for an instant..." She continued to sob until she gained control of her cries. All Alexander could do was watch helplessly as she wept, for there was no comfort for her kind of woe.

"And my eyes have seen, Alex, but I did not act...I did not act on what I think the truth to be...because I didn't want to have to believe it. I demanded proof and then I didn't stand guard. And now...I don't want to go against my word. I don't want to be the enemy. And I will have to be. I will have to withhold what I promised to give."

He clasped her hand tight, not fully understanding what she meant, "It was the frog waiter who poisoned you. He was a rogue assassin seeking revenge against your clan from the Old War. They caught him. He confessed to it. There was no way for you to know."

She shook her head profusely, "Not the poison, Alex. The drought. The famine. I think the lion king is behind all of it."

"What are you talking about?"

She suddenly noticed the broken post on her bed. "Why is my bed broken?"

"The lion king has nothing to do with it. The lands in The Den are dry. You saw them yourself when we went to sign the treaty. And forget about the bed."

"They shouldn't *be* dry! You're not listening to me, *wolf*! The rain has never diminished. It falls directly into the sea! It's just like you said...I walked straight into the lion's den."

Alexander shook his head, trying to make meaning of her shouts.

"You broke my bed, didn't you!"

Alexander stood in exasperation, "I'll fix it! Besides, if what you're saying about the rain is true, then all it means is that the amphibians are right. The sun has shifted direction to the lion king's side causing the water to evaporate faster."

Rebekah's eyes darkened to that of the raven. "The sun hasn't changed direction. I watch it rise from the same spot *every* day. And, besides, you can't fix anything! You're terrible at it!"

Alexander paced all around her bed, contemplating everything she had just said, "I'm not that bad. Besides, why would Gunthar go to all the trouble you are suggesting to create a famine? What would he gain by starving his own people?"

Rebekah remained silent, staring out at the sun. Her voice was barely a whisper, "He does not honor the Sun...Palimus knew...that is the answer..."

Alexander looked at her pale form lying limply on the bed. She shifted her dark eyes to him, and what he saw behind them made his blood run cold.

"I feel death, Alex. I've heard its voice and am now kin to its call. I know that of which I speak. The lion king was the one who poisoned me."

It was then that Alexander looked at the chessboard, remembering that Rebekah held the king piece in her hand the moment he found her.

"You're tired, Rebekah. You're not making sense. You need your rest."

Rebekah closed her eyes and breathed in deeply, "Where is Poe?"

Alexander moved to her side and knelt by her bed. He touched her forehead, "Poe is still unaccounted for; Skoll is looking for him. You need to rest, Rebekah. The recovery of your clan depends on it. *I* depend on it."

"I know, cousin."

Alexander gritted his teeth, "Don't call me that."

Rebekah opened her eyes and looked at him; her eyes had softened to gray. She gently laid her hand against his strong face. "You are kin. You will always be kin to me, Alex."

His jaw tightened as he rested his strong hand over hers, "I love you, Rebekah. And I almost lost you." Tears stung his deep blue eyes. "I will never lose you again. I'm never going to leave your side. I'm going to marry you."

"Alex…"

But he would not let her finish, "I know you love me. You don't know what you're saying. You need your rest."

Rebekah lowered her hand; she was exhausted, "Alex, your mother told me late last night while you slept that your wedding is in a month."

Alexander narrowed his eyes in confusion, "What are you talking about? I haven't signed the contract."

"Your father signed it for you when Mar brought forth that frog. Only a king can break the contract now."

Alexander was speechless. As her words set in, he rose from her bed; his eyes were wild with fury, "HE CAN'T DO THAT!"

Her eyes began to close. "It's done."

Before he could say anything more, she closed her eyes and fell into a deep sleep.

Nathan was alone in the Great Library pouring over a large volume that covered the history of the amphibians.

"Are you still reading about the toads?"

Without lifting his head, he answered his younger brother, "Yes, I am."

Marcus entered the enormous room and made his way over to

his older brother. He leaned over Nathan's shoulder to see what he was reading. "What does it say?"

"Lots of things."

"Anything about Chief Netapheha and his potions?"

Nathan looked up from the page and closed the book. He looked at his younger brother, "No."

Marcus moved over to the corner of the desk and rested his chin on his tiny hand. "What do you think he meant?"

"What do you mean?"

"When he said that I need to remember?"

"I don't know. He was a bit strange."

"Yeah. But it was really neat what he did with that stone. I wish I knew how to make potions with stones. Then maybe I could've saved Rebekah."

Nathan looked at his younger brother and could not help but smile. "You like Queen Rebekah a lot, don't you?"

Marcus nodded in reply. "She's nice." Marcus looked up from the desk, "Are you going to marry her?"

Nathan laughed, "Maybe. I have to ask her first, you know."

"Are you going to make heirs with her?"

"And what do you know about making heirs?"

Marcus shrugged, "Maximillian said for me to go to Gorilla Jungle to find out."

Nathan sat back in his chair and crossed his arms over his chest. "And what did I tell you about listening to Max?"

"Not to." Marcus moved over to the other side of the desk. "I want to go see Rebekah."

Nathan picked up the large book once more, "It's too dangerous. Father said you have to stay here for the time being."

Marcus let out a deep sigh. "How is it more dangerous now that everyone signed a peace treaty?"

Nathan smiled in sympathy at his young brother's predicament, "I'll tell you what...if you want to write a letter to Queen Rebekah, I'll take it to her for you. I'm going to see her in a few days."

Marcus furrowed his brow, "Why do you get to go?"

Nathan handed Marcus a piece of paper. "Because I know how to sneak out of The Den *without* the guard."

Nathan went back to reading.

Marcus laid the piece of paper down. He asked, "Nathan, what does it mean to make an heir?"

Without looking up, Nathan handed Marcus a pen. "I'll tell you when you're nine."

Rebekah stood on her balcony overlooking her kingdom below. The gardens were still. Not a single bird warrior was in sight; they were still recovering just as she recovered. Pale and weak, she closed her eyes and listened.

She heard absolutely nothing.

The moonlight shone brightly down upon her. Tears streamed down her face as she willed herself to hear a single chirp, caw, or word from any member of her clan.

"I'm sorry…"

But there was no reply. Only the wind answered her as it blew gently through her raven hair. She was all alone. With nothing but the silence to surround her, the queen stood there, staring up at the moon holding the king chess piece in her hand. She held it tight, knowing that she should have trusted her instincts from the beginning, with or without the proof.

What kind of kings am I dealing with?

She thought back to the day all the clans had travelled to The Den. She had looked at each of the kings on the other side of the realm, searching for truth, searching for light, searching for dark. What had she seen then? What had she felt?

The gorilla king seemed to desire her and nothing else. She had not felt a threat under his hulky exterior — other than to her virtue — but nothing that would warrant the feeling of a threat that he had wanted her to die. Besides, that did not seem possible, for he was a remnant too. He would know what it meant to kill a king or queen who was last in their line, and he seemed to respect the responsibility of that kind of duty. She could not see that he would be so ruthless as to annihilate an entire clan — even her own. He had even sent the toad chief to help her. Yet…he was loyal to the lion king.

The lion king.

Rebekah's insides twisted the moment she thought of him. She knew the moment he had linked arms with her that his sincerity was only for show. She could see the tension behind his eyes as they tried to smile a little too much at her, with a little too much joy. The moment she realized she had been poisoned, the only thought was that it was he. Gut reaction, sixth sense, call it what you will…she knew it was he.

And at that moment, all she could think of was Palimus.

"What did Palimus do?"

He had waited. He had paused. He had not engaged. Did he have the same kind of feeling she had the day she received the lion king's request to come to The Den? That feeling that says, "Don't believe it."

And when all eyes in The Den were on her the moment the lion king asked her, "What say you…" did he hear that voice that said, *"The way to live is not to be ruled by the wants of the world, but to live to a higher standard that emboldens you to become. Sign it. Sign it for the people. But don't sign it for him."*

How she wished she had had Palimus' confidence to know when to move and when to stand still. For she had failed. She had failed herself. She had failed her clan. She had almost killed them, her children, by allowing her guard to come down for a moment of joy at a ball — something she had relished in a little too much with the lion king's son.

Nathan...

And in that moment, standing in the moonlight, Rebekah realized she had gotten what she had asked for. She was different than Palimus, and it was the first time in her life she did not want to be.

Rebekah's eyes dimmed slightly as the thought of how easy a target she had proven herself to be. She could feel the heat in her body rising as she thought of the lion king throwing a ball in her honor...only to be twirled into demise.

I need Poe...

Her heart pounded inside her fragile chest as she willed the raven inside of her to awaken — she knew the shadow within wanted to be roused; it desired nothing more than the moment to be born, for it was a burning strength that she needed to call upon in order to decide her next move. And she abhorred what she was thinking. She raged over the idea and hated the realm for forcing the idea to even enter her mind. But anger can be tamed. Anger can give direction. Anger...could be productive.

She clutched the king piece in her hand so tightly, her fingernails cut into her skin, causing her to bleed. Why be a good queen when the world did not want your kind of kindness? Why champion peace to those who don't deserve it? Why share your gifts for a world that does not want it?

The medallion hanging from her neck began to glow.

Why be kind when you could be cunning?

The wind whipped all around her the more her anger rose. The moonlight continued to shine down over her medallion, lighting it aglow. The trees and the shrubs in her garden began to writhe and shift. She could not control it — the rage.

How do you want to be remembered?

Tears streamed down her angry face as she fought to decide between her will to rise above this without losing her conviction and the desire to act befitting to the gauntlet thrown down by the world. The fire deep inside her continued to burn. She could feel her entire body grow hot as the rage continued to mount. She clutched the railing of her balcony, lowering her head as she fought the battle within her.

"Build...your...house..."

Her head snapped up the moment the words were spoken. The wind had died down, blowing gently across her face. She could see the gentle breeze blowing through her gardens. Seeing its gentle sway, she seemed to calm, breathing deeper as she watched the flowers slowly move from side to side.

"My queen..."

Whatever anger remained within her died the moment Rebekah heard her eagle's voice. She turned around and saw Reginald walking slowly toward her.

"Reginald..."

Seeing his dilapidated form, she wept the moment she saw him.

She walked toward him. He knelt down on one knee and bowed his large head upon her approach. She felt so unworthy of such an act, she silently sobbed as she took his large eagle head in her hands as he exposed his neck to her. He was breathing hard; the very act of walking weakened him.

"I'm so…sorry…"

She buried her head in his shoulder. He closed his eyes and laid his head against hers. The sound of her cries brought tears to his own.

"No, my queen, do not cry. I will mend. And more important, you are well. I can feel the beat of your heart in mine and it is strong. You are strong, my queen."

"Oh, Reginald, I'm such a fool. I jumped when I should have stood still. I reached out when I should have waited to be approached…and I clutched on. I'm such a fool."

Reginald closed his eyes as she cried, knowing that she needed to speak her thoughts aloud in order to best heal.

"Peace, my queen, peace…you cry for more than just this moment. You cry because you trust no one, and you wanted to in order for others to know you could be trusted. That is not a vice, my queen, but a virtue others will soon come to admire. There is one valiant prince who already has."

She lifted her head, wiping the tears from her face. "You speak of the lion prince."

He nodded.

"He was most unexpected, Reginald. He has...great words, words that mirror my own."

She looked out at the moonlight, "But words are futile, Reginald, when dealing with kings and their sons. Yet, I cannot help but like Prince Nathan all the same." She looked at Reginald and smiled sadly, "I like him very much." She shook her head. "Why does the world show you such beautiful things only to sneak up on you to then bring you all its horrors?"

Reginald placed his eagle hand over his heart, "You are more than just fond of him. I felt it the moment he stood beside you on the dance floor. We all did...we felt the flutter in your heart. No man has ever made you react so."

Rebekah moved over to one of the chairs on her balcony and sat down. She suddenly looked extraordinarily sad.

Reginald slowly rose from the floor and sat beside his queen, "What is it?"

"It wasn't the amphibian that poisoned me." She looked into his beautiful raptor eyes. "It was the lion king."

Reginald's pupils dilated to the size of pins.

She smiled sadly, "So you see, admiration...and love...cannot be. Not for me." She looked at the king piece in her hand. "And yet, I need an heir to protect the clan so that you may all live on."

"And you are certain that is was the lion king who is responsible?"

She stared up at the moon. "Truth is a funny thing, Reginald.

You shy away from it when you stand before it, wanting it to be otherwise. To escape its gaze is so very easy. To look into its eyes can shake your core and shatter your world. And yet, truth sets you free. I know this truth. I've heard its voice, faint and small, and yet I did not face it, although it was staring straight at me all along. That's why I feel so foolish. I wanted what I've dreamed knowing that dreams are so very impossible. But I thought, just for a moment, how nice it was that not everything was so hard. That some things really could be that easy. I took the road that has been trampled upon instead of the one never travelled. That was my mistake. I turned away from truth, wanting so very much to live in the world instead of remembering that I am a queen of the realm. And with that, comes greater responsibility, and more discernment of what it is I am meant to do while I am alive. I failed once. I will not fail again."

Without looking at him, she continued, "Besides, I know you are tired from more than just this murderous attempt. I know you have only returned just now from your travels."

The feathers on his head stood on end. He looked down, unable to face his queen.

"You went to the swamps to see the toad chief."

"Yes, I did."

She shifted her eyes to look at him.

"So you know that I'm right."

Reginald ruffled his feathers, barely lifting his head to meet his queen's stare. "I wanted to know. And I knew you would need proof if you were to face the kings and queen on our side of the realm when you chose to reveal the truth to them. They would need it too, for such news is not easy to bear. It is as you say. I went there to ask the toad how he recognized the poison. He said…he recognized the symptoms. It was an old form of poisoning that had not been tried in centuries, but he knew. 'It was from a plant that only grows in the Lion's Den,' he said."

"And yet you knelt there in silence as I told you my thoughts. Why?"

He could not meet her stare. "I wish you to be happy, my queen. And the lion prince…has made you so."

Rebekah tapped her long finger on the armrest. "Correction. You want me to be married. You want me to produce an heir in order to insure the clan's survival."

Reginald swiveled his head in her direction, "There is nothing wrong with wanting my queen to be married!"

"There is when it is to the son of the king who tried to destroy my clan! I can see it in your eyes, Reginald."

"Because it reflects what I see in yours!"

She looked away from him and out at the moonlight.

"Yes, I want you married. After this episode, the clan has every reason to desire it. You are not safe. Who knows what the lion king will try next to finish what he started! There may be war! And we are too weak to fight!"

Rebekah continued to stare at the moonlight, her face was set; Reginald could see the tightness in her jaw, knowing she was angry.

"You could marry him. Gunthar would have to allow it, or he would be found out. The lesser clans would rise up to bring him down if they knew what he had done."

"Marrying the lion prince is not the answer. Besides, the ravens would never stand for it, Reginald."

Reginald felt a chill trickle down his spine as she spoke the words. "You are our queen. Where you lead, we follow."

She turned her head and looked him dead in the eye. Her eyes were completely black. What he saw behind her eyes was something he had never seen before, and it terrified him.

Palimus...

"Can you imagine how they would feel if I married the son of the king who tried to annihilate us? Would they honor any heir that I was to produce with the son of our attempted murderer? And once I produced the remnant, would the ravens not then try to murder their king? What then, Reginald? Eye for an eye is how the ravens have always lived. They do not turn the other cheek as the eagles do."

Reginald's body trembled at the wrath and venom in her tone. He had never seen this side of her before. He could feel the heat inside his heart rising, knowing that it mirrored her own.

"My queen, this is not how you have ever desired to live. You have never lived by the rule of the defensive. You have never bowed down to the blow of the weak. And the lion, as powerful as he may seem, is weak in the end. He does not bear the magnitude of grace. It is kings like him who have destroyed the realm. It is kings like him who have made the silent grow mad and the poor grow violent. He is not loved, Queen. The kings in the lesser clans despise him…you have seen it. I know you have. I saw your face as you stared at each of them, seeing their angry hearts within. You have seen many things in this world and had a greater vision of how it can become. You cannot live in darkness, Queen, when you have seen a great light."

"But…this world won't let me shine, Reginald! It tried to snuff me out. Whatever desire I had was naïve…"

"It was not naïve! For no one has ever seen it through! *No one!* It is only in our weakness that we can become strong! It is only when we fall that we can rise up again and bring others with us. It is only when we suffer that grace can abound. It inspires, Queen, when you keep the sanity amongst the pain and continue on the way you have always marched. And I follow you because of it. I stand at your side because I know it can be done and you are the one to do it. I have longed for the tide to turn in our favor, and the tornado has come. A hurricane has taken our peaceful sea and roused it into a storm. Be the wave, Queen. Pull back for now, but do not tremble at the idea of rolling toward the shore. For it is the shore that awaits the coming of the tide. Without it, the world shifts and plunders. Think of the clan, my queen!"

"I *AM*, REGINALD! But I must weigh my choices upon many things! Vengeance against those who wish to annihilate my clan...or mercy upon them! As you have said, we are weak! We cannot fight...I don't want a war like the last one. I'm still trying to change the outcome of it!" Rebekah looked out over her balcony. "And the world will not let me have what I want. There are too many men imposing their will standing in my way."

Reginald calmed, "What you want demands great risk — change always does. With the lion prince, you accomplish it, for he desires it too. The prince does not know what his father has done. He does not know, my queen."

Rebekah looked at him in silence. Her youthful face looked pale and exhausted, but her eyes had softened to a hazel-green. She looked at the king piece in her hand, setting it down on the table beside her.

"No, he doesn't, Reginald. But he soon will." She looked up at him, "And divided we will remain."

"Prince Nathan is not his father."

"I'm not so sure, Reginald."

He leveled his eyes at her, "Yes, you are. And when he finds out what his father has done, he will do everything in his power to right his father's wrong. He will unite the realm, and the only way he can do it is with you."

Rebekah and Reginald stared at one another in silence before the eagle finally spoke. "If you want this man, if you love this prince,

then have him, for he desires you. We all saw it. We all felt it —
even the lions. And a union with him would be something good. It
would undermine what his father began. It would turn the wrong
into a right. Leave the ravens and the crows to us eagles. We can
handle the dark and the fire of the clan. They will obey, Queen, for
the light of the sun wipes out the shadows of the night. Do not live
there, Queen. It is in the sun you shine best."

She sat there in silence thinking about his words.

"There is no greater weapon to demolish evil and hatred in the
world than love. It destroys any will of malcontent. And the heart
riots for it, especially mine. Love the lion...and let the lion love
you." His eyes bored into hers. "Be the change you wish to see, my
queen, not the one you think the world demands you become. We
trust you. I speak on behalf of all the lives under your wing —
especially the ravens."

Rebekah inhaled deeply as she looked at her eagle. "I think the
nearness of death has made you a much bolder eagle, Reginald.
And a much wiser one."

The crow cawed once — a visitor had arrived.

Reginald stood and peered over the balcony. "The lion is here."

Rebekah rose and looked into the gardens below. Nathan walked
through them holding a large bouquet of flowers in his hand.
Nathan looked up at Rebekah's balcony. The moment their eyes
connected, he smiled, and her birds' song was heard all across her
kingdom.

LOVE

XV

A wolf howled in the distance. Alexander threw off his cloak and gloves as King Ivan stormed inside his chambers, "Where have you been?!?"

Alexander sat down calmly, unlacing his boots, "As if it matters."

Queen Tatiana walked inside, "Alex..."

He tossed his boots into the far corner of the room and stared at his parents. "Why? Why did you sign that contract without telling me?"

Both his parents remained silent.

"Answer me!"

Ivan's eyes glowed, "Don't speak to me as if I were one of your pack! *I* am king! And I know what's best for The Lair!"

Alexander sneered at his father. "*The Lair*...what about what's best for me?"

Tatiana moved toward him, trying to console her son, "Alex, there is no reason for you to refuse to marry the princess. She is kind, virtuous…"

"You should have signed the contract before we left their kingdom over a month ago!'"

Alexander glared at his father, "I told you I didn't want to marry the mariner. I *told* you she was not a queen who could rule the pack. I told you she was not a queen *fit* for The Lair. Do you think that a spoiled princess living in the sea could lead a line of lethal warriors. Is *she* the one best suited for The Lair? Best suited for me?"

He pointed at Tatiana, "Mother could do it! But not that princess with her ladies in waiting basking in the sun in the center of the sea doing nothing for no one but what has already been done before."

"The realm needs to be unified once more. When the lion king sent out his treaty, the mariner king reached out to The Lair. He knew what it meant to lift his clan from a lesser one to a higher one. It's a sign of good will that we can be part of. One to be proud of. We wolves can leave our mark!"

Alexander rose from his bed and moved toward his father.

"YOU DON'T UNDERSTAND! *I'M BUILDING MY HOUSE!* Do you know what that means? That means I'm not merely interested in a gold star for a good deed on a single day. I'm thinking of all the lifelines long after mine!" He stepped to his father. "I want a woman at my side worthy to rule the pack, strong enough to walk The Lair against any foe. A woman whose iron will solidifies mine! The choice is not about convenient alliances of the present, but one to be weighed for my heirs! I want to build my house up as a force to be reckoned with! The mariner princess is not a cornerstone in that house!"

"And Rebekah is."

He looked at his mother, his tone softening a bit, "I have always loved her. You both know that. I'm with her every day. Why would you suddenly think I would choose to spend all the rest of them without her?"

Ivan shook his head, "Marriage isn't always about love."

"Yours was."

Ivan and Tatiana remained utterly silent. After several moments, Ivan simply said, "I've already signed the contract."

"Break it."

The wolf king's face turned lethal as his son issued him a command. "I will do no such thing. To even consider it would be an embarrassment to the clan."

Alexander's eyes glowed silver, "To marry into a lesser clan is embarrassment enough." Alexander turned and stormed out of The Lair.

"Flowers for the beautiful lady."

Nathan bowed before Rebekah, extending the bouquet of dandelions and daisies toward her. She smiled and took them from him.

"Thank you."

They sat down on a stone bench in the middle of her garden.

"Oh, and Marcus sends his regards."

He handed her Marcus' letter. She opened it and read the boyish print; she could not help but smile widely.

"Young lion…"

Nathan studied her face, memorizing the look of joy she now had, "You look well today."

Rebekah folded the letter and looked at Nathan skeptically, "I thought you said you were an honest lion. I don't look well at all, but I feel much better. The sun helps."

She closed her eyes and lifted her head to the sun, breathing in its rays. Nathan noticed her medallion hanging around her neck. It seemed to glow of its own accord, as if it were catching fire.

"That is a beautiful medallion. Did the critters make it for you?"

Rebekah lowered her head and opened her eyes, looking down at the golden orb. "No. This was given to me long ago. My father died when I was very young. Every morning he would rise just before the dawn. He would travel to Wolf Lake and stand on the banks in the woods near The Lair, waiting for the dawn of a new day. For he knew that no matter how desperate a moment seemed, or how hard your struggle was to bear, or how disastrous a mistake you had made, there was always a new day coming on the horizon; an opportunity to change it, a peace that wrapped its arms around you that wasn't there the day before, a little less heartache and a little less pain than what you felt the day before. He loved the Sun. He was an eagle through and through. And the Sun loved my father."

Rebekah's face was filled with peace as she spoke, never before having shared this memory of her father with anyone before. "I used to go with him. We would ride on our warriors to Wolf Lake and watch the sunrise — just he and I together. I don't know if I saw what he saw the moment the sun showed its face, dawn after dawn, day after day, but I wanted to. I wanted to feel what he felt — that peace, that knowledge that says life is hard but its pain is not your master. I think I mimicked him more than I understood what it was I mimicked, but you see, I loved my father. And because I loved my father, I loved the Sun."

She looked down at the bouquet in her hands and touched them gently. "When my father grew sick, I flew to The Lair and willed the Sun to rise. I spoke to it and asked it to shine down upon my father, to heal him from his pain, to send him the dawn of a new day that he believed in, the one I wanted to believe in too. But the Sun did not answer me, at least not in the way I wanted. My father died, and my mother soon after. All I was left with was the memory of him, standing at the lake, waiting for the dawn."

Rebekah looked up at the sky.

"And one day, almost as if he were speaking to me from the grave, I finally understood why he honored it. The Sun is life. It is the bearer of it." She paused. "Something so simple — to respect life — yet it had such a profound affect on me."

She looked at him, "And one I understood, I too, followed in my father's footsteps and have watched the sun rise, day after day, knowing that each dawn brings another chance to change what has been unchangeable. I want to live in the sun, Nathan. I want my clan to shine in the light as a beacon of hope that other kingdoms can count upon — to be the dawn of a new day."

She shook her head, "But these last few days, I have not seen the Sun. And I haven't wanted to. There's something to be said for moments in the dark. There's a comfort to pain, you know. It's another means to survive. Anger can be a gift, I've found recently. It can focus you like no other to rally your desires to a means to accomplish what you could not have done had you had no further opposition to make the impossible possible."

She laughed softly. "I'm sorry. I'm probably not making any sense, rambling this way. But it's a strange thing, Nathan, when you awake from death and see the dawn of a new day unlike you have ever seen before. I'm almost angry that it's there."

His voice was soft, "Why is that?"

"Because it did not protect me when I needed protection most — no matter how much I honored it. It let me down in some way, and I have yet to understand why."

"But it wasn't the sun that let you down, Rebekah."

She looked at him, his amber eyes boring into hers with complete understanding. "It was the darkness that embraced you and pulled you in. The shadow of an enemy clan. It was in the night when he showed his face. Without the light, how could you have seen it coming?"

She looked at him for a long time, studying his face as he spoke the words. He truly did not know.

"May I ask you a question?"

Rebekah nodded.

"How is it that you were able to heal my brother? Marcus told me you summoned the moonlight. If the night were the archenemy of the sun, how did you do it?"

"Without the sun, you can never see the moon."

He smiled softly.

"I don't know why I have the gift that I do. I don't use it much and I rarely speak of it to others, but it only came after my father died. It's almost as if it were compensation for the sun itself — an answer to my prayer that was meant to be answered on a different day. I don't know how it is that I do what I do, only that it pains me to summon the light in order to heal another. A strange adverse penalty for doing something good."

"Like signing a treaty."

Rebekah could not help but laugh at the irony of the statement.

"Are you able to heal yourself the way you did Marcus?"

She shook her head. "Although my gift comes from the sun's fire, its use is for the healing of others alone. It has the opposite affect on me."

Nathan's eyes narrowed, "What do you mean?"

"If I absorb all of the fire inside my body, it would kill me."

"You mean, you could kill yourself?"

She nodded.

His voice fells to a whisper, "You must never do that, Rebekah."

"Well, I don't ever plan to..."

He rose from the bench and looked out across her lands. "I've seen death in many forms, but nothing affected me as much as seeing yours almost come upon you. I have not been able to sleep. I have not been able to do anything since it happened."

He turned and looked at her, his eyes imploring, "Promise me you'll do whatever you have to as queen, but never end your life by your own hand."

She reached out and touched his hand. "I won't. I promise."

His shoulders fell an inch in utter relief.

"Nathan, I don't want to die — especially since I almost did. There is so much I have left to do. Nothing matters more to me now than to protect my clan."

Nathan looked at her pale form sitting in the sunlight. And weak or not, she appeared to glow, and something inside his heart broke as he looked at her. "Rebekah, I cannot bear to think of this world without you in it." He sat down beside her and touched her face. "You're all I think about. And now that I'm here with you, I don't want to leave your side. I don't want to go. Being near you brings me peace. I can't explain it. I knew it the moment I saw you. I knew I had to make you mine. I know what I want, Rebekah. I want you."

She remained silent as she listened to his confession; she knew he meant every word.

"If I've learned anything these last few weeks, it's that time is short...and I don't intend on wasting any more. I can court you, pursue you relentlessly, write a thousand letters to you over months or years, but my intent will be the same. I want to marry you. I want to unite the clans. And I want to do it all today."

Nathan held her face in his hands. "I've given many things away, but the one thing I've never given anyone is my heart. I'm giving it to you. It will never belong to any other woman as long as I live. That is my promise to you, should you want it, but say you'll have it. Take it...because it's yours. Marry me, Rebekah. Be my queen. Make me your king. Walk with me in the sun, dance with me in the dark. You have a champion in me — always. I'll never let you down."

She laid her hand over his knowing deep down his father would never allow it.

"Say yes."

Her heart fluttered at the thought.

What would Palimus do? Not this.

She looked deep into his amber-colored eyes, and felt her soul leap. "I'll marry you, Nathan."

His face lit up, "Yes?"

She nodded, "Yes."

Nathan took her face in his strong hands and kissed her passionately. All throughout her gardens, her birds sang loudly in reply.

Nathan grinned widely, "I like it when they do that."

He kissed her again. From the balcony that overlooked her gardens, there was one being that was not singing their song — Alexander watched them from above having heard all.

THE SHADOW
XVI

Skoll, Freki and a fox soldier named Reynard entered Raven Territory. Everywhere they searched, they saw nothing but slaughtered ravens. Small fires around their torched nests still burned bright.

Skoll took in the damage. "This was a planned attack. One the enemy knew would not be thwarted."

Reynard crouched down and saw footprints in the mud. "Bulls."

Freki sniffed the air. "And amphibians."

Skoll froze, having smelled a familiar scent, the one he was searching for. *"POE!!!"*

Skoll raced through the trees until he came to a nested home burning on the ground. Poe was lying on the heap of his dismantled home surrounded by the bodies of his wife and son. His son laid dead in his arms gutted by a dozen daggers. Poe himself was badly wounded. Skoll crouched down to him.

"Ssskoll...my ssson..."

Freki approached, "There aren't any survivors. The ravens...all but Poe...they are no more."

Skoll commanded his warriors, "Gather the pack." He picked up Poe in his massive arms. "Do you think you can ride me, old friend?"

"Yessss....take me to my queen."

Rebekah was seated beside a small fire, her chessboard was set for play. Reginald flew onto her balcony and stepped inside.

"There is no sign of Prince Alexander, my queen."

"And what of the wolf king or queen?"

He shook his large eagle head, "The Lair is empty. Wherever they went, they did not even bother to tell Rayford or Kahn."

"Will Rayford and Khan be here?"

He nodded, "Tomorrow morning. It will be a long day."

"No wolves." She looked at the fire, "The ravens would know. They would've seen them leave The Lair...and yet there's still no sign of Poe."

"The wolves will find him."

Rebekah continued to stare at the fire. "Tomorrow will be a

long day indeed. There is so much to say, Reginald, so much to tell them — and it is not going to be anything good."

"Your engagement is the one good thing."

"No, that is to remain a secret — at least for now. Nathan needs to speak with the lion king. And I believe for Nathan, it will be a long night." She breathed deeply, hypnotized by the flames, thinking of the wolf prince. "Reginald, do you know why I never wished to marry Alexander?"

"I have my thoughts on the matter."

She turned and looked at him. "To marry Alexander would be a comfortable choice of what I am already used to without any surprise of what to expect. He is the dark...and when I'm with him, I feel the raven's fire within me rising. It wasn't until I met Nathan that I recognized it. And Nathan is the light...he is the sun. When I'm with him, I feel the eagle's spirit thunder in my heart." She turned back to the fire. "I'd rather soar nearest the sun than dance in the dark, Reginald." She looked out over her balcony, "But there is no sun today and yet I feel burnt by it all the same. Something is wrong. I felt this way the day my mother died...I didn't see it coming. So many things I haven't seen coming these days...where is my Sun?"

"My queen, you are right to feel as you do."

Rebekah turned and looked at her eagle captain. "What is it that I don't know?"

"I have flown over the territories on the other side of Mariner

Sea, to the other side of the realm — the forbidden side — and I flew further in. I saw the water levels and followed the flow of the canals." Reginald continued, "The waters have risen. The mariner king has raised the walls of the dam to contain it. He has also restricted the water on the lion king's side...and *only* his side."

"The *mariner* king...what do you mean?"

"King Mar has altered the dam and blocked the canals to the Lion's Den and Gorilla Jungle. But the jungle's canals have recently been opened."

Rebekah slowly rose from her seat, her mind on overdrive as she deciphered the news.

Reginald breathed in deeply, "And he has had help from the lesser clans. Bull Valley and the Amphibian Swamps have food. Their lands are healthy. Only The Den and jungle are dry."

Rebekah's voice was faint, "The bodies...the bodies of the bulls and amphibians were hard before arriving...just like Poe said. Which means many more crossed in order to bring them here. Where did they go?" She continued to think; she looked at the king piece on the chessboard.

What kind of kings am I dealing with...

Her heart was pounding, "Reginald...if the mariner king controls the sea and the bulls and amphibians are on his side, they can march their legions upon me and take my lands."

"And he will control the valley."

"Correction." Her eyes darkened to that of the raven. "He will rule the realm."

"Like the Old War."

"Yes, Reginald…like the Old War."

"But what of the lion king?"

"I am not the only one who didn't see this coming. He fell for it. And yet he acted on his own because of it…against me, against my clan…"

Keneun, a thunderbird, flew inside. "My queen, the wolves have returned to The Lair."

Rebekah looked to her eagle captain, "Take me to them. Ivan and Tatiana must know. Tomorrow cannot wait."

"I will fly as fast as I can, my queen."

Reginald dove over the ledge. Rebekah gathered all the strength she could muster. She ran across the room and jumped over the balcony just as Reginald rose up; he caught her as she jumped onto his back. They soared across the sky to Wolf Lair.

Rebekah jumped off Reginald the moment they landed on Alexander's balcony. Alexander was seated by a large hearth, reading a book by the fire.

"Alexander…where have you been?"

Lackadaisically, he reached for the glass of wine on the table beside him. Without looking up from the page, he asked, "Missed me, *cousin?*"

She ignored the tone in his voice. "Alex, I need to speak to your mother and father at once!"

He lowered his goblet back down onto the table, "I'll bet you do."

He continued to read. When he did not speak another word, Rebekah walked swiftly toward the door. "I don't have time for this…"

The moment her hand was on the knob, Alexander finally spoke, "Tell me, Rebekah, if I told you I no longer had my marriage contract, what would you do?"

She lowered her head and turned around to face him, "What do you mean?"

He finally looked at her, "Would it mean something to you?"

"Alexander, I have to speak to the king and queen…"

"Answer the question!"

His shout echoed across his chambers.

Reginald stepped forward, "Prince!"

"I asked the queen a question, Reginald! She owes me an answer!" His eyes glowed silver as he stared at her. "Well? Would it?"

She stood there in her fragile state, having dreaded this conversation, wishing she could skip over it in order to relay the message she had come to reveal.

"I'm waiting."

Her whole body trembled as he stared at her. She knew this conversation would soon be coming, but it was not one she was prepared to have, although necessary.

"Alex…"

"Say it."

She swallowed hard. "I don't know what you want me to say."

Alexander hurled his book into the fire and rose from his seat. *"Say it! Say that it matters to you! That I matter to you!"*

She had never seen him this angry before. "Alexander, you matter…of course you matter…you mean the world to me…"

He turned toward the fire and shook his head.

Rebekah stepped closer to him. "Why are you so angry, Alex?"

He whirled around at her, glaring at her in utter hatred. Rebekah was taken aback by the fierceness behind his eyes. "Because I *don't* matter to you, Rebekah. I never did."

"That's not true!"

He stared at her for a long time with his hateful glare before he finally asked, "Why did you come here?"

"I…"

He narrowed his eyes, "You what? You have some good news to share?" He sat back down in his chair. "So share. I'm right here. So tell me. I want to hear it. I want to hear you say it."

"Say what!"

His eyes glowed, "I want to hear you say…how you love your lion."

Alexander saw the impact of his words written all over her face. "Oh, yes, cousin, that's quite a bit of news…a life-changing moment that not even a very large bird dared to share with me."

He shifted his angry glare to Reginald before looking back at Rebekah once more. "I want to hear you say it, because there are many things I've heard lately, but you loving Nathan is not one of them. So tell me, Rebekah. Tell me how the vision of your dreams will come to pass by marrying this man."

She looked away from him. "I don't have time for this, Alex. I need to speak to your mother and father."

"LOOK AT ME!" He clasped his hands tightly, looking down at the ground as he tried to contain his anger. He lifted his head, his eyes glowed silver as he looked at her, "Tell me you're only marrying him because I had my contract. Tell me it's him because you need a child!"

"What do you mean *had?*"

Alexander suddenly smiled. "Bird…you never listen to me." He stared at her for a long time before he finally spoke, "Nathan was married to Princess Lara this morning."

Rebekah stood there, stunned. Reginald stepped toward her, "My queen…"

Alexander sat back in his seat, never taking his eyes from her, "Your lion lied to you. He is not a man who is capable of keeping his promises. You've been duped again. *Nathan* didn't love you at all."

Rebekah was frozen to the spot, digesting all his words. He watched for her reaction, and what he saw was a darkening behind her eyes. She lifted her head and shouted toward the door. *"KING!!!!"*

Alexander cringed the moment she shouted for his father.

"IVAN!!!"

The wolf king burst inside Alexander's chambers. He was wearing a beautiful fur coat made entirely of wolf fur. It was one Rebekah had never seen before.

"Rebekah…"

She could not contain her emotions, "Is it true? Did King Mar break the contract?"

Ivan looked at Alexander.

"LOOK…AT *ME*!!! Is it true?"

He nodded, never before having seen her this angry. He had never witnessed the rage within her as he stood there, horrified by the black pools that consumed the gray of her eyes.

"To what end, uncle!"

She rubbed her chest, feeling a sharp pain near her heart. Reginald shifted uncomfortably, feeling the mirrored pain as well.

Ivan answered, "Gunthar chose to honor the treaty in unifying the realm by taking a neutral territory and making it equal to the rest. I agreed knowing how much Alexander didn't want to marry the princess. So, I broke the contract in order to give the lion king the same opportunity I had willed for my son." He looked at Alexander, "It was a stroke of luck to break the contract knowing that Alexander was so against marrying the princess."

Rebekah stepped toward Ivan, "Uncle, Gunthar doesn't want to unite the realm...he wants my lands. Gunthar was the one who poisoned me."

Ivan looked at her in disbelief. "Impossible!"

Reginald stepped forward. "It is true, king. The toad chief confirmed it."

Alexander slowly rose from his chair.

"Ivan, I came here to tell you there is no famine. There is no drought. It's all a lie." Rebekah's heart was pounding, she found it harder and harder to breathe, still in her weakened state. "Mar...has created a false drought and famine."

Alexander was finally hit with the full understanding of the news. Refusing to believe it, he replied, "The mariner king is not a player!"

Rebekah whirled around at him. "He is the *king* in this match, Alexander! Mar has raised the walls of the dam and restrained the water back from the canals on the lion king's side to make Gunthar think that there is a drought and famine! And the bulls and amphibians are in on it!"

Alexander looked at Reginald for confirmation. Reginald nodded in reply.

Rebekah grabbed onto a pillar in the room, leaning against it, trying to catch her breath, "They have always been allies to the mariners. Their prediction was false. It's the bulls and amphibians that have been slaughtering their own kind to make it look like their people have been crossing onto our territories to hunt for food. They haven't been hunting! They've been probing the borders for penetration! The lion king is a pawn in his own game. I thought he was the only one…but I was wrong."

Ivan took it all in in complete understanding, "Mar controls the sea…"

"He's a fool…just like Cassius." Rebekah's voice was breathless as she struggled to speak on, "By marrying his daughter to Nathan, the king of a lesser clan has risen higher than the rest. The lion king and his heirs will be dead by the end of the month. Mar will inherit Gunthar's lands, and no doubt he will lead the rest of the clans to overthrow mine."

Ivan shook his head, "No, Brutus would not allow it. He was furious when he heard the news you had been poisoned."

"I don't know which side he's on or what he knows. Ivan, all I know is that you have shifted the power of the clans to the other side by agreeing to break that contract. What did you get in return?"

His face paled at the question. He looked away from his goddaughter, unable to meet her stare. She noticed the coat made of wolf fur that he was wearing. Her face fell the moment she realized what it was.

Ivan answered sheepishly. "It is a relic. It belongs with my clan."

Reginald was breathing hard; he struggled to stand erect.

Rebekah clutched her chest, rubbing the muscle as it began to seize.

Reginald's body shuddered as he whispered to her, "I feel it my queen."

Alexander heard him, but his pride and rage consumed all his senses as he stood looking accusingly at Rebekah. "And you knew...all of this...and you were going to marry Nathan anyway." He slowly moved closer towards her until he stood right in front of her. "Why?"

Tears streamed down her face as she looked at him. "Because I love him."

Alexander's face completely changed the moment she said the words aloud. No matter how much he had prepared himself for it, it was a blow he was not completely prepared to handle. All blood drained from his face; his jaw clenched into a tight line as Rebekah's tears begin to fall.

"Don't...don't you cry, Rebekah, not in front of me and not over this...I told you. I told you to stay away from the lions. But you refused to hear! You refused to see! And now your clan will suffer for it because you chose to play harlot to the lion! You are no Palimus. You're not fit to be his heir. You are a queen to be despised. You're not fit to rule. You're nothing more than a stupid queen who allowed her emotions to get the best of her. *You*...are a disgrace to your clan!"

Rebekah struck Alexander hard across the face. His wolf eyes glowed in rage at the assault. The clouds gathered in the sky behind her, darkening rapidly as the minutes wore on. The wind blew violently through Alexander's chambers. Rebekah backed up slowly. She could barely breathe as she looked between her godfather and the prince, suddenly feeling desperately alone.

"Perhaps I am to be despised, Alex. Perhaps I deserve this." The tears continued to fall, "But then again, perhaps the realm deserves what's coming to them too."

She whirled around to the end of the balcony and ran off the ledge. Reginald dove down after her, catching her, swooping up swiftly, soaring to Bird Kingdom as the sky continued to darken.

Alexander watched her fly away, hating himself for what he had said, hating her for what she felt and did not feel. His anger and pride collided with all his disappointment and sorrow as he stood paralyzed watching her fly into the darkening sun, knowing that what he had just said, he could never take back — no matter how much he wanted to.

Reginald flew as fast as he could toward the castle gates. His strength was wearing thin. Lightning struck all across the sky. Reginald soared over Rebekah's balcony and into her chambers. She slid off of Reginald just as Skoll and Freki entered her bedroom carrying Poe.

The moment she saw her raven, Rebekah ran to Poe's side. Falling to her knees, Skoll laid Poe gently down onto her lap.

His wilted, ebony head rested against her pale form. She caressed his head as she took in his massive wounds.

"Poe..."

He looked up at her; a pitiful chirp escaped his black beak. *"My queen...you are well. I knew you would be...you... are better than them all. You cannot let them beat you, my queen, the lionsss, marinersss, amphibiansss and bullsss...let your fire burn, my queen...let it burn...tok...tok...tok..."*

His eyes closed and he fell unconscious. Reginald approached and knelt beside her, seeing the devastated look on her face. It was a look he had seen before in the lost and forsaken. Too many blows too quickly drove people to desperate measures they never would have taken had there been spaces between the pain. He had no idea what his queen would do.

"My queen…"

But she was not listening to him. Rebekah held Poe's head in her lap, stroking it with a far-off look on her face. She was deadly silent as she held Poe close.

Reginald turned to Skoll. "What happened?"

"The Raven's Nest was attacked. Bulls and amphibians penetrated the borders. Queen, the ravens...they were slaughtered. Poe is now the remnant of his own clan."

Her eyes blackened to the color of coal. Skoll's fur stood on end the moment he saw the change. Her voice was low, yet calm, "Return to your lair, wolf."

The wolf captain bowed and leapt from her balcony and raced

with the rest of the pack back to the Wolf Lair.

A crow cawed three times in the distance sounding the arrival of an enemy.

Reginald rushed to the balcony. His feathers stood on end. "My queen! The bull and amphibian armies are here...and the gorillas are with them."

LIVE AND LET DIE
XVII

Skoll and Freki burst inside Alexander's chambers. "*KING!!!*
The armies of the lesser clans are marching upon Bird
Kingdom! And the gorillas are leading them!"

Ivan rose from a chair beside Alexander in shock and alarm,
"*NOW?!?*"

Alexander immediately vaulted from his balcony and bounded
down through the woods of The Lair, storming toward Bird
Kingdom. Skoll and Freki were immediately at his side. Skoll
howled for the Wolf Pack, his summons echoing through the
woods. The wolf, hyena and fox warriors emerged from the
shadows in the trees and joined their prince as they charged to Bird
Kingdom.

The thunder roared across the sky.

Reginald took in the number of warriors down below. "There are too many. We are weak, my queen, we cannot fight them."

Rebekah laid Poe's head gently onto the ground. She walked slowly over to Reginald, looking out from her balcony at the land beyond her gates. She stood there in silence for several moments; her face was set as she took in the sight of the enormous army. She looked back at Poe lying unconscious on the ground.

How do you want to be remembered?

She looked at Reginald, seeing his weakened form breathing hard from his flight from The Lair. His feathers were half gone, having wilted away from her recent sickness. There was nothing more to say. Nothing more to do as she stood between her eagle and her raven.

Better than this day.

She looked to the sky and searched for the Sun. She closed her eyes and willed it to answer her, willed it to protect her as the tears streamed down her face.

Better than the rest.

She knew what she had to do. And the moment she felt a single ray of light shining down on her from amongst the clouds, she knew it would be done.

To be…different than Palimus.

She opened her eyes. Rebekah was at peace even as she looked out at the armies below. And for the first time, Rebekah's heart went out to them, for what she was about to do would be far worse for them than what Palimus or any other king or queen had ever done before, but it needed to be done.

"Reginald...I need you to do something for me."

Rebekah slowly unclasped her medallion that hung around her neck, holding it gently in her hands. It glowed ever so slightly. She looked up at Reginald, her eyes completely gray as she spoke the words.

"What is it my queen?"

Rebekah extended her hand. The moment he saw the medallion, his eyes dilated to that of pins. "No weapon formed against us shall prosper this day. The Sun...he will protect us."

She handed Reginald the medallion. "Be my eyes. Be my remnant."

Reginald was overcome, "My queen..."

"Do this for me, Reginald. For there is nothing more I can do. And I will not go down this day. Not for any man. Not for any reason. I will not fail the clan again. There is a time to move and a time to stand still. This, I have learned from your tale of Palimus." She looked out at the approaching army, "They will not capture what is not theirs to possess. They will not master what is not theirs to rule."

Reginald took the medallion in his hand, "My queen, what are you going to do?"

Her eyes slowly dimmed. "I'm going to give them what they thought they wanted. I'm going to give them what they thought they had. I'm going to feed them their lies. The Sun…he will answer me. And so will his brothers…and the sister. The world will not bow down to the desires of these kings, for it is not for these kings to rule this way. In the dark, I have seen a great light, I have seen my Sun, and he is with me. This is what I know. And for the first time, I am not afraid."

Reginald looked up to the moonlight. "The Sun and his fire…the elements…"

Rebekah looked out at the warriors below. "We need time to heal. Fly to the White Mountain near Ume's side. You will be safe there until I see you again."

He knelt down before her and lowered his regal head, exposing the back of his neck to his queen. Rebekah leaned down and kissed it. Reginald rose, tears stung his eagle eyes. "I'm sorry that I told you to hold out for the lion."

Rebekah touched the side of his face, "I'm not. I aimed to marry a king, and he was only a prince without any power yet to do anything but obey. There is a great irony in obedience, and a great virtue. Nathan has it. Now fly…"

Without another word, Reginald dove over the balcony and soared toward the mountains. His eagle cry echoed across the cloudy sky. Rebekah turned toward the armies collecting at her gates — and it was then that her eyes went completely black.

This is not how I saw my life playing out. This is not the kind of day I ever saw coming.

The pain in her chest began to stab at her from all sides. They were daggers of anger, daggers of woe, daggers of frustration and helplessness, daggers of strength.

How do you want to be remembered?

Queen Rebekah looked out over her balcony and shouted to the clans below, "ARMIES OF THE REALM! YOU SHALL HAVE YOUR FAMINE! YOU WILL HAVE YOUR DROUGHT!"

Alexander heard her voice raging across the sky as he raced toward her kingdom. "No, Rebekah…"

Ivan and Tatiana, dressed for battle, raced beside him with the Wolf Pack all around them. Alexander charged even faster.

Rebekah leaned over the ledge, looking out across her kingdom. "YOU WILL NEVER HAVE MY LANDS! YOU WILL NEVER HAVE PEACE! RESTLESSNESS SHALL CONSUME YOUR CLANS! YOUR ONLY HOPE AGAINST ME SHALL BE YOUR HEIRS!!!"

She spread her arms wide. The lightning touched her fingertips.

Alexander saw the light shining brightly against the moon. He knew what she was about to do. "No, Rebekah…"

Rebekah looked up to the sky, speaking to the elements around her, "Fire…Wind…Ice…Earth…protect my clan."

Alexander and the Wolf Pack were almost to the edge of the woods, but the wind blew all around them, slowing their pace.

Rebekah lowered her eyes to the kingdom beyond. "Only a noble heart…"

And in one fell swoop, the bird queen slammed her hands together. The lightning struck through her body and out through her hands, sending its electricity forth…and out onto the realm. The entire bird clan cried out the moment the lightning struck their queen. Their thunderous voices were heard all throughout the kingdom.

The lightning exploded from her castle, and a massive shockwave burst forth from her gates. Like a tidal wave, it rolled out across the realm. Alexander, Ivan, Tatiana and the Wolf Pack rocketed back into the trees on impact.

The gorilla, mariner, bull and amphibian armies were leveled to the ground off of the force of the massive shockwave. Vines burst forth from the ground and immediately rose up, gathering all around the castle gates. And they were no ordinary vines. They were arms as they reach out toward the soldiers, viciously pinning them down. They wrapped around their arms, ankles and torsos, binding their limbs and weighing them down like chains. The vines whipped their bodies around, forcing them down to the ground.

It was the sister.

The soldiers of the lesser clans roared and screamed in terror as the vines grew over them, covering their bodies, burying them alive. So tall did they grow that only an eagle could rise so high — so thick were its walls that no gorilla or bull could charge or attack. Roses rapidly bloomed on the outside of the gate, their petals forming a phrase, *"Only a Noble Heart."*

And as the shockwave rolled across the realm…it headed for Mariner Tower.

THE MARINER KING
XVIII

Nathan sat beside Princess Lara at the head of their wedding table in utter silence. All around them, the clans celebrated as they dined and drank in celebration. Gunthar sat beside Brutus and Mar; he was stone drunk. He looked across the hall for his son and roared, "Nathan!"

Nathan slowly turned his head in reply. His father raised a goblet to him. "To an alliance worthy of the clan!

The room erupted in shouts and applause.

Nathan rose from his chair. "Excuse me, Princess Lara."

Lara looked up at him as he rose, sitting in silence as she watched him go. Seated all alone, she looked around at all the drunken clan members surrounding her halls. Her eyes moved to her father's. He nodded to her in silent communication, shifting his eyes to Nathan's goblet in front of her. Her face went pale. Mar turned to speak quietly with Brutus as they eyed Gunthar. Lara looked at Nathan's goblet in front of her and stared at it for a long time. She suddenly rose and fled the hall without another word.

A frog waiter passed by, and snatched the goblet from the table, disappearing into the crowded hall.

Nathan walked toward a building at the end of the dock closest to the sea. He heard Apollo and Roman speaking with other members of the Lion Guard inside. "The frog didn't have any idea what was going on. He was simply a waiter told to give the queen that goblet on his tray. Our king was the one who ordered her death."

Roman scoffed, "Our prince is a fool to think The Den would ever join with the birds again."

He stopped talking the moment he saw Nathan standing in the doorway.

Apollo bowed, "My prince."

The remainder of The Den bowed to him. He looked at all of them in silence, finally resting his amber eyes on Apollo. Without another word, he stepped back from the door and shut it. From inside, the Lion Guard heard the metal latch come down. Within seconds, they saw smoke seeping in from under the door. They roared, colliding into the building, fighting to get out.

Nathan stood outside its door, watching the building burn; the torch was still in his hand. Mariner soldiers vaulted out of the sea, landing beside him.

Nathan merely stared at the door without emitting any emotion.

"Let it burn. Should any of them break free, kill them."

He tossed the torch down onto the building and turned to walk down toward the boats.

"Prince Nathan..."

Nathan turned and saw Lara approaching.

As she came closer, he could see the tears streaming down her face. "I cannot stand to be here any more than you can. Take me with you. Please. I cannot bear it. Send me where you will, but take me with you."

He looked at the sorrowful look on her face, knowing it mirrored the pain in his own heart, "You loved the wolf."

"As you loved the bird."

He offered her his arm in comfort. "Come on."

She looked up at him in gratitude and took it. They walked down toward the dock together, each lost in their own world of the brokenhearted, understanding each other's pain.

"Nathan! Wait for me!"

Marcus and SinJin came running down the dock. All four of them gathered in the boats to head back toward the Lion's Den.

The mariner king was focused, waiting for the right moment — and that moment had finally come. He nodded to all of his guards around the hall — it was the signal they had been waiting for. They

quickly shut the doors, locking the nobles of the lion clan inside. Brutus moved closer to Gunthar and lifted the lion king's drunken head just as a frog waiter handed Mar a goblet of wine.

Gunthar looked at the gorilla king with red-rimmed eyes. "Brutus...ask your toads how many grandchildren I will have. Here...here's a stone."

Gunthar placed a rock onto the table and smiled widely in his inebriated state. Brutus took his bone scepter and swiped it viciously across Gunthar's head, issuing him his deathblow. The mariner soldiers closed in, attacking the lion clan and nobles, slaughtering them at the wedding tables; they were too drunk to defend themselves. Mar sat on his throne and watched it all in apathetic satisfaction. He picked up the goblet recently delivered, and swallowed it all down.

Nathan helped Lara out of the boat, having reached the Lion's Den side. The wind whipped wildly all around them as the thunder and lightning continued to strike down over Bird Kingdom.

The ground beneath them began to shift and quake. SinJin growled as Marcus jumped out of the boat. The waves in the sea began to roll faster and faster, rising higher and higher. Nathan looked to the lightning. Feeling the ground shifting beneath him, his eyes grew wide. Out of sheer instinct, Nathan threw Lara down and jumped on top of Marcus.

That was when the shockwave hit.

It rolled out across the realm, demolishing everything in its path. It rolled out toward Mariner Sea pulverizing the dam. Slamming against the stone, the dam and canals crumbled on impact...and the sea was unleashed on all sides of the valley.

Brutus swung his scepter down, bludgeoning the lion queen. He turned his head toward the sound of the crumbling dam. Mar rose from his throne as his fortress began to shake. Everyone rushed to the tower windows and looked down at the sea.

Brutus and Mar watched as the sea rushed forth, flooding the entire valley. Mar still held the wine goblet in his hand as he witnessed the destruction of his kingdom.

Brutus cried out, *"MY JUNGLE!!!"*

Mar clutched his stomach. He immediately fell to the ground, struggling to breathe. He looked at the goblet resting at his feet. As his body began to convulse, the realization of whose goblet it was collided onto his face, *"No..."*

Nathan slowly sat up, "Is everyone all right? *Marcus?*"

Marcus nodded as SinJin held onto him tightly.

Lara grabbed hold of his arm. "Nathan! My father and the gorilla king sent a legion to march on Queen Rebekah's kingdom. They are there...*now!*"

Nathan's face shifted to one of pure fury. His eyes slit to that of a cat, and a roar thundered from his chest as he called to The Den. He rose and raced toward Rebekah's kingdom.

Lions and tigers roared in reply having heard the call of their prince. Jumping down from The Den walls and storming out of the gates were jaguar, tiger, panther, lynx and cheetah warriors of every kind. They followed their prince as Nathan charged toward Bird Kingdom.

Marcus cried out, "*NATHAN!!!*"

Marcus' eyes slit to a cat as a cub-like roar erupted from his tiny chest. He charged after them with SinJin at his side. Lara was left all alone, watching them go. She turned her head toward her sea and watched the waves rise and fall higher than they ever had before.

"Father...what have you done?"

Ivan and Alexander slowly sat up after the shockwave hit. Alexander was looking out toward Rebekah's kingdom when he heard his father cry out, "*TATIANA!!!*"

Alexander shifted his gaze as Ivan raced toward the queen. Tatiana's body lay broken on the ground, having smashed upon a tree. Ivan fell to his knees; a mournful groan escaped him, and his wolves howled in reply. Alexander looked down at his mother's broken body. In stunned silence, he stood and walked toward Rebekah's kingdom. A few members of the pack followed.

The moment they reached Rebekah's gates, they watched in horror as the vines shot up from the ground, intertwining like clasped hands as they formed a solid wall. Alexander looked all across the width of the gate.

Skoll shouted to his master, "My prince!"

Alexander looked and saw roses growing on the outside of the vine doors. Skoll nodded to Freki and a few coyote, hyena and fox warriors, "See if you can chop your way inside. Dig your way underneath."

The coyotes began to chop and the foxes began to dig.

Alexander's eyes glowed silver. "Stop."

They kept going.

"*STOP!!!!*"

His pained voice was like a shockwave all its own. Alexander stood and stared at the roses. He looked up to see how far they reached. His jaw was clenched as he spat out the word, "*Coward.*"

Kahn, the reptile king, approached with a legion of reptile warriors. The Critter Chief Rayford and his band of warriors were beside them. They saw the wall of vines fortifying the kingdom. Rayford looked at the bodies on the ground. "What does this mean?"

He turned and looked at the wolf prince. "Where are the birds? Where is the queen?"

But Alexander did not reply. There were no words for what he was feeling at this moment.

Rayford, Kahn and the rest of the clans began hacking away at the vines, while Alexander read the writing on the wall. He turned away from the gate, away from his father holding his dead mother in his arms, and headed back toward The Lair, leaping beyond the trees with ferocious speed, carrying his pain and rage with him. Skoll watched him go.

Freki approached his captain, "Did you hear it? Before she cursed them?"

Skoll touched the gate, feeling its solid foundation. He looked up at it. "What do you mean *them*?" His eyes glowed yellow as he looked at Freki. "She's cursed us all."

Freki was still breathing hard in fear and trepidation. "But did you hear it?"

Skoll nodded, looking at the vine wall, "And they answered."

THE DAM
XIX

Nathan and the Lion Guard reached the gate. They slowed as Nathan took in the vines and the roses. Marcus was beside him.

SinJin approached, "My prince…"

Nathan turned and moved toward SinJin. He looked down and saw the faces and limbs of various lesser clan soldiers buried underneath the vines.

"She has protected the clan."

Nathan and Marcus whirled around as Reginald landed in front of them. He was wearing Rebekah's medallion around his neck. Nathan saw it immediately.

"Reginald, what happened here?"

Reginald's eyes grew cold. "Tragedy and grace."

Marcus was in a panic, "Where's Queen Rebekah?"

Reginald looked up at the massive vines. "My queen is behind these walls, but she is neither alive nor dead. Only the noble of heart may seek to rouse her now."

Marcus turned and ran at the gate. He frantically tried to pull the vines apart. "*I* will awaken her!"

He was about to swipe at the gate with his sword when Reginald reached out and stopped him. He knelt down before the prince.

"No, young lion. These vines have many thorns. They will slice your limbs in two."

Marcus looked into Reginald's eyes, "Not if she finds me noble! I will be protected."

Reginald lowered his head, "She does not find you noble, young prince."

SinJin growled lowly at Reginald, but Marcus simply stood there, devastated. His proud chest fell several inches as tears filled his amber eyes. "It's because of I killed the squirrel warrior, isn't it?" He reached inside the pocket of his vest and pulled out Ratatosk's compass. He extended it to Reginald, "She said I should keep it! Take it! I don't want it. Make her come back!"

SinJin stepped up and put his arm protectively around his prince. "Come, my prince. Let us leave your brother with the captain."

Reginald rose and turned to Nathan.

Nathan's face was filled with anguish, "Is this my fault?"

Reginald looked at him for a long while. "This was a battle you could not possibly win. My queen was too weak to fight. This was the only way she knew to live."

Nathan's face was pained. "But she wouldn't have done this if I hadn't married the mariner."

Reginald's feathers stood on end. "Kings in the realm were to blame for this outcome. My queen would have done this with or without your marriage. She would have had to in order for the clan to heal."

"You're a bad liar, Reginald."

Reginald lowered his head, "King, those who are truly responsible for this will feel the aftershock of pain far exceeding any threshold of mercy they thought they could bear. Even you."

"I am no king."

Reginald lifted his large head and leveled his eyes at Nathan. "This night you are. Look to the sea."

Nathan paled at the eagle captain's words. Reginald launched into the sky just as Nathan turned to a jackal soldier. "Sphynx! Take a squadron to Mariner Sea. Find my mother and father."

Sphynx nodded and charged forth with a band of warriors on his tail. Nathan looked back at the gate and saw Marcus standing before the roses with SinJin at his side. Marcus held a rose in his hand. Nathan's jaw clenched in anger, sadness and pain.

"SinJin, take Marcus home. He is not to leave The Den."

SinJin nodded to his king. Nathan turned toward the sea. He

ran, his charge gaining speed as the rage emerged on his face until he could not hold it in any longer. And as the lion king charged toward Mariner Tower, his roar echoed across the realms of time.

TWENTY YEARS LATER...

THE SHIFT
XX

My beloved queen,

Today I write a tale of tragic news that has reached me high upon my mountain I have come to call my Hole of Hope. King Ivan has perished from the plague. Its vicious wave of death has been swift, reaching out to everyone, everywhere, without preference to whom its tide consumes as it devours both man and beast all across the realm.

And because of this, there are rumors, rumors of abomination and horror on the horizon stemming from the lesser clans. I can barely stomach the idea as I write these words. We need you, my queen, we need you stop what is coming. The realm is without food. What little that was left to be hunted or gathered has ceased in supply some time ago. All life that once flourished from clan to clan, has now withered and died, returning to the earth as dust and bone.

The clans are truly starving. The famine is real this time. And because of that, many have ventured forth to our gates, attempting to climb their way over them, or burn their way through in an attempt to find food from the crops within our land. But they have not been successful, for the Creators will not allow it. The sister strengthens the gate and the brothers extinguish the flame by wind, water or self-consuming fire. And for that, the wolves, reptiles, and critters feel the weight of this hellish life, as if they too were somehow guilty for the closing of your gates by the mark of the intertwining vines.

As for me, I do not starve but have what I need. The sister has been good to me, bringing me a gifted morsel day after day from behind our gates, sustaining me in all ways through and through.

But it is hard, my queen.

It is hard to see what the realm has become. You would not recognize it. What was once a picture of majestic beauty has now become a dried out portrait of death and decay. You can see the land whither and die minute by minute, you can feel the dread of death, and you can smell the decay. It's the rotting stench of corpses, Queen, that has infected the realm.

It started with the mariners. Your lion wiped them out, leaving their bodies to rot in open field. Without the vultures to devour the carcass, the plague soon set in, but not like the wave of death we now see. Bodies are dropping every day from either starvation, exhaustion, or fever from the plague.

That is where the rumor has come, finding its way to my door.

Chief Rayford and Kahn have been guarding the borders, for there are whispers on the wind that the beasts and their kings on the other side of the realm welcome the idea of cannibalism — and they have set their sites on the men and beasts on our side to accomplish it.

But they have not dared attempt to cross our borders just yet, for fear of The Lair. King Ivan has ruled our side well, even through all the heartache and pain. But now with his death, I don't know what will happen, for Prince Alexander…you would not respect the man he has become. I have neither seen nor heard from the prince in quite some time, although his actions and whereabouts have not escaped my attention. His pack will want to know the news I have just recently learned. It is this news, along with the news of King Ivan, upon which I will travel this night to The Lair on behalf of the clan, my queen.

But before I go, I wanted you to know, I have seen your lion. He has become the kind of king you always knew he would one day be. King Nathan and Princess Lara's son, Matthew, is expecting a child any day. Prince Matthew looks just like Nathan, but with his mariner mother's eyes. It is quite a shame she never got to see their shining blue behind them, having died bringing his life forth.

So much tragedy, my queen, and so much grace. My only wish for you is that your dreams be of happiness while you sleep, and that your mind be filled with peace. I have a feeling you are, or I believe I would have felt your angst stirring in my heart, a stirring I would gladly welcome, for I know it would mean your return. And for that, as much as we need you, I know the time for your return is not now. When it will be, I can only ponder. May the Noble One rise up soon, mirroring the dawn so that all may enter your gates.

Your beloved servant,

Reginald

Alexander stood in front of a large pyre. The glow from the bonfire reflected off his steely wolf eyes as he watched King Ivan's body burn upon it. He was even more handsome after all these years, having eluding the aging of time.

Alexander held the coveted wolf coat in his hand, swearing to destroy the one relic that reminded him of the worst day of his life. He tossed it into the fire and watched it all burn. Skoll and Freki were beside him, their once powerful frames now gaunt from the lack of food and game that once existed before the birds had disappeared. All around them, the woods were barren. No snow covered the ground, having melted away long ago from the rising heat of the sun.

Freki sniffed and lifted his nose skyward, "My king, the eagle approaches."

Alexander did not respond, but Skoll could see the slightest tensing in his king's form. Reginald landed down beside them and bowed to Alexander, "I have come to pay respect to your father, King."

Alexander did not even bother to look at him. He had not

looked at much these last few years, feeling that when he truly chose to focus, all he saw was pain, pain he knew he could do nothing about. So he had chosen to live life looking at an unfocused world, one where he could distance himself from the day to day trials he was powerless to change. Hearing Reginald's voice, however, anchored him to truth, and it was not the truth he wanted to hear at this moment.

He answered Reginald with an angry retort, "You've come to pay your respects to the great wolf king…have you really?"

Reginald rose and took in Alexander's unshaven and disheveled form.

"I would rather think you'd relish in my father's death after what he did." Alexander stared at the cherished wolf coat burning on the fire. "He was never the same after my mother died. He was the walking dead, hating himself, hating Rebekah, hating the world day after day for taking love from his life." He looked at Reginald. "The great irony, Reginald, for him trying to do the same to me. And yet, I understand him more than I ever did before. We are all the walking dead."

Reginald looked at Skoll and Freki. They exchanged a look between them. Alexander looked back at the fire and watched as the coat burned over his father's body. Reginald turned toward the fire and stood beside Alexander in silence.

He could not stand it. Feeling the eagle so close, Alexander could not take it knowing that Reginald lived as Rebekah continued to live. How it was possible, he did not know. All he understood was that she was protected by the elements — a power he never knew they were willing to wield, but a power he despised for it did not include him in it. He had been thrown into the same predicament as the rest of the realm, feeling the wrath of punishment he did not believe he should have been dealt, for he had always honored Fire. He had always honored the Sun — he and Rebekah — always. The unfairness of the world he was forced to live in was more than he could bear.

It was then that the wolf king finally spoke, his face contorted in anger, "I cannot...I cannot bear to have you beside me without her here. What are you to me without her?"

He could not take all this pain. The pent-up emotion he had been carrying inside for years suddenly exploded. Alexander growled viciously and lunged at Reginald, "SHE CAN'T JUST LEAVE ME HERE!!! OPEN HER GATES, REGINALD!!! *WAKEN HER!!!*"

Skoll and Freki jumped in front of their king to protect the eagle captain. Fighting with his pack, they rolled and swung at each other, keeping their king at bay. Alexander's wolf eyes darkened as he seethed, lashing out at Reginald.

Skoll held him back. "My king! It is not the eagle's fault. It is not his doing."

Alexander fought his pack off, glaring at his captain. He spat at Reginald's feet and walked into the darkness and out toward

Gorilla Jungle with no further word. His warriors watched him go.

Skoll turned to the eagle captain. "Forgive my king, Reginald. He is changed by the loss of so many loved ones. He has not been the same since your queen shut him out. He shares his thoughts with no one and wills himself to die. Our queen is dead. My king burns upon the fire. And now our future lies in the hands of a remnant who drowns himself in the bed of the enemy."

Reginald answered knowingly. "Gorilla Jungle."

Skoll turned to Reginald and looked at the queen's medallion hanging around his massive neck. "We are at the mercy of our kings and queens, are we not?"

Reginald's eyes dilated to that of pins, "Wolf, it is on the wings of mercy that I say these words to you...go get your king. Bring him back to his lair. Drag him out of that jungle if you must...and bring his daughter with him."

Skoll's wolf eyes glowed. Freki's fur stood on end. "The birth of the remnant."

Reginald continued, "Born in the gorilla jungle out of the loins of your king's angry heart. He does not know. The mother, whoever she was, is dead from the fever." He grabbed Skoll around his muscular shoulders. "We are only at the mercy of our kings and queens if we choose not to hold them accountable for their actions *for*...or *against* the clan."

Skoll howled and barked, calling to members of the Wolf Pack. Jackal, fox and coyote warriors gathered around behind him.

"To the jungle to retrieve our king!"

They howled, barked and growled in unison.

Skoll asked, "How will I know her?"

"You will know." Reginald laid his enormous raptor hand over his own heart. "She is the cornerstone of your existence. You will feel the power of her heart."

They nodded to one another in respect as the Wolf Pack headed out into the woods and toward Gorilla Jungle.

THE HEARTBEAT
XXI

Alexander lay asleep in a large bamboo bed with three gorilla clan women; they were all asleep. Limbs intertwined, they were unaware in their drunken state that King Brutus was in the room with them. Still handsome after all these years, the only change was to his massive frame; it had atrophied over the years from malnutrition. His warriors, although gaunt, were still strong; the only sign of change was their thinning hair and leaner frames.

Brutus tapped the bamboo bedframe with his bone scepter. No one stirred. Brutus' silverback and baboon guards stood beside him carrying torches in their gigantic fists. The gorilla king looked down at the wolf prince.

"Find the girl."

The silverback nodded to the baboon. He swung from the bamboo bed and out toward another part of the jungle. A chimpanzee soldier entered the room excitedly whooping just loud enough to mark his entrance. He spoke to the silverback, "*Wolves*...the pack is here..."

Brutus was still looking down at Alexander's unconscious form. "Don't deter them. They're here for this mess."

They marched out, leaving the wolf king in the dark.

Alexander was dreaming. He was laying on his stomach in the exact same position he was just in, but the room had changed — he was laying in his own bed in The Lair, fast asleep. A gentle breeze blew through the room as the moonlight shone down upon him from the balcony beyond.

"*Alexander...*"

Alexander stirred at the sound of his name, but he did not awaken. A woman's hand gently touched his dark, wavy hair, running her long fingers through it. The woman lowered down and spoke softly in his ear, "*Alexander...*"

Alexander opened his eyes. He slowly turned and saw Rebekah. He looked at her face, deciding whether or not to believe she was real. He suddenly rolled over and grabbed her face in his hands. Alexander took in her presence in stunned silence willing himself to believe that what he saw was true. His face fell into one of pain and sorrow as he held onto her.

"I didn't mean it. I didn't mean for you to go."

"Alexander..."

He kissed her as he spoke, "Don't leave me here, Rebekah.

Take me with you...wherever you go."

She caressed his sad face. He wrapped his arms around her. "You have to stay..."

Alexander rolled on top of her. "I won't let you *leave* me here..."

She held him back and looked deeply into his sad wolf eyes. "Alexander...do not forget who you are and what you wanted. You must build your house."

He clenched his jaw.

"Do you hear me, wolf? *Build...your...house...*"

Alexander looked at her and lowered his head onto her chest. "I cannot build it without you...you are my cornerstone."

The moment his head rested against her body, Alexander felt nothing but the satin sheets. He looked up. Rebekah was gone — vanished from underneath him. He lowered himself back down and buried his head in the sheets, grabbing onto them in his powerful fists. He groaned mournfully, compelling his thoughts to bring Rebekah back once again. "Don't leave me..."

While Alexander dreamt, the wolf pack had arrived in the jungle. They stood in the darkened room, surrounding the bamboo bed. The pack was silent as they stared down at their king groaning in his drunken sleep. Skoll took a large bucket of water and poured it all over his king.

The gorilla clan women bolted upright. Seeing the wolf pack, they screamed and covered themselves in shock. Alexander, however, did not stir. Skoll turned his wolf eyes on one of the women, growling lowly. "Woman, you have stirred him once this night. Stir him again."

All three women tried to shake Alexander awake. He moaned and threw their arms off of him, never opening his eyes. Suddenly, Alexander was yanked violently out of bed by his ankles and thrown against the wall. He was awake now seeing his pack before him. His eyes glowed silver as he growled and attacked the members of his pack. He was too drunk, however, and his movements were clumsy. It took no effort whatsoever for Skoll to pick up his king and toss him to the other end of the wall.

Alexander fell onto the floor. Freki tossed another pail of water on him. Alexander's fury rose, and this time, his clarity helped his movements as he launched straight for the captain of his guard. He was almost upon him when Skoll pulled his sword out and aimed it at Alexander's neck. Alexander stopped cold as the edge of the blade rested less than an inch from his jugular.

"I would put that down if I were you, Skoll. You kill me, you kill us all."

Skoll challenged his king, "I thought you wanted to die."

They stared at one another.

"I do... but not here."

Skoll lowered his sword. The women scattered out of the room. The pack surrounded their king, growling angrily at him. Alexander took in all their enraged faces.

Skoll continued to glare at his king, "We will all die one day, my king, but unlike you, I desire a death of honor. One where the pack may march upon my grave and say, 'He fought so others may live.' You disgrace us."

He turned his back on his king and barked to the pack. They moved to gather behind him, leaving their king.

"You came all this way to leave me here."

"No, we came to see if you would lead us home."

They raced on.

Alexander was left all alone amidst the empty bottles of wine and disheveled bed. He sat on the edge of it, clutching his pounding head in his hands. A gentle breeze blew through the room.

"Build…your…house…"

Alexander lifted his head having heard the words.

"Bird, I hear you…I always hear you…"

He slowly gathered his shirt and left the room. He ran through the jungle after his pack. And as he ran through the bamboo forest, his step suddenly slowed. With his wolf-like hearing, he turned his head.

He had heard it.

Alexander shifted his body in the direction of the sound. The wolf king walked slowly forward. His eyes remained fixed straight ahead as he continued moving, following the source of the sound.

It was the slow beat of a heart.

Alexander continued moving forward; his eyes were raised on a single point. The wolf pack was gathered at the edge of the jungle staring up at the gorilla king's fortress — staring at the same fixed point Alexander was looking at. Alexander moved between the pack and past them, looking up at Brutus' kingdom. Alexander moved in front of the pack, never blinking, never speaking, his wolf eyes never moving from its focus on the beating heart of the remnant.

Brutus was seated on his throne. A little girl with raven-colored hair and wolf-colored eyes rested on the gorilla king's knee playing with a bamboo flute.

Brutus smiled upon seeing Alexander and the Wolf Pack approach. "Alexander. It's good to see you up and about. I was sorry to hear about Ivan's death. You have my condolences."

Alexander looked at Brutus, shifting his eyes stoically to the little girl. Several moments passed before he spoke, "Is that her?"

Brutus continued to smile, "So the women say..."

A female servant brought a tray of goblets. He took one and toasted Alexander.

"Welcome to the clan, King."

He drank deeply. The servant offered a goblet to Alexander, but he ignored her, refusing to take his eyes off of Brutus.

"Disappointed that she's not part bird?"

Skoll and the pack growled lowly. Brutus looked down at the little girl.

"You know, I could easily pass her off as one of my own daughters if you don't want her — a playmate for my son, Byron."

"How do you know she's mine?"

Brutus tossed the goblet across his floor. He rose from his throne.

"Well, you can never be too sure. There's only one way to find out."

He set the little girl down onto the floor. He reached for his bone scepter.

"One less female in the world makes no difference to me."

Brutus swung his scepter around to loosen up his muscles. He looked at Alexander. When it appeared Alexander was not about to stop him, Brutus came up behind the little girl and raised his scepter high above his head.

The pack went wild, crouching down to attack, growling viciously. All the while, Alexander did not move a single muscle; he merely continued to hold Brutus' stare. The coyote and jackal warriors yelped loudly as the heir to the throne was about to be bludgeoned.

Brutus inhaled and brought the scepter down.

"Stop."

The scepter stopped just above the little girl's tiny head. Alexander lifted his wolf eyes to the gorilla king. "What do you want?"

Brutus chuckled low and deep, "*King...*" He moved Bane to his side. "My clan is starving."

"*All* the clans are starving."

Brutus sat back against his throne measuring up the wolf king. "Remove your protection on the critters and the reptiles."

They held each other's stare.

"Done."

Alexander stepped swiftly forward and picked up his daughter without any further discussion. He turned away from the gorilla king and marched out. Brutus slammed his bone scepter down, sounding the thunder of drums all across the jungle. The joyous whooping of gorilla clan soldiers filled the kingdom.

The wolf pack followed quickly behind their king. Skoll rushed up alongside Alexander, "My king, *we* are the critter and reptile clans' guardians!"

Alexander kept walking swiftly, never breaking stride. He did not bother to look at Skoll. "The Bird Clan is guardian to the critters...and they are not here."

"But they will be slaughtered."

Alexander turned his wolf eyes to his guard, "For every critter and reptile fed upon..." He looked at Skoll, "Feast upon the amphibians and bulls."

THE NOBLE ONE
XXII

Marcus, now a handsome young man, looked down at a map of the seven kingdoms, studying the different pathways that led outside the realm. He had sent out several squads to the world outside The Den, hoping they would find food or some other means to bring the rain. So far, upon every return, there had been nothing to find — only more land that had nothing but inedible foliage to bear.

SinJin suddenly burst through the doors to the Great Library. "My prince!"

Marcus did not bother to look up. "Do you know how to knock? I hate it when you do that."

SinJin bowed lowly. "It cannot be helped. The prince's son has been born!"

Marcus put the map down. A huge smile spread across his handsome face. "Matthew has a son…"

His eyes slit to a cat as he vaulted from his chair and out through the library doors; SinJin was right behind him.

Marcus entered Matthew's chambers. Upon seeing his uncle, Matthew jumped up and rushed to scoop Marcus up in his massive arms. "Uncle! I have a son! Ha!"

Matthew set Marcus down and rushed back over to his wife, the Cheetah Princess Tara. She was cradling their new baby in her arms.

Marcus grinned, "Your heir…"

Matthew glowed with pride as he gazed at his son. He motioned for Marcus to come to the bedside to get a better look.

"We named him Daniel."

Tara smiled at Marcus. "Would you like to hold him?"

Marcus nodded shyly. Tara held him out to him. The moment Baby Daniel was in his arms, he began to smile and coo.

Tara touched his muscular arm, "I think he likes you."

Marcus smiled widely as he took in his grandnephew.

Matthew and Tara exchanged a look as they watched him holding their child. "Uncle, we've been talking. We think you need a cub of your own…and soon."

Tara added, "And I know just the cheetah woman willing to do it."

Marcus' eyes grew wide in panic. "No! No more cheetahs, thank you. The last female you introduced me to attacked me on our stroll."

SinJin roared in laughter.

Marcus looked at his guard, "What are you laughing at?"

There was a slight roar in his undertone. SinJin swallowed his laughter immediately. Matthew looked at his beautiful blonde wife, with her almond shaped eyes and asked, "Martha?"

She nodded.

"You sent him up with *her*???" Matthew roared in laughter.

Tara shrugged off his reaction, "I suppose she's a *little* aggressive."

Matthew added, "She's an absolute beast!" He looked at Marcus. "I'm sorry, uncle. I thought my wife liked you."

Tara hit him in the rib. "Stop it. I thought it would be a good match since Marcus is so slow to make the first move."

Matthew grinned at his uncle, "So what did you do to fight her off? It couldn't have been easy. I've seen her in action."

Tara looked at him quizzically, "You mean…*Jeremy?*"

He nodded in reply. "Uh-huh. He couldn't walk for days."

Matthew and Tara looked back at Marcus.

Marcus shook his head at them, "You set me up with the jaguar baron's hand- me-down? *Tara…*"

She shrugged his comment off again, "Beside the point…what did you do to her, Marcus? I must know…"

He handed Baby Daniel back to her. He took a deep breath, "I had to pin her down…"

Matthew was stunned, "Whoa! Pin her down?" He covered Baby Daniel's ears.

Tara shook her head at him. "Not a good move, Marcus. She likes that kind of thing. Sent the wrong message."

SinJin started laughing once again.

Matthew narrowed his eyes, "Now I *have* to know."

Marcus sighed in resignation. "All right. I pinned her down and told her that…as attractive as she is…"

"She's not attractive, Marcus."

Tara hit Matthew in the ribs again. He grinned mischievously.

Marcus continued, "That my heart belongs to another."

Matthew looked from his uncle to his wife, "That's it? Oh, wait…I get it. I get your strategy, uncle. Tell a woman your heart belongs to another…good one. Using my father's line."

Tara rested her head against her husband's muscular chest, taking his hand in hers. "Do you know how many women pine away for your father? He's so handsome. And to know that he watches the sun rise over the bird queen's kingdom every day…waiting for her…*oh*…"

Matthew looked at Marcus and pointed to his wife. "Exactly…but I still don't get it."

Tara eyed SinJin. She touched Matthew's arm. "Dearest, would you go find your father and tell him the good news? I promised him I would send you to tell him once I delivered."

Matthew was looking at SinJin.

Tara lifted her head. "Matthew?"

He turned and kissed her and Daniel's head. "As you wish." He walked over to SinJin and whispered to him, "You're coming with me to Bull Valley. I want to hear what really happened."

Matthew charged out the room. SinJin looked at Marcus. He coughed nervously off Marcus' look and used it as a means to exit. "Not feeling well, my prince. I need some air." He charged out of the room after Matthew.

Tara looked down at her son, coddling him, "I'm going to send for a pup from my clan to be your protector. You will have your own cheetah warrior by your side."

"And what's wrong with a lion?"

She looked up at Marcus, crinkling her nose. "Too clumsy. Matthew has a lot to learn. So tell me…who was she?"

Marcus shook his head. "You cheetahs…such questions."

"It wasn't just King Nathan's line you were using. I want to know. It would help me know you better…so I can fix you up with someone more your type. Besides, I know what really happened with Martha." She smiled. "It's her own fault…rolling on top of you once she was pinned down. Served her right knocking herself out by hitting her head against that boulder. So tell me…who was this love of yours?"

Marcus gave up. "All right. I fell in love when I was eight. She was the most beautiful woman I had ever seen. She was kind...funny...she saved my life."

"The bird queen."

He nodded. "When Nathan married the Mariner Princess, I *knew* I was destined to marry Rebekah. Just a boy with a dream-filled crush. So I don't think it really counts as love. All I know is that I never felt the same way about any other woman again. So why marry?"

"But you're still so young. You're only ten years older than Matthew."

Marcus shook his head. "There's too much to do, Tara. There's so much suffering, so much pain. My focus is elsewhere. I'm determined to find either food beyond the kingdoms or a way to bring the rain." Marcus looked down at Daniel. "So your son can live...and live free."

Tara smiled lovingly at him. "I'm glad you are what you have become, Marcus. Matthew loves you so...if you hadn't been in his life, he'd be a different man and I'd be a different woman. A woman without a son."

Marcus grabbed her hand and squeezed it tight. "Then promise me you won't set me up with any more cheetahs. I may not have what I thought I wanted, but I have what I need. You, Matthew, Nathan, and now this little cub here...that's more than enough for this lion's heart."

"Marcus, you're the most noble man I know."

Marcus' smile slowly faded the moment she spoke the words. He looked down at Baby Daniel, taking in his innocent face, "Perhaps the noblest of us lions in The Den has yet to come."

A KING FOR A KING
XXIII

Alexander's daughter was playing with the chess pieces on the floor in his room, nibbling on them as she teethed. Alexander watched her every movement with a stoic face while sitting on a chair beside her. After several moments, he lowered down onto the floor and placed her in his lap. He stared into her wolf-colored eyes, seeing his own in hers. She grabbed his handsome face in her hands and smiled. She pulled at his hair with her tiny fists and giggled. Alexander closed his eyes and rested his forehead against hers, relishing in her innocent laugh. When she continued to pull at his hair, he could not help but smile. It had been a long time since he felt moved enough to do even that simple gesture. As he opened his eyes to take in her beautiful little face, he felt a sense of peace that he had not felt in years — not since Rebekah had ruled her side of the realm.

His smile slowly faded the moment he felt a large shadow looming over him. He did not bother to turn his head, knowing whose form it was.

Reginald carried in the carcass of a critter warrior — a beaver named Quill. The eagle captain dropped the body down in front of him. His armor was tarnished and stained with blood. His eagle eyes were wild with fury; his pupils were the size of pins, and his feathers were standing straight up in utter rage. He did not even see the little girl staring up at him with her innocent eyes.

"*This* is how a king rules!"

Reginald stepped forward. Alexander shifted his wolf eyes toward him; a low, threatening growl rumbled in his chest.

Reginald stopped.

Alexander eyed him, "They are not mine to rule, eagle."

"They are kin to our clans!"

Alexander rose and stepped to him, "To which *your* clan is to protect! But your queen is not here. Had she done her duty, she should have frozen the critters inside her kingdom along with the rest of her birds! Were *we* kin, she should have done the same for mine!"

He turned back to his daughter.

Reginald was breathing rapidly. "And the reptiles…"

Several moments passed before Alexander spoke, "My pack is starving. My responsibility is to them first before all others."

"The bodies are piling up along *our* borders now! The carcass rots openly across the desert and country. Disease is spreading to our people! The vultures…"

"They aren't here, are they! If you want to put a stop to the chaos, Reginald, awaken your queen! Soar through her gates and out toward its fields! Bring us food from within it, for the only food here is the kind we can kill!"

Alexander glared at Reginald. "Ah, that's right. You can't do it. She has shut you out as well — surrounding herself behind walls so high no eagle can fly. Rebekah left us *all* to rot across the plains, Reginald, and don't you forget it."

He turned his back on the eagle captain.

"*WOLF!!!*"

Alexander gritted his teeth, but he did not turn.

"I came here to speak to a *king*. I shall go and seek another. My queen was wise in her choices — especially in refusing you!"

Alexander whirled around; his eyes glowed silver but Reginald was not swayed.

"I'm going to The Den. The lion king has not yet heard of your pack feasting upon the bulls under the protection of *his* domain."

Reginald ran across the balcony and dove over it, soaring to the east. Alexander stood there in anger. He was about to cry out in rage when he heard his daughter crying. Alexander looked down and saw her sitting in front of Quill's dead body. All fury vanished from his body the moment he saw his daughter's tears. He bent down and picked her up, holding her close to his heart. "Don't cry,

Alexandra. I can't stand it when you cry. It's all going to be all right. I promise."

Brutus, the Bull King Rom, and hunters from the gorilla and bull clans had entered Critter Clan Village. Hacking away at critter homes, squirrel, possum and raccoon warriors and their families, there was nothing but slaughter to the left and to the right. Critters were being dragged from their homes, thrown into caged carts, only to be wheeled away to Gorilla Jungle and Bull Valley to be massacred if they had not already been so.

Brutus commanded his brood, "BURN THEM OUT! ROM! TAKE THE CAPTURED ONES TO THE VALLEY FOR FEASTING!"

Rom shouted to his warriors. They grabbed hold of the carriages and carted the critters out toward Gorilla Jungle and Bull Valley. Orangutan guards tossed torches onto the thatched roofs to smoke out any remaining member inside.

In a surprise attack, the Critter Chief Rayford led a small band of squirrel and chipmunk warriors out from the trees and down upon the gorillas and bulls. With their smaller frames and weakened forms, the critters were no match for the other clans, but they bravely fought on.

Rayford raced toward the gorilla soldiers, skidding underneath them, rushing past them and on toward the gorilla king. *"BRUTUS!!!"*

The moment Brutus heard Rayford shout his name, he swung his scepter around to face his foe. As Rayford raced forth, gorilla clan warriors charged after the critter chief to attack. Out of nowhere, vines burst up from the soil, ripping the gorilla soldiers off the ground, strangling them back against the trees, tossing them into the fires they themselves ignited. The vines continued to protect Rayford as he continued to charge forth.

Brutus cried out, *"THE SISTER!!!"*

He took his scepter and hurled it out past the trees. Rayford continued to plow straight for Brutus; his sword aimed directly at the gorilla king's heart. He was almost on him.

Rayford jumped up, raising his sword high, when the bone scepter wound back around. It slammed into Rayford; the point of the scepter piercing his tiny body all the way through the critter chief's chest. Rayford fell to the ground.

Brutus walked over to Rayford and looked down at the mighty chief's body. He closed his eyes in deep regret at what he had just done, clearing his conscience for what he felt he had to do. He stepped on the critter chief's back, ripping his scepter out from his back. He bent down to Rayford, still seeing his tiny chest move up and down.

"You know this was necessary, chief. It's the only way my clan can survive."

A lion growled lowly behind him.

Brutus swiftly turned and found himself face to face with King Nathan and the Lion Guard. Staring into the lion king's cat-like eyes, Brutus could not help but notice that the years had been good to Nathan, making him more handsome and more fierce as the years wore on, marking his powerful presence as one to be reckoned with. Especially since he held the tip of his sword against Brutus' jugular. The gorilla king swallowed hard, and dropped Rayford's head from his grasp as he slowly rose to face the lion king. The tip of Nathan's sword, however, never moved from its spot.

Reginald swooped down from the sky and rushed to the critter chief's side to tend to him.

Brutus took in Nathan's lean, yet powerful form, still seeing the mark of strength lining every inch of his form. "Well, well, well, if it isn't the noblest of us all." Marcus and Matthew stood on either side of Nathan. "There's a bit of hypocrisy going on here. Planning on doing more slaughtering of your own, lion?"

"Maybe."

Brutus took in the severity of the situation. "Lower your sword, King."

"Why? Perhaps the critters are hungry."

Brutus' face paled at Nathan's words. He tried another approach. "Your father is kin to my…"

Nathan roared, "YOU DARE SPEAK OF MY FATHER!"

He moved closer to Brutus so that he spoke directly into his ear, "I know what you did. You like to smash things, don't you, King — skulls most of all. My father's…my mother's…"

He slammed Brutus on both sides of the face with the hilt of his sword. He grabbed the gorilla king by the back of the neck and forced him down to the ground, pinning his face down upon it. Nathan tossed his sword aside and took Brutus' scepter. He held it roughly against the gorilla king's face.

"This wouldn't be the scepter, would it?"

Brutus was breathing hard, "You wouldn't do it! My clan…"

"Your clan will survive without you; you have a son. Congratulations. Now, don't move."

Nathan rose and swung the scepter around.

Brutus shouted, "*KING!!!*"

Nathan lifted Bane high above his head. He slammed it down onto Brutus' spine. The gorilla king roared in agony.

"I missed."

Nathan raised the scepter again.

Brutus raged in pain, "*WAIT!!!*"

Nathan slammed it down onto Brutus' hand. "Are you moving?"

Brutus could barely speak through his pain, "You…you…don't have a heart."

"Not today."

Nathan brought the scepter down upon the gorilla king's head, smashing his skull in two. He handed the bone to Sphynx. "Toss it in The Lair. It's the wolf king's only warning."

Sphynx nodded to his king. Nathan turned to the rest of his guard and gave the order, "Leave no gorilla warrior alive except one. Send him back to the jungle as a message to his clan."

The Lion Guard roared and charged toward the burning critter village. Matthew gripped his sword. "I'll go after Rom."

Nathan put his hand in front of his son; he was looking down at the critter chief. "No. By the time the bulls get to the valley, the meat will be rotten. Once they eat it, the meat will do the work for us. Follow me."

They walked on leaving Marcus alone with Reginald. Rayford was breathing hard. He grabbed onto Reginald's hand and gripped it tight. "The Sister…she…tried to protect us…the vines…did you see her vines?"

Reginald smiled faintly, "I know, my friend, I saw them."

Marcus looked out at the colony and saw the gorilla soldiers' lifeless bodies hanging from the trees. He turned back around and knelt down beside Reginald. Reginald's eyes never left Rayford's as the critter chief breathed his last breath. Reginald's eyes filled with tears. "Oh no…" He looked up at the last of the critters still standing all around them. They looked back at Reginald with wide-eyed looks, wondering what would happen next.

That was when their bodies dropped — and the entire critter clan fell.

Marcus was stunned as he saw all the bodies spread out across the landscape. Reginald looked to the sky and let out a painful cry. He dropped his head in agony, "Oh, my queen…"

Marcus looked down at Rayford. "He was a remnant."

Reginald tried to hold his emotions inside, "Yes, young lion, he was."

Marcus was completely overcome as he stood amongst the demolished Critter Clan. He pulled out Ratatosk's compass from the pocket in his vest, still carrying it with him after all these years. He stared down at it, holding it in his strong hands as he took in all the critter bodies surrounding him and the eagle captain. "Queen Rebekah…she told me…she told me there was a difference…that the future of my clan depended on it. They *aren't* just animals to hunt, Reginald. They're people — like me. People who don't want to die. But they *are* dying! And I can't make it stop! I don't know how!"

Reginald looked at Marcus; he struggled not to weep. "Loss, as unbearable as it is, is necessary, young prince. It is the great risk of truly living. To engage in life, you encounter all its odds, all its chances, all its pain and miracles…" He looked at Rayford. "And its tragedies."

Marcus shook his head, "All its evil! I know what my father did to Rebekah! I've seen what my brother has done! Everyone around me does nothing…but *kill!*"

Reginald lifted his head to look at the pained expression on the lion prince's face. "And what is your answer to what you see and what you know?"

"To change it."

Reginald nodded to him. "You think exactly how my queen thought."

Marcus finally met Reginald's eye. "But how? No one is trying to find the answer. Nobody cares, Reginald."

"Young lion, it's not that they don't care. It's that they're tired and afraid. They don't want to lose what little they have if there is no guarantee of victory. The only energy they have to spend is the one that protects them from the hope they never think they'll get. That is why they don't engage. They need others to do it for them.

"And when the battle is fought and won, it is then they will march in that victory parade as if they were the ones who fought in the battle all along. But the irony is…they…are…marching. And in that march, they join the cause and will not allow the idea of loss to occur…because they have their champions. They've been given a glimpse of victory…hope…and they use that energy. They engage. The people need their champion."

Marcus took in his words.

"And if you wish to see change, then *be* it, young prince. It is you who must be the victor over the vanquished. You must give the people a parade upon which they can march. Equip yourself with the knowledge you need to bring your victory about, and act on it. Never let your words contradict that action or you will lose from the very beginning. I have great faith in you, young lion, as did my queen."

Marcus continued to stare at the compass in his hand. "What if I fail?"

Reginald rested his hand on Rayford's chest, and looked at all the dead critters.

"To never have what you thought you wanted, to never be what you dreamed you could be, to give everything you had and get nothing in return…it is a choice you have to make. Do you engage?"

Reginald craned his neck around and looked at the lion prince. "You may fail, prince…but the better question to ask is…what if you *win?*"

THE LITTLE PRINCES
XXIV

Minotauro ran through the forest. His head was lowered as he charged on, weaving between the trees. His seven-year-old body moved fast and furious. From behind, two Black Angus warriors chased after him, winding between the trees. They were almost on him. One of the two warriors grabbed him from behind and threw him over his shoulder. Minotauro tried to fight his way out of the bull's hold but to no avail.

The bulls turned around and charged back in the direction they came. Minotauro lifted his head and looked back at the trees. He fixed his eyes on the destination he almost reached — a small tree house up ahead. Minotauro kept his eyes on it, knowing he would soon be running to it again.

Rom and other bull warriors hacked up the critter meat, roasting it over a large bonfire. Rom used a meat cleaver to cut off a critter's thigh. He threw it into the fire while other members of the clan surrounding him feasted. The Black Angus warriors approached, carrying Minotauro. The moment Rom saw his son, his eyes glowed red. He threw the meat cleaver down onto the table and stormed toward the bulls. He grabbed Minotauro and hurled him onto the ground.

Minotauro tried to get up, but Rom pushed his heel into his son's back, pinning the little prince down. Rom motioned for one of the warriors to toss him a piece of critter meat. The moment he had it, Rom bent down and grabbed the back of Minotauro's head.

"EAT!"

Minotauro clenched his mouth shut. Rom shoved it in his face.

"*EAT!!!*"

He forced his fingers inside Minotauro's mouth and shoved the meat inside. Rom moved his son's jaw around until he started chewing. Rom threw his son's head down and rose from his bench. Minotauro choked on the meat and spat some of it out. The moment Rom saw what his son had done, he raged and picked Minotauro up by the shirt and dragged him over to the table where the critter carcass lay.

"You ungrateful little brat!"

He shoved Minotauro's head next to the head of the critter.

"He died *because of you*! Many bulls in the herd died trying to get this *for you*!"

The whole time Rom held Minotauro down, Minotauro kept his

emotions buried deep inside. Rom hovered over his son and whispered in his ear, *"Eat it."*

He placed a raw piece of meat down in front of his son. Minotauro saw the meat cleaver in front of him. He slowly lifted his hands up onto the table. He grabbed hold of the meat and brought it to his lips.

"That's it."

Minotauro bit down and began to chew. Satisfied, Rom rose and released his hold on his son. He turned to grab another piece of meat when Minotauro grabbed the cleaver. He spat the meat at his father and slashed Rom on the arm with it. Rom roared. Minotauro dove under the table as his father and the other bulls dove underneath it to grab for him. He swiped at the warriors and raced out from under the table and charged toward the forest once again.

The bull warriors raced after him. Minotauro ran with everything he had within him when, suddenly, another young boy swung down from the trees a few yards away. He whispered, "Minotauro!!!"

"Byron!"

"This way…"

Minotauro raced for the other boy — Brutus' son — the gorilla prince. Byron reached out for him and helped him climb the tree. Silently, they waited, listening for the bulls.

From up above, they could see the bull warriors approach. The little princes clung to the branches, hoping the shadows of the trees would cloak them from view. The bulls searched all around for Minotauro, snorting in anger as they wove through the forest. Byron turned and saw that Minotauro was holding onto a meat cleaver. Tears streamed down Minotauro's face; he was breathing hard, but no other emotion could be seen on the young prince's face.

The bulls moved on.

Byron commanded, "Come on!"

Minotauro followed Byron through the trees until they came to the tree with the tree house. They moved quietly inside. The amphibian prince, Sebastian, was huddled in a corner; his arms were wrapped around his tiny legs. He looked up in relief the moment Byron and Minotauro climbed inside.

"Minotauro!"

Sebastian moved to Byron and Minotauro. He wrapped his arms around their shoulders, holding them close. The three little princes rested their heads against each other, sitting in silence as the violence continued all around them from the outside.

A wolf howled in distance.

The three princes quickly separated and moved to different parts of the tree house and looked down at the forest below. Various members of the Wolf Pack raced by. Skoll stopped running the moment he reached the tree house. He sniffed rapidly and barked to the sky. He raced on. As soon as he left, the princes saw a tall, muscular man down below — it was Alexander. He stopped just underneath the tree house and looked up. The boys quickly backed away from the windows, hoping against hope that they had not been seen. Minotauro was still holding the meat cleaver in his hand, gripping it tight. They looked at one another. Sebastian's heart was pounding, "Do you think he saw us?"

Byron whispered back, "I don't know."

They heard a light knock coming from the bottom of the tree house door.

The princes looked down at the latch that rested right beneath their feet. They looked at one another in fear.

They heard the knock again.

Sebastian whispered, "What do we do?"

Minotauro gripped the meat cleaver even tighter; his whole body was shaking.

"You can open the door, young princes. I'm not going to hurt you."

They hesitated.

"I give you my word. Now open the door."

Byron nodded to Sebastian. He unhooked the latch. Alexander pushed it open and climbed inside. The boys scrambled back away from him. Byron had his hands spread wide to protect Minotauro and Sebastian. Alexander crouched down and looked at the three little boys. His face softened at their disheveled, starved appearance. He could see that they were terrified. He crouched down in the far corner of the house and focused on Byron.

"You know who I am?"

Byron nodded.

"Good, then you know why I'm here. We must speak you and me — a king to a king."

Minotauro and Sebastian looked at Byron.

"I have something for you."

From his side, he pulled Brutus' bone scepter out. He handed it to Byron. Byron quickly took it and placed it in front of his group, using it as a shield. Minotauro and Sebastian gathered closer behind him.

Alexander studied the frightened, malnourished boys trying to act unafraid. It was clear they were close and protective of one another. There was no doubt in Alexander's mind that they would continue to be and do so till the end. Something about their age and their loyalty to one another reminded him of when he and Rebekah were children. Thinking of her while sitting in a shack-like tree house, staring at the little princes as they hid from the chaos he had caused, he finally understood what he had done — and something in his heart began to ache.

"You know, I have a daughter a few years younger than you. And she's been crying. She's very afraid of what she sees — all the hunting, the killing, the feasting. I don't like it when my daughter cries. And I don't want her to be afraid."

His wolf eyes moved to Byron.

"King...I've come to tell you that this night, my pack and I will end the bulls' feasting. The lions are out tonight and we've decided to join forces with The Den against the bulls for this purpose alone. I need you to keep the gorillas in the jungle with you. And if you give me your word that you will keep your gorillas home, then I will give you mine...no more bulls hunting, killing or feasting ever again. What is your answer?"

Byron looked at Alexander and thought for a moment. He lifted his bone scepter and slammed it down.

"You have my word, Wolf King."

Alexander nodded. "There is one more thing I need you to do before I go. You three have to promise me you'll stick together. Don't leave the jungle tonight. Stay with the soldiers and your women. Do not come out until the sun is bright. Do I have your word, Kings?"

They looked at one another and nodded to Alexander. Byron answered for all of them, "We give you our word."

"Good." Alexander lifted the latch and jumped down from the tree house, racing through the forest. The moment he was gone, Sebastian quickly locked the door. He looked at his friends in fear, "He called us kings. Minotauro and me are only princes."

Byron looked down at the bone scepter resting in his small hand. He squeezed his father's weapon tight. "Let's go. We have to get to my jungle."

Byron swung out from the branches outside the tree house with the other two kings following closely behind.

A NEW TREATY
XXV

Matthew silently crept through the abandoned forest near Bull Valley. Tara was right beside him dressed for battle. She moved on Matthew's instruction, as did the rest of the Lion Guard.

Matthew quietly scolded his wife, "I told you to stay home, woman."

They crept forward.

"You forget, my love, we met on the battlefield."

"Those were drills, Tara."

Tara smiled at him coyly, "So you let me choke you out for fun?"

Matthew's eyes twinkled brightly as he looked at his wife. "It was the only way I could get you to put your hands on me."

She eyed him.

He winked at her. "You know I like it when you dominate."

Marcus chimed in, "Would you two shut up already?"

Matthew and Tara answered in unison, "Sorry, uncle."

"Sorry, Marcus."

They heard movement to the right. They shifted direction. Marcus, Matthew and Tara's eyes slit to a cat. They crouched and listened. Suddenly, all around them, buffalo soldiers burst forth, winding through the trees.

The Lion Guard roared.

Tara and Matthew immediately slashed the soldiers on all sides as the buffalos raced by.

Marcus rammed a bull warrior, charging into him, knocking him into a tree before lifting him up and slamming him back down. He lifted his sword and drove it into the bull warrior's heart. A ram soldier was directly behind Marcus. His battle-axe was ready to swipe; Marcus turned just as a spear drove through the ram's neck. The soldier dropped. Behind the ram warrior stood a muscular, female, cheetah warrior.

Marcus nodded to her in gratitude, "Martha."

She nodded back, "Marcus."

They moved back to their ends of the battlefield. Lions, tigers, buffalos, bulls and rams battled it out with one another. A buffalo warrior charged toward Tara. He turned his head sideways and collided into her, knocking her to the ground. Matthew roared and charged after the buffalo. The buffalo immediately spun on his heel and wound around a tree. Without thinking twice, Matthew followed.

Marcus spotted Tara lying wounded on the ground, *"Tara!"* He rushed to her side. He suddenly heard the sound of wolves howling through the trees. It was a sound he had not heard since he ventured into The Lair so long ago, and it was a sound he would never forget. The moment he looked up, wolves, coyotes and hyenas raced through the woods, attacking bull warriors as they pounced. Alexander led the wolf pack, fighting his way through the forest, following Matthew's footsteps.

Marcus quickly turned his attention back to Tara. Her side had been ripped open by the buffalo's horn. A pool of blood surrounded her tiny form. Tara looked up at Marcus as he cradled her dying body in his arms.

She held his hand tight, "Raise him, Marcus. Raise my son. Teach Daniel to be a man of honor. A man who stands up and fights when everyone else lies down. Teach him to act nobly…" She placed her hand on Marcus' chest. "Because, my son…he has a mighty heart…"

Marcus felt her body shudder before it went still. "Tara…" Marcus stared at her still form, unwilling to believe that she was truly dead. All around him, the Lion Guard battled it out with the buffalo soldiers. But even in all the fighting, he could not move, and he had no desire to rise and engage.

Matthew raced through the Old Forest. Broken bridges and

thatched homes surrounded him. He rapidly looked around, searching for the buffalo warrior, when he caught sight of the soldier winding around the trees. He turned toward it just as another soldier ran the other way. Matthew turned again. Three more buffalo soldiers emerged from the thatched homes. They charged toward Matthew.

The Bull King Rom emerged from the largest thatched home in the village. He saw Matthew, lowered his head and charged. Matthew saw Rom and turned around to face him. Swinging his sword, he placed it inside his sheath and raced forth. The other two buffalo soldiers joined the other three soldiers as they wound back around the trees. Like a herd on a stampede, they raced toward the lion prince.

Rom and Matthew were almost upon one another when Matthew jumped up. He dove over Rom, but before launching his body directly over him, he grabbed hold of Rom's waist with his muscular arms. Matthew flipped over and wrenched Rom's body backward and over him, slamming Rom into the ground. Rom's head bashed against a boulder; he was out cold.

Matthew immediately jumped up and whirled around toward the oncoming herd. He ran and stepped onto a tree trunk lying on the ground. He vaulted up and over the herd, front flipping over them as they ran past. He grabbed onto a branch above him, and hurled his body weight back around and down upon the herd. Matthew landed on the back of the last soldier. He ripped two sabers from his sheaths and stepped on his back, severing the head off the soldier to his right; he then slashed the head off the soldier to his left. Their bodies dropped as the soldier at the front of the shrunken herd wound around the trees to the left.

The soldier Matthew was riding, fought to buck him off as he thrashed to and fro, colliding against the tree trunks, but the lion prince held on. That was when Matthew saw the other soldier wind around the trees. The beast was about to pass him when Matthew swung his sword down upon the soldier, slicing his head clean off.

Matthew replaced one saber into the sheath on his back. He took the other one and plunged it straight down into the crown of the buffalo soldier he was riding. He grabbed the horns of the soldier and turned the soldier's body around the trees as it collapsed and skidded into the ground upon its death. The buffalo soldier's body came to a halt the moment it reached the heads and bodies of the other dead buffalo soldiers.

Matthew was pulling his saber out of the warrior's head when Alexander raced forth. The wolf king took in the sight of the mound of buffalos on the ground. He lowered his sword and looked at Matthew. "Nicely done, lion…"

Matthew looked around for Rom, but the bull king was nowhere to be found. He eyed Alexander. "So…you *are* still alive, wolf."

Alexander kept his eyes on the movement of the forest, "The days of walking death are behind me, prince."

Matthew lowered his head, "Not true. I will gladly kill you should you step foot outside your lair again."

"Well then, we shall battle on, lion, for your bulls have crossed into reptile lands. But I do not wish to fight against The Den but alongside it...but only until the dawn."

"Why? Do wolves lose their stamina in the day?"

Alexander smiled. "No..." He looked around the village. "We perform at any hour. But the bloodshed ends tonight."

Matthew continued to watch him. "I hope so, King. There's been far too many deaths. And we need a better way to live."

"Agreed." Alexander's eyes suddenly glowed silver, "Rom is here..."

Matthew looked all around the forest. "He was."

"*Is.*"

Matthew put his last saber behind his back. It was then that the mound of bodies behind him suddenly moved. He did not see it — but Alexander heard it. Alexander whirled around and hurled his sword straight at Matthew's head. It sliced through the air as it spiraled toward the lion prince.

Alexander roared, "*GET DOWN!!!*"

Matthew's eyes grew wide. But before he could move, he felt a sharp pain in his chest. He gasped, and looked down to see two blades sticking out of his ribcage. He looked up at Alexander in shock; he dropped to his knees just as Alexander's sword cleared his head.

The sword missed Matthew, but met its mark with Rom. Rom

was standing directly behind Matthew, having dealt his final blow upon the lion prince. The moment the sword reached the bull king, his head was severed clean off. Rom's body hit the ground — the bull king was dead.

Alexander leapt across the grounds and landed beside Matthew, taking in his wounds. "Ah, lion…"

Skoll and the pack raced through the forest. They stopped the moment they saw the heads and bodies of the buffalo soldiers. Seeing the dismembered body of the bull king on the ground, and the lion prince lying beside their king, they lowered their weapons.

Skoll barked out the words, "My king…it is done. The bulls have surrendered."

Alexander looked down at Matthew, "Yes, but not soon enough."

Nathan cradled Baby Daniel in his muscular arms. Staring down at his grandson, the lion king felt a sense of wonderment as he took in Daniel's blue eyes and golden hair. He remembered the day Matthew was born. It was a day he had mourned simply because it was a reminder of where his life had led, but it was a day that had turned the storm brewing in his heart to a drizzle of tranquility.

Looking into his grandson's peaceful face, he had hoped that the world he was shaping would be one where his grandson could thrive. One where the realm would come to life and live as it once had before. For there had been far too much blood, far too much pain, and far too much hatred for any generation to bear. It was time for happiness, it was time for peace. And Nathan's only hope was that it would begin this day for his young grandson by ending the violence with the bulls.

He looked out at the Great Mountains far in the distance thinking of her, thinking of the queen. He wondered if she saw him standing in The Den with another heir, wondering if she was happy, or wondering if a sight such as this brought her pain. There was not a single day that went by that he did not think of her, willing her to awaken, hoping that it was he that could undo what had been done. But he knew that such a wish was not meant to be granted, but he wished it all the same.

Nathan continued to walk through the courtyard, lost in his own reflective thoughts, when Marcus entered through the courtyard gate. Nathan slowed his step the moment he saw the look on his younger brother's face. Nathan's eyes shifted to SinJin and Sphynx carrying Matthew and Tara's lifeless bodies inside The Den — that was when the lion king roared.

Nathan sat in the dark, sitting alone in the confines of his own room, resting his head in his hands. His heart was heavy as he grieved in solitude, holding back the pain, stuffing it down deep inside. He wanted nothing else in the world at this moment but to be left alone.

He heard the door to his chambers creak open. Without lifting his head, he commanded, "Get out."

"I wish I could, lion. But I can't let you sit where I have lain...in the darkness of sadness' embrace. It's far too comfortable lying in grief's arms. And she desires nothing good."

Nathan slowly looked up from his desk to see Alexander standing directly across from him. He leaned back against his chair in both annoyance and disbelief.

"Alexander..."

"And you...my living symbol of what I lacked in the eyes of the woman I loved." Alexander smiled. "How I've hated you. Ironic that it is you that have taught me my greatest lesson."

"And what is that?"

"That it's never too late to alter your course. You who slaughtered the mariners now defend the weak that I turned my back on. I got your message."

Nathan remained silent as Alexander took in the portraits lining the walls. He stopped the moment he saw the one of King Luther.

"Children are the guardian's of humanity's soul. I look at my daughter and see the world differently through her eyes. I don't want to see her cry. And the child-kings in the swamps and jungle…it is on their shoulders as to how this realm will stand or fall. With scarred hearts there will be no beat of solace in the kingdoms. That is why it all must change."

He turned and looked at Nathan; his wolf eyes began to glow.

"I have come to tell you…you will never see my face again. My pack will not prowl outside The Lair unless there's a need. And I suggest you do the same with your den. It's the only way to protect all that is left of us that still lives."

Nathan took in his words.

"You've done your job, King. You've protected and fought so others may live. But you can't go on doing it forever. It is my daughter and your grandson who must now be protected first and best above all. Solidify The Den. Keep all others out. The bulls are no longer your responsibility. They severed the tie long ago when they joined with the gorillas. Let them stay in that valley to rot."

Marcus entered the library. Neither king acknowledged his presence as they continued to hold each other's stare.

"I know you're still waiting for her, King, but she's never coming back."

Nathan shifted uncomfortably in his chair.

"I know you watch the sun rise every day as it ascends over her kingdom. Look to the sunrise in the youth you have living in this den instead, and let all else fall where it will. Let it be nothing to us if my pack and your den hunt for food amongst those who sought to do it first. What are they to us anyway?"

Marcus looked at both kings in horror. "What are you saying? You can't allow the one thing we've been fighting to stop from happening...*happen!* My scouts haven't come back yet! There could be a way! Nathan, listen to me...there could be food elsewhere."

Alexander ignored him, never taking his eyes off Nathan. "Are we agreed, King?"

The lion king weighed this moment; it was no easy decision. He finally looked at Marcus. "Twenty years without rain. Ten years of scouting the lands outside the realm and still no answer." He looked back at Alexander. "We are agreed."

Without another word, Alexander swiftly turned and left Nathan's chambers. Marcus was absolutely stunned. He approached his older brother — and his king. "Never in all the years since you've been king have I ever disagreed with you, Nathan..."

"Then stop while you're ahead, Marcus. I don't want to hear it."

"You *need* to hear it!"

Nathan lowered his head in his hands. "You don't want to go down this road with me, brother. Not today."

But Marcus was not listening. "This dishonors Matthew! *Tara!* They died trying to stop the cannibalism! And now you've agreed to let it go on! This is not the way a king rules!"

Nathan lifted his head; his eyes slit to cat. His face contorted into one of absolute rage. He pounded his fist into the desk; its blow echoed across the den. "*I* RULE THIS DEN!!! A den of prowlers, hunters and killers! That is what they do! My men...*dead!* My daughter-in-law...*dead!* My son is *dead!*"

Marcus pleaded with Nathan, "And they fought for you because you were doing what was right!"

"I didn't fight because I thought it was right, Marcus! I only stepped in to help the critters because they were *hers!* I don't blame those kings for what they've done! They did what they had to do...for their clans!"

Marcus was stunned by his brother's admission.

Nathan shook his head as he took in his brother's accusing face. "Oh, to be you, Marcus. You stand there and judge me and everybody else...you who have never truly risked anything to understand what is to lose. What have you ever led? You send out your guard to scout the kingdoms, but you don't go with them. Maybe they've never found anything because they don't have someone to lead them to it!"

"That's not fair, Nathan. I couldn't go. I stayed here and helped you. I helped you raise Matthew. A kid raising a kid to be a man when I didn't even know how to be one!"

Nathan sat back and stared at his younger brother in utter contempt. "You didn't raise my son. All you have ever done is weep. You have wept for everyone and everything...but you, my brother, you have never wept for me. I'm the one who had to live with a woman I didn't love and didn't love me. And we created a son that we didn't want but had to have. A remnant for the clans! Who else was going to do it? *You?* I knew you would never marry. You wept for Rebekah like she was someone you lost when you never had her love to begin with. *You never had her.* And *I'm* the one who consoled *you.* When Mother and Father died, I had to hold you and The Den from falling apart. Who was weeping for me then?"

Nathan shook his head.

"Oh to be you, Marcus…to have been you staring at Rebekah's gate, ramming against her doors night after night, shouting up at her to let you in. To be Alexander, wallowing in self-pity and despair. To have had the freedom of being either of you. To be you is easy. Writing down all you see and judging it instead of being the words on the page itself."

He looked out at the moonlight.

"Every day, I wait for that sun to rise. And for a split second when the darkness is about to turn to light, I get a glimpse of peace. Of silence without the cries. And I can breathe. Every day I think…this could be the day that peace stays with me. Every day, I say she will come home to me. And every day, I say…this is the day when I will run free…because I've forgiven myself for what I've done. And every day that sun rises and the peace never comes…and *no one* weeps for me."

Marcus could not speak.

Nathan looked back at his brother. "I had to find within myself a way to raise a son I never wanted with a woman I barely knew. And…*I loved him*…I loved him, Marcus…"

Tears streamed down the king's strong face.

"So you can judge me and hate me, brother, for what I've done and what I'm about to do. But it's because I cannot take it…if anything happens to Daniel…one more blow to my heart will be the end of me. And I can't fall apart just yet…"

He leveled his eyes at his younger brother, his voice dropping a lower octave, "Because I have a brother who lives in The Den…and he cannot lead it. Now go and do what you do best, Marcus…*go hide behind your library doors.*"

Several moments passed before Marcus turned and left leaving Nathan all alone. He had meant what he said to his brother — every word of it. And it angered him that he finally had to say it. Nathan lowered his head in his hands and tried to hold back his rage, but he could not hold it back anymore. He roared in grief, pounding his fists into his wooden desk again and again and again. He had to get out of the room. The weight of sorrow he felt in his heart was too much to bear. The rage in his heart was overwhelming. He rose from his chair and tore his room apart. He ran toward his window, bursting through it, shattering the glass as he crashed down onto the courtyard below. He looked out at the hills and began to race toward them when his den was suddenly upon him. His Lion Guard warriors held him back, surrounding him on all sides.

Chester, captain of the Lion Guard, held his massive paw against his king's chest. "Peace, King…peace…."

They huddled around him and held him still as they grabbed onto him, feeling his grief and his pain as it flowed through their king's veins.

"Stay with us, King. Don't go just yet. Stay, King…stay…"

They lowered their heads and rested them against their king — and as he stood amongst them, it was the lions that wept for their king.

REPENTANCE

XXVI

Alexander stood over his balcony looking up at the sky. He whistled sharply in the same way Rebekah used to do so long ago.

Silence.

He whistled again.

"Come on, Reginald…"

But there was no sign of the eagle captain flying amongst the clear, blue sky answering his summons. Alexander's face fell in disappointment. He was hoping he would have the opportunity to make peace with Reginald. He *needed* to make peace with Reginald. Reluctantly, he turned back around to enter his chambers, when he found himself face to face with the eagle captain.

Reginald did not utter a single word as his fierce, regal face looked down at the wolf king. They stared at each other for a long time.

Alexander let out a heavy sigh, "I'm sorry."

Reginald did not reply. Alexander knelt before him and lowered his head.

"I'm sorry, Reginald. I knew better...and I did it anyway. I'm just so...I miss her..."

And for the first time in his entire life, the wolf king broke down and wept.

"I'm so *angry*, Reginald. And I took it out on the ones I was supposed to protect. If Rebekah saw me now...I can't undo what I've done...but from here on out, I can do it better." He looked up at Reginald. "I need you to forgive me."

Reginald looked deep into the wolf king's eyes. He knelt down in front of Alexander and lowered his head, exposing his neck.

"King..."

Alexander raised his hand and lowered it onto Reginald's neck. He scratched it as their heads rested against each other's. Further inside Alexander's room, they heard Alexandra laugh. Reginald swiveled his large eagle head in Alexandra's direction. Alexander breathed in deeply at the sight of his daughter, feeling an overwhelming sense of peace.

Reginald's eyes dilated to that of pins. "Remnant..."

Alexander nodded as he fought to hold back the tears that would not stop. "Alexandra."

Reginald smiled at the wolf princess. "For every death there is life. You have a daughter."

"Nature's vengeance upon a man like me."

They stared at her in silence.

Reginald took in her dark, raven-colored hair. "She reminds me of my queen. When she's old enough, King, I'm going to teach her to fly."

Alexander pulled his head up. "I don't think so. I saw how Rebekah flew."

Reginald chuckled softly, remembering the adventurous spirit of his queen. "She'll be safe with me, King, as was my queen."

Alexander looked at the eagle's peaceful face, "Do you feel her, Reginald?"

Reginald closed his eyes and breathed in deep. "Yes. I can feel her heart. She's at peace, King." He turned his head toward Alexander and looked deep into his eyes. "We would not have survived had she not cried out to the Creators. You need to know that. The lesser clans and gorillas would have slaughtered us completely. Many blame and hate my queen for the state of the realm at this moment. I can hear their curses and cries on the wind. I've even heard yours."

Alexander's jaw clenched tightly as he tried to hold his emotions deep inside. "I couldn't help it, Reginald. I've loved Rebekah every day of my life. I almost watched her die. Holding her in my arms at that moment, I felt my life and my dreams dying with her. And when she lived, I swore I would never hold back from what I felt or what I wanted ever again. I told myself that I would fix the mistakes no one knew I was making, that I would fight for what was important to me no matter what the cost. Life changed for me at that moment as I imagined myself on the path to being a better man — more noble and respectable." He laughed at the thought. "And she didn't want me, anyway. What I wanted didn't matter in the end." He shook his head at the memory. "I said awful things to her that day, Reginald. Things I knew would bring her pain. I wanted to hurt her. There's not an hour that goes by that I wish I could take it all back. I've relived that moment over and over again, thinking about the look on her face as I said those things to her."

"King…"

Alexander looked at Reginald with tear-filled eyes, "You said she's at peace, Reginald. Do you think that means she's forgiven me too?" The tears streamed down his face. "Because I can't forgive myself, you know."

Reginald's chest suddenly seized. He quickly grabbed his heart, feeling it throb in pain.

Alarmed, Alexander grabbed hold of Reginald. "What is it? What's wrong?"

The pain dulled just a little. "She hears you, King. Your cries have made her grieve. I feel it. I have not felt a stirring like this in quite some time." He looked at Alexander. "She wants you to be happy. She wants you to…"

"Build...my...house." Alexander looked out at the sky and smiled sadly, remembering his dream. "I hear you, bird. I always hear you." He turned and looked down at Alexandra playing with the chess pieces. "Second chances come in many forms, even if we don't deserve them."

"That they do, King. But yours is more deserving than most...you're not afraid to make the wrong things right with the second chance you've been given." He nodded toward Alexandra.

Alexander bent down and picked up his daughter, holding her close to his heart. "I wonder how much Rebekah hears as she rests behind her gates." He looked out at the sky speaking softly to himself, "And how much she sees." He moved out onto the balcony and looked out at the Great Mountains feeling a sense of peace. He looked down at his daughter and said, "My cornerstone..."

Alexandra giggled as Reginald stepped out onto the balcony to join them. The wolf princess reached her tiny arms out to the eagle captain, hoping to be held. Reginald looked at Alexander.

"Go ahead."

He reached out and took the tiny princess in his massive arms. Looking into her beautiful face as she smiled up at him, Reginald could not help but smile back.

"She does that you know...makes you smile."

"Just like my queen."

Alexander nodded as he looked out at the mountains once

again, "Yes, just like the queen."

Nathan stood on the hilltop watching the sunrise over Bird Kingdom. For years he had come to this very same spot, feeling a connection to Rebekah as he mirrored her ritual day after day. There were nights when he would come just to remember their few moments together, while there were others where he would talk to her on the wind. He had not spoken much since Matthew had died, keeping to himself as the weeks wore on, turning a blind eye as his den hunted the Amphibian Swamps and Bull Valley. The gorillas would attack the Lion Guard from time to time, protecting the beasts from the lesser clans, but more often than not, the jungle remained still.

He had heard that the wolves and the reptiles had sworn an oath to one another only to eat what had died, and to protect all that was living. Alexander had even begun building a wall to surround his kingdom from one end to the other. Nathan believed that the wolf king would remain true to his promise — that he would never see Alexander again.

He heard the sound of dried grass crunching from behind. Nathan did not bother to turn as Marcus stepped up beside him. Neither one had spoken to the other since the day Matthew and

Tara had died.

It was Marcus who spoke first, "I've been thinking a lot about what you said. You have always told me the truth when no one else would. It's something I've always counted on. And what you said the other day was absolutely true. I haven't done anything with my life. I haven't become anyone important. I have not engaged. I've merely despised the world I live in, sickened at what it's become because others have made it so. And I've been forced to live in the world of their making, forced to abide by the unmaking of rules that should never have been broken, only to find myself forced to accept new ones that make everything worse. I took too long to react. I was silent when I should have spoken. My timing has been off for far too long.

"And I can't live this way, Nathan. I can't live in this world the way it is now. I can't accept the change of believing that what truly matters, no longer does. I long for the way the world was before — it seemed so much simpler then. There were much clearer lines."

He pulled out the small compass from his vest pocket. "I came here to tell you that SinJin and I are leaving. I am going to travel outside the realm to see what others have seen, and hopefully see something different."

Nathan turned his head and looked at his younger brother.

"It's something I should have done long ago. I don't know if it's useless or not to really try now, but seeing you standing on this hill everyday gives me hope…that sometimes the noblest desires of the heart will finally be met. And hopefully we'll both succeed: me in finding a means to bring life back to the realm, and you to finally live again."

Both brothers stood there in silence for some time before Nathan finally answered. "What do you hope to find that others have not?"

"I don't really know. But I've been thinking a lot these last few weeks, and there's some things I have recently remembered. Actually, it came to me in a dream. I was in Rebekah's room with the old toad chief. He turned to me and said, 'Watch, watch…you need to remember….this borax stone is from outside the realm….a gift, a gift, a gift for me…it is what the earth gave to me. Remember, young lion, you will see…' And then I woke up. Perhaps, there is something out there that can only be found if I am the only one seeking it." He turned and looked at Nathan. "I guess there's only one way to know." He smiled softly, but Nathan did not reply. Looking at his brother with his gaze focused on Bird Kingdom, Marcus suddenly felt a wave of sadness wash over him as he stared at the image of his brother standing on the hilltop all alone. He began to see his brother in a different light, wishing there was something he could say to ease his brother's pain. But he knew there was nothing that could be done.

"You know, you said something to me once when I was a young boy, something I've never forgotten. I asked you why Rebekah did not find me noble, why she would not let me inside her gates. You said, 'I think it's because Rebekah didn't want you wasting your strength running against her doors, but using it to barge your way into opening others. What's behind these vine walls has nothing to do with you, Marcus. It's what's out there…beyond them.' And now I'm going to go."

He waited for a moment to see if Nathan would reply. And when he did not, Marcus lowered his head and placed the compass back inside his vest. "I just wanted you to know."

He turned to walk back down the hill when Nathan finally stopped him.

"You forgot one other thing that I said." Nathan turned and looked at him, "You *are* braver than me. You always have been, Marcus."

Marcus did not know what to say. But before he could, Nathan turned back to face the mountains. "It's hard to believe that one clan gone changed it for all the others, and that it was the bird clan that changed it. It just goes to show that you can never underestimate the power one person can make until the first domino falls. Never forget your power, Marcus, the power of one."

Marcus continued to stand there in silence.

"You should take Sphynx with you. SinJin isn't all he used to be."

"None of us really are."

"That's the beauty of it, Marcus. The road to what you can

become."

Marcus stood there a moment longer, taking in his brother's stature as he stood on the hilltop staring out at Bird Kingdom, memorizing it for all time. "I hope Alexander was wrong. I hope Rebekah does come back, and that she opens her doors for you, Nathan."

Nathan turned his head slightly. "She opened her doors for me before, Marcus, and I walked through other ones. But if she ever opens them again, I'll be there on the other side."

"And what if she doesn't?"

"She will, Marcus. In her absence, I have learned something quite valuable. It's why I stand on this hill every day. It's something Rebekah taught me. Because of my love for her, I have learned how to honor the Sun." Nathan looked up at the shining orb as it rose up over Bird Kingdom. "And the one thing I wish for, he will give to me."

THIRTY YEARS LATER…

TO RISE AGAIN
XXVII

*M*y dear queen,

We have reached the point in our existence where there is no hope anymore. I myself have grown weary, feeling the weight of a tortured existence as I live on in your absence. I cannot even feel you anymore, and wonder what that means. Yet knowing I live on, I try to remain anchored in the world I am in, instead of feeling like I am floating in a kind of limbo as I continue to wait for your return. I have stopped asking when that will be, for I have given up trying to figure out the answer. I have even ceased in wondering who it will be that will open your gates, for there are none who venture toward them anymore. Even the idea of you has been forgotten somewhere in all this pain.

But I have not forgotten, neither has Alexander nor the lion king. Alexander has made sure that your memory lives on, retelling the tales of your adventures together as children to his daughter — even demanding that I tell her everything about you as well. I have recently been reminded of a forbidden Fire Dance you learned one night in the woods. I am not smiling as I write these words, and Alexander was not smiling when his daughter asked him if she could learn it.

The princess Alexandra seems to relish in our tales, asking question after question about you and all the other clans as she and I fly over our side of the realm night after night. She is an excellent flyer — just like you, my queen. I find that flying with her brings me a sort of peace, helping me deal with my former life and prior existence as I stood by your side amongst my brethren in the clan.

Some time ago, Alexander recanted his doubts of your return, reminding us all that today could be the day. He has grown into an optimist, showering his daughter with unceasing love and wisdom to see her through her years. He has grown old, my queen, and I can sense he knows his years are short. It matters to him most that his daughter rule the pack well when his time finally comes.

As to your lion, I visit him in the den from time to time, but flying across the realm leaves me in despair. My visits have grown scarce because of it.

The realm is in shambles — a graveyard of dust and bone. The trees surrounding Wolf Lake have become diseased and rotten. All that remains are barren lands, desert landscapes, and haunted forests of the long dead still wishing to be mourned, still waiting to live on, not to be forgotten.

The waters surrounding Mariner Sea have receded to the size of a small, blackened lake that runs red from time to time. Most of the land that was underwater has now become an ivory beach that covers the bones of the dead.

The Amphibian Swamps have become a prison fortress of its own making. The young king that rules there commanded his soldiers to erect bamboo bars around his fortress to hide and protect its *inhabitants somewhere in between.*

Gorilla Jungle has grown silent. Its caves have grown dark, and the only form of life can be seen once in a long while when a warrior ventures forth to either hunt plants and insects, or be a sacrifice itself to the lions in order to keep the peace.

The plains outside the Lion's Den have turned to mounds of soiled dunes. The...

Reginald suddenly stopped writing. His eyes dilated to that of small pins as the feathers on his head stood on end.

He had felt it.

The eagle warrior rose from his chair and exited his cave to stare out at the moonlight. He could feel the heat in his body rising.

She was angry.

Was it the words he was writing, or was it something else? He winced again as a sharp pain stabbed him inside his chest. The last time he had felt this kind of pain was the night the queen healed the young lion prince when he ventured forth into The Lair. They had all felt it.

The pain shot forth again. Reginald gripped the side of the mountain with his taloned hand, trying to breathe deeply as the pain throbbed inside his chest.

She was trying to talk to him. She was trying speak.

Reginald looked up at the fading moonlight as the sun began to rise. And what he saw in the dawn, made all the pain in his chest cease to die. Tears filled his eyes as he fell to his knees, seeing the glorious rising of the sun.

"My queen…"

Alexander looked out over his balcony, seeing the strange reddish hue. He had never seen the sun look the way it did at this moment in all his life. A rush of excitement flooded his veins as he relished in the idea of what it could mean, and if today was finally the day.

"Father!"

A faint smile formed on the corner of his lips at the sound of his daughter's voice. The Wolf Princess Alexandra entered her father's chambers. She had grown into a beautiful young woman with her long, lean frame and exotic eyes. Alexandra approached her father, wrapped her arms around his old, tired shoulders, and rested her chin in the crook of his neck.

Alexander sighed deeply. "Beautiful, isn't it."

"I've never seen the sun look that way."

Alexander leaned his head against hers, "It has the autumn tint of gold."

"What does it mean?"

Alexander's eyes glowed as he looked north toward Bird Kingdom. "Hope."

Alexandra moved away from her father and scoffed, "Hope." She turned back around, "Father, the pack is starving. Within a year, they will all be dead. I cannot bear to look upon their gaunt faces and thinning fur. I find every excuse not to be around them, for fear they ask me to give an answer I have no means to give." She shook her head in despair. "There isn't any hope — not even on that horizon."

Alexander leaned against his cane, and looked at his beloved daughter; his eyes were filled with compassion, "My daughter, you must always hold your head high and lead whether there be many or few. If the pack was to see this look on your face, you would strip them of their last glimmer of hope, for the people always desire to know that change will happen and it will wrap its arms around them. And those arms are yours and mine. Famine is out of your hands, Alexandra. Thirst cannot be quenched by worry."

He stepped in front of her and lifted her chin with his withered hand. "All the kingdoms of the realm share this heartache. We all face the same obstacle. We all share the blame for how this came to be. The tide will turn."

"How?"

He looked out at the crimson sun. "On the call of nobility it shall be done."

Upon the wolf king's proclamation, the wind suddenly began to blow.

I *have dreamt of her face...*

And she danced before me in my dream, dressed in the color of the darkest night, dancing in the moonlight. Shadows of large creatures danced beside her, moving and gliding to the sound of a lone drum. They danced side by side, dancing as one, dancing before the fire that blazed red like the sun. "Who are you?" I asked her.

She turned to face me, uttering the words with the softest of sounds, "The one that is forgotten, the one who honored the Sun."

She faded then, in and out of my dream.

"Tok...tok...tok..."

Rising from the shadows on her right and on her left there came an eagle and a raven, whose eyes glowed red, red like the sun. The bird warriors turned away from the fire — one faced east while the other faced west. Upon their movement, the flames grew higher as the woman swayed before the flames. She turned swiftly then, so that we were eye to eye. "Only a noble heart..."

She slammed her hands together so that the two became one. And then, I awoke, dripping sweat in my bed, haunted, summoned, feeling more alive once again.

Who are you?

Like a blank canvas without a muse, I have painted the portrait of her image with each brushstroke, mixing and creating the colors of pigment to form and shade each line and curve of her face without any reference to it but the confines of my subconscious mind — and she is beautiful. I imagine her in the day, wondering if what I have thought her to be is true to her likeness, or quite possibly insulting to her actual memory. I daydream about her in the night, relishing in the legends of her flying across the realm on the backs of her eagle captain and raven assassin. But all I have are imaginings. There are no paintings of her, no carvings etched in stone. And yet, I can see her standing clearly before me — a goddess shrouded in a moonlit glow, her hair flowing down her back long and dark — "as black as her raven's," the Tiger Chief once said.

"Her eyes were the color of her eagle's — the reflection of the farthest insight, penetrating with the deepest wisdom." At least, that is what the elders in the Panther Clan have uttered.

Even Cheetah, my warrior guardian, has shared the stories of her from his clan, "She was a force of thunder that could call down lightning to her fingertips. Your Uncle Marcus knows all about it — he has seen her do it. Ask him to tell you the tale of the night he spent in the Wolf Lair." But Uncle Marcus never did. I asked him about it once, what she was like, what The Lair was like, but he never answered. He always ignores my questions, as if in acknowledging them he were confirming that the bird queen and the other clans outside the Lion's Den still actually exist.

The Wolf King Alexander.

The Critter Chief Rayford.

The Reptile King Khan.

Even the kings in Gorilla Jungle, Bull Valley and the Amphibian Swamps are silent within the realm — but the stories are there...and I aim to know them all.

Who are you? And should I be afraid?

"WHAT ARE YOU DOING IN HERE?!?"

Prince Daniel jumped, startled by the angry tone in his uncle's deep, baritone voice. He looked up and saw his Uncle Marcus standing in the doorway with his eight-foot-tall guard, SinJin, beside him. Both of them held a large amount of scrolls in their dust-marked arms, standing side by side like a couple of vagabonds.

"Uncle! I didn't know you had returned."

He slammed the journal shut, knowing full well that he was not supposed to be in this room, let alone writing in his journal while being in it.

Marcus stormed inside the grand room, bringing all the roadside dust with him as his boots thundered over the wooden floor. The library was one of the grandest rooms inside the Lion's Den, the kingdom Daniel called "home." Its walls were filled with an overwhelming number of books, reaching from the floor to well over twelve stories above their heads. In every nook and cranny, there were strange relics from outside the realm, rocks and stones unlike he had ever seen. Daniel loved this room. There was knowledge here. History. Adventure. His grandfather had told him that the Lion King Luther built it over two hundred years ago, for "there was power in wisdom" he once said. It was a room Daniel would one day inherit, but for now it was true — this was Marcus' territory.

"It doesn't matter if I am here nor there. This library is off limits!"

"Well, it *is* a library, uncle. I was simply reading." He quickly stood, tucking both his journal and another book beneath the crook of his arm.

"It's not just *a* library. It is *my* library. If you wish to have one your own, have your grandfather build you one!"

Marcus moved swiftly across the room, covering the distance from the doorway to the desk in four great strides.

"But you have all the books."

"*Out!* SinJin and I have work to do."

Daniel maneuvered swiftly around the desk just as Marcus marched up toward it, dropping the scrolls down onto the flat, wooden surface. Seeing all the papers spill across the desktop from end to end until no piece of oak was left to be seen, Daniel wondered what tales were rolled up within them. He reached for one of the long bits of paper hoping to get a glimpse just this once, but just as his strong fingers touched the parchment, Marcus snatched it from beneath his fingertips.

"*OUT!*"

Daniel frowned at his uncle, hating to be chastised like he was a young child when he was anything but.

"You know, uncle, I may be of some use to you if you actually shared with me where it is you go and what it is you're doing every time you step outside The Den."

Marcus looked up from the scroll he had snatched and suddenly roared in laughter. "You? Share with you what it is I'm after! You're not equipped for life outside this den. You have no life skill of survival upon which to draw upon. You would be a hindrance to me, Daniel. Nathan has sheltered you behind these walls with no other image of the outside world than the one you see every day. And you have no one but your grandfather to blame for that!'

Without another word, Marcus pulled a monocle from the inside pocket of his leather travelling vest and immediately began examining the drawings on each of the sheets of paper, unraveling the scrolls one by one. He mumbled to himself, "Now, now…let me see…no, not this one…" He set the long sketch down and reached for another.

Daniel moved toward the door, feeling frustrated and utterly useless. Marcus was right. He would have no clue as to what to expect the moment he stepped outside the walls of the Lion's Den. What would he see beyond the desert plains as he moved toward the borders of Gorilla Jungle, Bull Valley and the Amphibian Swamps? And if he dared to cross over to the other side of the realm, what would he see as he travelled through the Critter and Reptile Kingdoms and into the Wolf Lair and lands of Bird Kingdom?

He had heard that the Wolf King Alexander was still alive, but why it was that he and his grandfather, the lion king himself, never crossed paths, no one would answer. Well…not all.

"It was because of her."

"It was because of the bird queen."

That is what the cheetah warriors once said.

Daniel was about to close the doors behind him, when he suddenly decided to turn around. He looked all about the room, seeing the enormous amount of scrolls piled into every corner, every cabinet — making the library look more like an archaic museum of unwarranted scrolls than the greatest library of knowledge the realm had ever known. Seeing the portraits of his ancestors on the walls between the twelve-story-high bookshelves, Daniel wondered what each of them would have said or done to change the destiny of this time, and rule The Den during this existence. His eyes stopped short the moment they fell onto his great-grandfather, the Lion King Gunthar. From what the Lion Guard had shared, Gunthar was a legend — a king that was just as ruthless as he was passionate about the love he showered over his den — and his family.

He watched his uncle, taking in his lean muscular build, his callused hands and the wisdom behind his amber-colored eyes as he examined each and every scroll. His uncle had been places. He had seen many things. He was living life just as his ancestors had done. Unlike Daniel who was merely waiting to live his.

"SinJin, I need the sketch of the waterfall."

Daniel dropped one of the books he was carrying, overcome by his shock. "A waterfall! Uncle! You found another waterway outside the realm?"

Marcus slammed the scroll down onto the desk and shouted, *"OUT!"*

"But…"

Marcus stormed toward him, finally noticing the weathered book lying on the floor between them. Before Daniel knew what was happening, Marcus bent down and picked up the large journal. He immediately began flipping through it.

"What is this?"

Daniel tried to grab it from his uncle's grasp, but despite the age difference, Marcus was remarkably quicker, pulling the book from Daniel's reach.

"I don't like to repeat myself, Daniel. Answer the question."

It was not his journal. It was the other book he had been carrying with him. Daniel exhaled deeply. "It's a book Reginald gave me."

SinJin immediately lowered his large feline head and looked at him intently as well. Marcus did not say another word but merely stared at Daniel for what seemed like an eternity. Daniel did not even know if he should breathe let alone ask for the book back.

"What did he write about that was important enough to give to you?"

Daniel could feel the hammering in his chest once more. He knew what kind of reaction his answer would bring, for he had seen it amongst the Lion Guard and Tiger Warriors any time her name was mentioned. No one was supposed to know that he had the book. Reginald had given it to him, entrusting it to him after one of his many visits with his grandfather.

"You have asked many questions of me about my queen and all the other

kings and queens in the clans on my side of the realm. I made a promise to your grandfather long ago that the history of how things were and how they have become would be to his telling alone. But since he has never shared with you any knowledge related to it, I feel something must be done. For how shall you treat my kind and those that are kindred to my clan if you are left to wonder instead of truly know? Would you hate and despise them? Would you fear them as is expected of you? Or would you listen to them and help them if there was a need?

"I shall keep my promise to your king, but instead of my telling it to you, I shall let my queen tell it to you in her own words, how she came to know it. I am giving you a gift — it is one of the many books I have written about my most beloved queen. I have written down all my memories of her, including the things she felt and thoughts she once shared. I believe you will find what you are looking for. Keep it beside you always. Learn from it. See past the words itself for the things she was truly saying as she said them. For there will come a day when I shall ask for it back, but today is not that day."

How disappointed Reginald would be if he learned how short-lived his book had remained in his hands undetected. There was only one way to fix this. Daniel took a deep breath and blurted out the words, "The history of Mariner Sea."

Marcus raised an eyebrow from behind his monocle, "Daniel, you are the worst liar the clan has ever seen. Now what is the book about?"

"It's about Rebekah."

SinJin began growling in reply. Marcus froze at the sound of her name. "That's _Queen_ Rebekah." In a gentler tone, Marcus turned to his warrior companion, "SinJin…"

SinJin's growl quieted down. But even from where Daniel stood, he could see the fur standing straight up on the old chief's back. Marcus turned back to Daniel with a much softer, kinder tone in his voice than Daniel was used to hearing. Even the look on Marcus' face seemed to soften a bit, revealing a much more boyish quality he must have had long before the years grew harsher with the drought and famine that had infected the realm.

"Reginald wrote about when you met her in The Lair."

Marcus smiled faintly. "Yes, when I was a young boy." He looked down at the journal in his hand, "I can only imagine what it is Reginald has written about his queen. You are lucky he trusted you enough to share in them."

Without another word, he handed Reginald's book back and walked over to the large desk; his walk just a little bit slower now that Rebekah's name had been mentioned. Daniel took the journal wondering why it was he was getting it back so easily. "You mean, you don't want to read it?"

Marcus looked over his shoulder and narrowed his eyes at his nephew, "If he had wanted me to read his words, my dear nephew, Reginald would have given the book to me. He has given you a privileged bit of education you may one day need if you ever meet his queen."

Daniel shook his head in confusion. "But that could never be, uncle. She's been dead for over fifty years."

SinJin's eyes began to glow the moment Daniel uttered the words. Even Marcus' eyes appeared to slit to a cat. "That is where you are wrong, Daniel. She is not dead. Queen Rebekah is very much alive."

Daniel looked between SinJin and his uncle. "But I don't understand."

Marcus let out a heavy sigh and turned back toward the enormous desk. "I know. That is why I continue my search for what you do not understand." Marcus pulled out the small compass from inside his vest and stared at it for a long while.

Daniel simply stood there waiting for either SinJin or his uncle to say anything more. "Answer me! How is she alive?!?"

Without turning, Marcus answered, "Go ask your grandfather. He has made us all swear an oath to keep from you all matters of the past."

"I don't care!"

"You *should* care! Do you know what it is to swear an oath? It is to curse yourself should you break a promise — especially when that promise is to your king!"

"Why would he demand such a thing?"

"So you do not go looking for her. You may be killed by any member of the lesser clans should you venture forth from these walls."

"Uncle…"

Marcus looked at him dead in the eye, "Don't ask me any more questions about the queen."

Daniel looked at SinJin for any other kind of response. All he saw in the warrior's eyes was fear and loathing. "But if she were found, she could revive the realm. Her birds could bring the rain!"

Daniel waited for his uncle to slam his fist into the desk in reply, but all he saw was his uncle's shoulders slump down in exhaustion instead. Marcus turned around and, with tired eyes, simply said, "No, Daniel, she would not bring the rain — not to this side anyway." He looked at the book in his nephew's hand. "I'm sure you will read the news soon enough in that book of yours, that it was our clan who tried to kill her, Daniel. She cursed the kingdoms after a cunning move of my father's brought about his own demise. Those words of pain are phantoms of a past life that still echo forth amongst the living. You are the future of The Den. If anything ever happened to you..." And it was then that Marcus realized, "The noble heart..."

SinJin alone heard his master's tone; his fur stood on end as Daniel continued on, "Reginald said she was a good queen, a kind and wise ruler to her clan. He said her lands were plentiful with food — food that the people need now. I have seen her in my dreams. She calls to me, uncle...as if she were beckoning me to awaken her."

Marcus stared at the young prince as Netapheha's words suddenly came pouring out of the cobwebs of the memories of his youth, *"Angry she will be…wrath of the raven cannot be…good queen, good queen, peace…"*

Marcus' tone was low and lethal, "Don't even think it." Then he remembered Poe.

But Daniel was not listening. "Famine would end."

Marcus slowly rose from his chair as Daniel continued on, "Slaughter and cannibalism would cease to exist."

He grabbed Daniel by the shoulders, "If she is awakened, there's no telling what she'll do! Vengeance or mercy…she could annihilate us all with her army of birds! Stay away from that kingdom! Stay away from the queen!"

The Lion Guard roared from the grounds below, sounding the arrival of their king.

Daniel and Marcus stared at one another. Marcus looked his nephew dead in the eye, "Speak nothing of this or your dreams to your grandfather. Do you understand?"

Daniel nodded in reply.

"Promise me you will not venture outside The Den."

Daniel remained silent.

"Promise me!"

"All right…I promise."

Marcus breathed a sigh of relief and released his hold on him.

"I want to be alone. Make sure the guard is aware of it."

Daniel nodded to his uncle and fled the room. Marcus walked over to the window and looked down at his brother Nathan. Even in his old age, the king's physically fit form and still-handsome face bore great strength and power of his youth. Marcus looked up at the sun and saw that it was strange hue of red and gold. He had never seen the sun look that way before.

Marcus spoke softly, "Rebekah, I beseech you...haunt the prince no more. Peace, good queen...peace..."

ONLY THE NOBLE
XXVIII

None of it made it any sense. How could Queen Rebekah still be alive? Why had nobody told him? How could the entire den swear an oath and keep a secret like that?

Daniel stormed throughout The Den looking for his grandfather, angered at being so sheltered to the point of being kept in the dark.

"CHEETAH!"

His seven-foot-tall guardian vaulted over the wall and glided toward him. Upon approach, he let out a low howl.

"Cheetah, where is the king?"

"He is making his rounds through The Den."

"The moment he returns, I want to know it!"

Daniel continued to storm down the halls not knowing exactly where to go, only knowing that the walls inside The Den seemed smaller than they had this morning. He could barely breathe as he rounded out the corners to each and every hall, finding no means of calming himself as he reached the four corners that bordered The Den.

He had reached the furthest wall that bordered Gorilla Jungle. He looked up at its height knowing that it was a well-built form of defense to keep members of the other clans out, but staring at it now, he felt more like the sole purpose it was built was merely to keep him in. He was angry. He felt like such a fool. How could he have settled all this time for unanswered questions? At first it was a comfort to know that there was a mystery to the knowledge that awaited him as time progressed, as if each stage of his life would be the key to opening a door to that knowledge. But with each passing year, the key was merely dangled in front of him, a key without a single door.

Daniel leaned back against the massive wall and looked up at the sky wondering if there were other princes or princesses out there. And if there were, did they feel the way he did? Were they sheltered from the world and kept behind walls for fear of...*fear of what?*

And as the lion prince stood staring at his own walls, the wind suddenly began to blow. He breathed in its essence, feeling a sense of calm and a sense of purpose.

The realm had a chance to survive...and it lay behind the bird queen's gates. Feeling the anger settling within, the lion prince felt extremely motivated to move. And it was then that he decided there was only one place to go. Promise or no promise, the lion prince began to climb.

Nathan burst inside the Great Library and grinned widely the moment he saw his younger brother. "Marcus! It does me good to see you, brother!"

Nathan bear-hugged Marcus and held him tight. When Marcus returned the embrace with barely a pat on his older brother's back, Nathan released him and looked deep into his eyes. "Not to worry if you did not find anything this time around. There's always another day to prove the impossible."

Marcus shook his head, "That's not it." He stepped back and leaned against his large, oak desk. "Daniel asked me today about the queen."

Nathan's jaw clenched into a tight line. "What did you tell him?"

"It's not what I told him, but what Reginald has. He gave your grandson a book…and it was all about the queen."

Nathan's face suddenly paled. "Does he know about the prophecy?"

Marcus looked down at his weathered hands, unable to meet his brother's stare.

"Does he?"

"I don't know."

Nathan whirled around and shouted to the den, *"GUARD!!!"*

The lion captain, Chester, burst through the library doors. "King…"

"Find the prince! He may have breeched the courtyard doors!"

Chester growled low and raced through the castle halls, calling to other members of the guard.

Marcus shook his head and looked at his brother. "I don't think he left the den, Nathan."

Nathan turned and looked at Marcus; his eyes were slit to a cat. "He is a *lion*, Marcus. It's his instinct to prowl outside the kingdom doors. If anything happens to him, so help me…I will hunt down that eagle and kill him myself."

Daniel stood on the hilltop that looked out over Bird Kingdom. He did not know exactly where it was when he first began walking outside The Den, but knowing that it resided north of his home, he knew it would not take much to find it. His adrenalin was on overdrive as he crossed the border to the Great Mountains. He never knew the land, even as lifeless as it was, could be so beautiful. He suddenly felt alive and free, as if he had been living behind a prison that framed his existence. Never again would he allow himself to be locked inside again.

The lion prince stood there looking at the castle rising up over the hill, taking it all in when he suddenly heard the sound of dry grass crunching behind him. Daniel spun around, grabbing the hilt of his sword, when he saw his guard Cheetah approaching.

"My prince, forgive me for sneaking up on you, but it is foolish to roam these hills unprotected with hunger amongst the clans. I saw you as you jumped from the gate. You should have told me you were going. Where you lead, I follow."

Daniel nodded and turned back toward Bird Kingdom. "I know, Cheetah, but I felt the need to come here all the same, and I didn't want anyone to stop me. There's something in the air stirring me deep inside. I can feel it; that energy from elsewhere calling to me from some unknown place. I am meant to be here at this moment."

Cheetah looked at his prince, studying his determined face. "A noble heart."

"What?"

"Only a noble heart may enter. That is what the bird queen's gates said after she cursed the clans. No one has been able to enter her grounds since that day."

Daniel thought about the vision of Rebekah in his dreams. "Perhaps, she finds me noble. That's why she comes to me when I sleep, calling to me."

"She has found no one noble in fifty years, my prince."

Daniel turned and looked at his guard. "And of those who tried to enter her gates, what happened to them?"

"Nothing. They never got in."

Daniel looked out at the bird clan fortress. "Then I have nothing to lose." He started walking down the hill toward Bird Kingdom. He stopped and turned to Cheetah. "Well...are you coming?"

Cheetah growled at him and quickly followed. From the hill above, a gaunt, yet powerful Black Angus soldier stood guard, watching Daniel and Cheetah run toward the bird clan gates. A silverback warrior was at his side. The bull lowered his head and snorted, *"To our kings!"*

Daniel and Cheetah reached the enormous gates made of walls of intertwining vines. The vines were as green as they were the day they burst forth. Daniel reached out to feel a leaf, never before having seen a plant as green as this. Upon touch, it curled upon itself and disappeared behind another vine. Cheetah nervously searched their surroundings, distrusting even the sound of the wind. Daniel waited, staring at the gate, but nothing happened. He turned to Cheetah. "Is there something I'm supposed to do?"

Before the warrior could answer, two vines suddenly burst forth from behind the gate. They wound around Daniel and pulled him

backwards through it. Cheetah roared and dove through the vines after him. The vines rocketed Daniel through its gates, throwing him across the royal gardens. Cheetah jumped and pounced on top of a fountain just behind Daniel. He was crouched and ready. The vines slithered back into the gate, locking the doors once again.

Daniel slowly sat up and looked all around the gardens. Every square inch of it remained lush and green with flowers of brilliant colors filling the grounds. The lion prince rose in stunned silence and walked toward the land beyond. What he saw, brought him to his knees.

"Cheetah…"

Cheetah himself was in shock as they looked out and saw thousands of acres of cropland as far as the eye could see.

"There's food…Cheetah! There's food!" He could not believe it. "Has anyone ever gotten this far?"

Cheetah shook his head as he stared at the food, "No, my prince."

Daniel turned and moved through the gardens and up the stairs into the massive castle. Bird statues filled the grounds, standing over eight feet tall. Daniel and Cheetah took in the sight of the stone figures, memorizing their powerful builds and muscular forms. "There's so many different kinds of birds…."

The continued to move through the castle and down its massive halls. Paintings of the bird clan family covered its walls. Daniel stopped right in front of the portrait of Palimus. "It's the king, Cheetah, the one from the Old War."

His guard hissed in reply. As Daniel rounded the corner, two golden doors came into view. A slight breeze blew as Daniel stared at the doors.

He did not know how he knew it, but the lion prince felt the stirring. Daniel whispered, "She's here."

He pushed against the massive doors. The moment they opened, Daniel saw a grand ballroom. He took in the enormous room, seeing it filled with marble pillars lined in gold. He gasped as he looked around the room. Instead of stone sculptures of bird warriors, inside this room were large figurines of bird soldiers encased in glass: owls, crows, falcons, and eagles.

Daniel walked all the way across the floor until he came to a small staircase. He looked up and saw a large music box on the top of the stairs with a human-size ballerina inside. There was a large glass dome that encased the ballerina. A brass key was at the bottom of the box. Daniel climbed up the stairs until he was eye-to-eye with the dancer; only the glass separated them. He looked at her features, studying her face.

Cheetah cried out, "Do not touch it! There are spells on this castle. Spells and curses."

Daniel was spellbound as he stared at the human-like being. He whispered his thoughts aloud, "I have dreamt of her face." He lifted his hand to touch the glass. It was cold to the touch, almost as if the ballerina were frozen inside.

Cheetah hissed exposing his fangs, but Daniel did not heed his warning. "Like a portrait taken after death. Cheetah, it's the queen."

He stepped back from the glass and looked down at the brass key. He looked up at her one last time, kneeling down in front of her. "May you find me noble."

He turned the key several times.

CLICK...CLICK...CLICK...

Cheetah growled in horror and leapt up onto the stairs, racing toward Daniel. The moment the key was completely tightened, Daniel lifted his hand.

CLICK.

"MY PRINCE!!!"

The glass dome surrounding the ballerina suddenly exploded. Cheetah tackled Daniel to the ground, rolling behind a marble pillar as shards of glass flew all around the room. They looked up as soon as the debris had settled, looking back at the frozen dancer.

It was then that the sun's rays began to shine through the ballroom windows, honing in on the dancer. A warm glow surrounded the ballerina, as the sun continued to shine down upon her. The key to the music box slowly began to turn, and beautiful chimes echoed forth from the massive music box.

Daniel and Cheetah watched as the ballerina slowly began to

move. Beat by beat, she slowly moved her arms and head to the music, twisting and turning mechanically while her lower body remained routed on its pedestal. Her torso lowered, and her head turned from side to side as she looked at her hands, almost as if she were seeing them for the first time. She held them palms up, lifting them close to her face. The dancer's eyes suddenly blinked in recognition as to what they were. Her torso lifted as the music continued, moving more fluidly as each chime sounded. Her torso rose and fell as her arms and hands swung about, until her eyes zeroed in on each of her legs. She moved her head from left to right looking from one foot to the next. As if on command, the left leg moved from its pedestal followed by the right. The ballerina moved awkwardly and mechanically down the steps, dancing to the music as the sun's rays shone down on her.

Cheetah was terrified. He grabbed hold of Daniel, trying to pull him away from the pillar. "We must go!"

He fought his guard off. "No!"

Mesmerized, Daniel ripped his arms free from Cheetah's. He watched as the ballerina's dance became more fluid with each step as she continued to glide, pirouette, and spin across the dance floor. As she spun, her demeanor and costume began to change. Her hair came undone from its bun until long, tendrils of dark hair spilt down her back. Her dress darkened with each turn of the dance, and the color of her skin went from a frozen hue to a lifelike tone, revealing olive skin.

Just like the king in the painting...

The music began to slow as the key to the music box ceased to turn. And before Daniel's very eyes, the sun's light shot brilliant rays down upon the ballerina as if it was lightning itself. With each burst of light, the dancer arched backward. And when she fell forward, the light burst forth from her body, shooting out at all the bird figurines behind the domes of glass, shattering their casings with every burst of light she brought forth. The music chimed once more, and the ballerina's body was thrown forward by a burst of light. Her arms shot forward, and the light exploded onto the bird paintings covering the ballroom walls. The walls turned from gray to a golden hue as bird warriors came to life, bursting forth from the painted portraits, and stepping forth from behind their glass casings as alive and well as the lions in The Den.

Daniel and Cheetah were overcome by the powerful warriors that cawed and trilled as they stood amongst the room, reaching heights of eight and nine feet tall. The lion prince looked back at the dancer. It was then that the wind funneled through the kingdom halls, flowing all around the ballerina, spinning her body rapidly like a tornado as she danced to the music, changing her body and bringing it back to life. And as the dancer's body slowed with the last chimes of the music, Daniel saw the final change.

The music died and the wind died with it. And as the dancer slowed in her final spin, Daniel saw a woman of impeccable beauty standing in the center of the ballroom floor as alive as any woman could possibly be.

Daniel whispered her name, *"Queen Rebekah…"*

With jet-black pools behind her eyes, the bird queen had awakened.

ABOUT THE AUTHOR

Corina Marie Zurcher is the author of the children's books *Growing Up Claus* and *Hailey the Courageous*, the Christmas book *Snow Falls* and the fantasy trilogy that includes *Archangels*, and *The Father of Lights*. She is also an actress, screenwriter, producer and the owner of RowanMeir Films. *Legacy* is the first of her newest fantasy trilogy and is the novelization of the screenplay.

You can follow Corina on Twitter, Facebook, WordPress and Tumblr. You can also hear her podcasts on iTunes and watch interviews on the RowanMeir-NeverMore YouTube channel.

For all other information, visit: www.corinamariezurcher.com.

ABOUT THE ILLUSTRATOR

Scott Edward is a freelance illustrator specializing in concept art and storybook illustrations. Trained in traditional art techniques, Scott converted his skillset to digital art and uses Adobe Illustrator, Photoshop, Artrage, and Sketchbook Pro to bring his original style and artwork to life. Scott illustrates novels, graphic novels, and storyboards. He is currently working on various children's books including the series *Hailey the Courageous*.

Freelance and aspiring writers are encouraged to contact Scott to conceptualize their projects at www.scott-edward.deviantart.com.

www.ingramcontent.com/pod-product-compliance
Lightning Source LLC
Chambersburg PA
CBHW030637260626
47157CB00007B/2371